Black Listed

By Shelly Bell

BENEDICTION NOVELS

Black Listed

Blue Blooded

Red Handed

White Collared
Part One: Mercy
Part Two: Greed
Part Three: Revenge
Part Four: Passion

Black Listed

A Benediction Novel

SHELLY BELL

red
AVON
IMPULSE
An Imprint of HarperCollins*Publishers*

EPub Edition MARCH 2016 ISBN: 9780062396501

Print Edition ISBN: 9780062396525

AM 10 9 8 7 6 5 4 3 2 1

Chapter One

He sucked in a breath, the tightening in his chest becoming more pronounced as he watched her glide across the dance floor with a glass of champagne in her hand. She'd changed since the last time he'd seen her. Gone were her halo of white blonde tresses that spilled down her back and those round silver irises that looked at him with what he'd believed was love. Like a chameleon, she'd adapted to her environment, her chestnut hair cut into a sleek bob and an air of sophistication clinging to her designer-clad body.

With a smile on her face, she had everyone at this wedding fooled, but he knew the truth. She was a cold-blooded whore, a con artist who had stolen millions from unsuspecting men and women. At the drop of a hat, she could become someone else, fade into the crowds until she turned invisible, only to return moments later as someone new. And no one would ever guess the truth.

She'd mastered the art of disguise, her ability to convince someone of her love and devotion worthy of an Academy Award. Just when she had you wrapped completely around her finger, she'd disappear without a trace, taking your money and your heart with her.

But she'd grown careless when she'd allowed herself to be photographed, the picture on the front page of every major newspaper. She'd been in the background, barely discernable to most. But not to him. Never him. He'd know his chameleon anywhere.

She had no idea he was watching her.

Stalking her.

Hunting her.

His chameleon had forgotten to use the reptilian sense that warned her of impending danger. If she had, she wouldn't be here at the wedding of one of her closest friends, but instead would have left her cozy life as a publicist and disappeared into the mist once again, shedding her old skin for a newer one. She didn't deserve to live like a powerful lion when she was more befitting as a lion's dinner. She might believe she was a predator, but she was now the prey.

His prey.

He slipped his hand into the pocket of his pants, moaning at the feel of her cool silk camisole caressing his flesh. Her scent had disappeared from the fabric years ago, but when he closed his eyes, he recalled it with vivid clarity. She smelled like summer and freedom and money and *her*, all mixed together and packaged into one beautiful girl. When she left, she took it all away, leaving behind an empty shell of a man longing for someone he both loved and despised. Summer had become an endless winter, freedom turned into a virtual prison cell from which he couldn't escape, the money dried up like an empty well, and the memories of *her* grew hazy without his daily reminder.

Sweat dripped down the back of his neck, and black spots flickered in his vision. He shook his head as if clearing the cobwebs from his mind. Didn't she understand he needed her? After everything he'd done for her, she owed him. It was time for her to repay her debts.

Time and fate had kept them apart for far too long. But now that he'd found her, he was never letting her go again.

She loved to play her games.

He smiled.

A game was what they'd play.

Chapter Two

WEDDINGS USED TO make her break out in hives.

All afternoon, Lisa Smith felt as though eyes were tracking her every move as she set up the wedding reception. Resisting the urge to flee, she laced her fingers together and took a deep breath. She was being paranoid.

No one was watching her, but old habits died hard.

She schooled her worried face into one of pleasantness. Today it was all about the bride and groom. With guests including federal agents, police officers, and private security agents, the backyard of the sex club, Benediction, was probably the safest place to be at the moment.

It wasn't the idea of marriage that bothered her. It wasn't the dressy clothes or the tiered cake or the hundreds of dollars spent on gifts that the bride and groom would never use. It wasn't the officiant's references to commitment and God.

No, it was the damn photographers, and the way they didn't respect the boundaries of the guests. No matter how hard she tried to avoid having her photo taken, the photographer always managed to get at least one of her. She had to weigh the consequences of having photographic evidence against drawing too much attention to herself when she avoided the camera. Luckily, it hadn't happened too often.

But as the wedding coordinator of her friend's special day, Lisa couldn't avoid it. Already married, Danielle and her Master, Cole DeMarco, had repeated their vows for their friends and family in the backyard of their mansion, which also housed the sex club, Benediction. While the vanilla guests would remain outside, members of Benediction or those interested in kink could go inside to partake of the club's offerings.

Lisa got her first taste of what all those offerings entailed when she'd added some special wedding touches to the dungeon. She could only imagine how a sadist would use fresh roses with their thorns still attached. Her past experience with kink hadn't been in a club like Benediction.

Moisture pooled in her panties as she was bombarded with memories of being spanked over a desk and handcuffed to a chair. The way her Master's soft hands would turn rough on her skin, darkening it from a blush pink to a rosy red. One night he'd be her royal prince and the next her captor. And although they'd negotiate the scenes beforehand, he'd always surprise her with his ability to take her further than she could've ever thought possible.

He could've been an actor with his rugged good looks. Blond hair long enough that she could grab onto as she rode him to climax. Copper-colored eyes that seduced the hearts of women across the country. Those eyes had been full of hope when she'd met him. And then they had been full of love. For her.

Until her Master, she'd never known love. Her parents had taught her and her two brothers that love was a weakness they couldn't afford, not even for each other. They were told to look out for themselves, because no one else would. Of course, after her mother died, her father had expected Lisa to give up her life for the family.

And she had. Not in the way he would've preferred, but in the only way she knew how.

But her family and her Master were all in someone else's past. Lisa Smith, on the other hand, came from a good family, with a mother who was a teacher and a father who worked as a mechanic. They didn't have money, but the love they had for each other made them the richest people in their small Ohio town.

Too bad they didn't really exist.

Just like Lisa Smith didn't really exist.

Honestly, Lisa didn't know her legal name. Her family had called her Annaliese and told her their last name was Hunt. But from city to city, from con to con, it changed. Annaliese became Annie or Anna, and Hunt had changed to suit the different nationalities and ethnicities of their marks. Hair had been cut and dyed, styles of clothes altered, accents and personalities transformed. Once she'd had to gain twenty pounds to seduce a guy who liked his women on the voluptuous side. She'd enjoyed every moment of those two months, as she'd gotten to gorge on cookies and milk shakes.

Tonight, if she was lucky and got to eat dinner, she'd dine on risotto and white wine. Narrowing in on the caterer, she crossed the dance floor, her shimmery silver dress's organza overlay blowing with every swish of her hips. She needed to check that everything was on schedule for the evening.

From the corner of the dance floor, Danielle caught Lisa's eye and smiled widely at her before she and Cole strolled over. She threw her arms around Lisa. "Thank you so much for organizing this wedding for me. It's everything I could've ever imagined." She moved back and placed her hands on her swollen belly, laughing as it shook from the force of the baby moving. "Okay, maybe I didn't picture being pregnant at my wedding."

Cole slipped his arm possessively around Danielle's waist. "Then I guess we'll just have to do it again after you have her."

Danielle looked up at Cole lovingly. "Him. And no, two weddings is plenty. I thought nothing could top our wedding in Arizona, but here, with family and friends all around us, I'm overwhelmed with love for you."

Lisa ignored the pangs of envy she felt as she observed Danielle and Cole together. There was once a time she thought she could have that kind of love, but like everything else in her life, it had been a mirage. But she didn't begrudge Cole and Danielle their happiness. After everything they'd gone through, they deserved a lifetime of happiness.

"Still don't know the gender of Baby DeMarco yet?" Lisa asked. "I was sure Cole would get it from the sonogram tech when you weren't looking."

Danielle shook her head. "No, Cole would never…" She stopped, staring at Cole, whose lips had tugged up slightly on the sides, as if he was suppressing a full grin. "We're having a girl?" Danielle shocked the hell out of her by bursting into tears.

Cole took her face in his hands and gently wiped her tears with his knuckles. "I am so sorry for ruining the surprise. I was kidding around. I didn't mean—"

Pressing a hard kiss on her husband's lips, Danielle laughed. "These are happy tears. We're having a girl. I'm going to have a daughter." She wrapped her hand around the locket she always wore around her neck. "Now the day is perfect."

Feeling a bit voyeuristic, Lisa glanced at her bare wrist as if looking at her watch. She didn't need a clock to tell her it was time to start the dancing. "If you're ready, I'll have the band leader announce you."

Danielle raised a brow suggestively at Cole. "Right now, I'd rather skip the dancing and go straight to the honeymoon."

"Later," Cole said, taking Danielle into his arms. "First, I want to dance with my wife and my daughter. And you need to eat. It's been a long day, and I promise you, we're going to have a long night." They kissed, oblivious to Lisa and the rest of the guests. Or maybe they didn't care. They were exhibitionists, after all.

Lisa coughed, but Cole and Danielle remained in their own little world. "I'll just…yeah." She backed away, giving them a moment to enjoy each other. "I'm giving you a five-minute warning." She turned with the intention of speaking to the caterer, but her friend Gracie stopped her before she could take more than a few steps.

On five-inch heels, Gracie wore a sparkly red sheer dress that looked more like a baby-doll nighty than a cocktail dress, the fabric barely covering her upper thighs. Previously one of Cole's slaves, she was now without a Master but had been given a job overseeing the education of sex slaves at Benediction.

"Squee! You look amazing." Not having many boundaries, Gracie ran her hands down Lisa's sides. "Wow, why haven't you ever shown off that figure of yours? You're always wearing those business jackets. I never even knew you had boobs."

Lisa shook her head, used to Gracie's exuberant behavior. "Having fun?"

"Best. Time. Ever. But I can't wait until the dungeon opens." She sighed wistfully, her gaze landing on Roman, Danielle's stepbrother, who was talking with Cole's parents over by the hors d'oeuvres. "There's something that's so sexy about being beaten by a man wearing a tuxedo."

"Are you and Roman finally…?" Lisa asked.

The two had stuck up a strange friendship when Danielle had moved back to Arizona after having temporarily broken up with Cole. Gracie had taken it upon herself to call Roman daily, saying it was to check up on Danielle, but Lisa had a feeling that wasn't the only reason for the calls.

Gracie pulled her gaze away from Roman. "No. We're still just friends."

Even if Lisa couldn't find love, she wanted it for her friends, especially Gracie, who went above and beyond for everyone.

Apparently her thoughts must have registered on her face. Gracie shook her finger. "Don't give me that sad expression. I do not have feelings for Danielle's step-brother. He's not my type."

Lisa couldn't help herself. "You have a type?"

"Until I find the right person or persons looking for a full-time slave, I'm only looking for sex. If I scene with Roman, we'll lose our friendship, and these days, he needs all the friends he can get." Gracie smiled. "Besides, he could never handle me."

"No one could handle you."

"Ed and Serge handle me just fine. They're meeting me tonight in the Jungle Room. Two Tarzans ready to swing me from the ceiling and go primal. What more do I need?"

"What about love?"

"I'm not holding my breath that I'll find someone who wants a full-time slave and also will fall in love with me." Her friend squared her shoulders. "But enough about me. Now that you've been inside of Benediction, aren't you a bit curious about what it's like during business hours?"

Kate, one of Lisa's best friends, sidled up beside them with a glass of red wine that she held out to Lisa in offering, knowing from their weekly girls' night she preferred wine over liquor. "Gracie, stop trying to recruit Lisa." Kate looked positively radiant in her black dress and her blonde hair in a messy bun with tendrils framing her face. "Do you need any help tonight?"

Lisa gave her a smile of gratitude for both her offer and her rescue from Gracie. "Between the hired help and Cole's slave trainees, I think I've got it covered."

"Of course you do. You're the most capable person I've ever met. Nothing flusters you," Kate remarked.

A couple of years ago, the two of them had met at a law firm, where Lisa had worked and Kate had interned. But they hadn't become close until they'd lost a mutual friend. During the crisis that had followed his death, Kate hadn't understood how Lisa had kept her composure, surprised that a legal secretary could organize a funeral, field phone calls from the press, and coordinate the entire law firm's public relations without shedding a tear or breaking down from sheer exhaustion. That's when the idea of Lisa opening her own public relations firm was born.

Now, Lisa represented several hockey players, a handful of local businesses, and one large credit union. Oh, and when the need arose, she also represented her friends, most recently criminal defense attorney Logan Bradford and television reporter Rachel Dawson, who had been framed for the murder of a local mobster.

Kate was right. Lisa didn't fluster easily. With her background, she'd learned early on how to keep her pulse steady and to maintain eye contact even while lying through her teeth.

But what her friends didn't know about her could get them all killed.

Without a date or anybody to play with inside Benediction, she was here simply to work for the rest of the night. Maybe that would help the envy snaking its way into her heart as she watched all the lovers laugh and kiss around the tables.

She cleared her throat. "I need to speak with the caterer and get the band leader to cue the first dance, so why don't you both go enjoy yourselves."

Walking away from her friends, she took a sip of wine and headed toward where she'd last seen the caterer. Not spotting him, she stopped and scanned the crowd.

"Lisa!" called Rachel.

Lisa turned and caught sight of Rachel walking toward her with two men by her side.

It took only a moment for it to register.

The long blond hair she loved to tug on during rough sex.

The stubble lining his jaw that used to scratch the skin of her inner thighs as he worked her over with his mouth.

The roguish and lighthearted appearance he maintained in public and the dark dominance that lurked beneath the surface.

It was him.

He was here.

Her *Master.*

He had found her.

She blinked a few times, trying to see if maybe she was imagining that the man she'd run from four years ago was suddenly only feet away and talking with her friends as if he knew them. That was impossible, right?

Her heart galloped a wild beat, and the sounds of the crowd disappeared under the roar of her pulse.

She wanted to run *from* him.

She wanted to run *to* him.

All the sorrow and regret she'd buried deep down inside came rushing back with a force that nearly bowled her over. And when the ghost from her past stood right in front of her and looked at her like a stranger, the glass of red wine slipped from her shaking hand onto the green grass, the liquid pooling beneath her heels.

Seemingly oblivious to her shock, Rachel smiled, a twinkle of mischief in her eyes. "I'd like to introduce you to Logan's friend, Sawyer Hayes. Sawyer, this is Lisa Smith."

Logan's friend? Sawyer was Logan's friend? This was the man who had helped Rachel and Logan in Las Vegas when they were framed for murder and running from the FBI?

"Hello," Sawyer said cordially, standing so close she could feel his body heat radiating off him and smell a scent that reminded her of the best days of her life. "It's nice to see you again, Annaliese."

Her mind was a jumbled mess.

Like she was prey caught in the sights of a hunter, she became entrapped in his eyes.

She couldn't breathe.

Couldn't speak.

Couldn't move.

"You know each other?" Rachel said, her brows wrinkled in confusion.

"You could say that," Sawyer said slowly, still holding Lisa captive with his eyes. "She's my wife."

"Lisa is the woman who conned you?" Logan asked incredulously.

Shame heated her cheeks, and she suppressed the threatening tears. Her friends would hate her when they discovered what she'd done. Not that she deserved any less.

And what did it matter? She was about to lose everything. She wouldn't be surprised if she was arrested at any moment.

Rachel took her hand, but she still couldn't look away from Sawyer. "I'm sure if she did, she had her reasons."

Yes, she had her reasons. Dark, dangerous reasons that sometimes woke her out of her sleep in the form of violent nightmares.

And now with Sawyer's appearance, her nightmares were one step closer to becoming true.

Chapter Three

Five Years Ago...

"Marry Sawyer Hayes, and you'll never have to pull another con again."

More than a month after Annaliese's father had uttered those words, her body still trembled in both apprehension and excitement as she stood outside the front door of the nightclub. Tonight she'd finally make initial contact with the man who would change her life.

For years, she'd dreamed of having a normal existence. And now, it would become her reality. She could go to school. Make friends. Fall in love.

As long as she was able to get the country's youngest billionaire to marry her.

Without a pesky pre-nup.

No small task.

Once she divorced him, her share of the fortune would be worth more than she could spend in ten lifetimes, even after she handed the majority of the money over to her family. But she'd give every penny she had just to be free of her father.

He'd never required her to go as far as marrying a mark. But the more she learned about Sawyer Hayes, the more she realized why her father had determined she marry the man. With his high IQ and military experience, he wouldn't fall for her usual schemes. There was only one way a man like Sawyer Hayes would marry.

Love.

And that meant she would have to find her way into his heart. Nothing in the file her father had given her would help her figure out how to accomplish that.

So she'd followed him.

She thought back to the moment she first laid eyes on him. The man oozed masculinity with every step he took and every clench of his fist as he sparred in his gym against the owner, a man who had trained for twenty years. Sawyer met him blow for blow, punch for punch. Sweat had glistened on his bare chest, his nipples hard as if he knew she watched from a distance.

He hadn't known, of course. She blended into the woodwork. Just a plain Jane with large glasses and frumpy workout clothes. While his thighs had flexed and bulged, the muscles of his throat growing taut as though he had gotten stuck mid-swallow, she acknowledged that her mark could never fade into oblivion. Even though he'd once tried, he was back now, and that made him a target.

Her target.

Annaliese had never heard of BDSM before researching Sawyer. Sex was something she tried to avoid, and when she did it, she rarely enjoyed it. It was hard to find pleasure when you were running through who you were supposed to be and what you were supposed to do.

Orgasms required her mind to drift away, and for someone like her—a grifter—that meant losing control. Control was key to every good con, and after being in the business practically all twenty years of her life, she was as good as it got.

Once men and women trusted her, she'd turn on them and breach that trust. She didn't know how to live any other way. It was all she had ever known.

The problem with this particular mark was that he needed control. He lived for control like she lived for a con. In order to lure this man, she had to pretend to be a submissive. Give up control to him. And from everything she'd read about it, he would know if she didn't. At least, if he was a good Dominant. Aside from the con artists she called family, she didn't know anyone who could read others well enough to know if they were lying.

Hell, the people she'd been with hadn't even known she had faked her orgasms. Guys she understood, but women should know when another woman had a climax. The way the muscles tightened and shook before the spasms of release. But the women she'd slept with had been oblivious to anything other than their own pleasure.

Maybe that's what made it so easy to take their money and run.

If she didn't, she'd lose everyone who was left. Her mother was dead. Now she only had her father and her two brothers, Mitch and Asa. She feared if she didn't succeed with the con, they'd leave her behind and she'd never find them again. For someone who had shuttled from place to place her whole life without being allowed to make real friends or real connections, she couldn't risk losing her family. Even though aside from Asa, she didn't like them very much.

Not that it mattered. She didn't like herself much either.

When her father had told her she'd be going to some sex club in Arizona, she thought he'd lost his mind. But no, apparently sex clubs did exist outside of movies and books. So she'd read up on everything she could about domination and submission. Watched movies. Read a couple romance novels that made her wet and giggly at the same time. Saw images on the Internet that confused her, like the ones of people with bruises and red welts all over their bodies. Why did it both scare her and arouse her at the same time?

She'd studied what made a good submissive until she realized all the studying in the world wouldn't be enough. She needed to know what her limits were before she approached Sawyer.

She'd needed to experience it.

Mistress Kay had taught her about those things that couldn't be learned through books. For an exorbitant fee, the professional Dominatrix had not only dominated her, but for a month, had become her teacher, her psychologist, her priest, and her closest friend.

Surprisingly, that first week all they did was talk. She learned that BDSM wasn't about sex. It was a power exchange in which the relationship between Dom and sub was one of trust, and honesty and communication were paramount. For someone like Lisa, who had spent her entire life lying, both came difficult for her.

Because of Annaliese's past, her Domme had introduced impact play cautiously. To Annaliese's shock, she loved the pain brought by the blow of a flogger and the whack of a cane. Craved the feel of her Mistress's hand slapping her thigh or face. It didn't make sense to Annaliese. How could she enjoy being hit after suffering her father's abuse?

Mistress Kay had explained that when Annaliese submitted, she consented to the acts that resulted in pain, giving her a power she hadn't had with her father. Annaliese's masochistic tendencies had nothing to do with her abusive past.

By the end of the month, Annaliese had a much better understanding of both BDSM and her sexuality. But would it be enough to win Sawyer's trust and, eventually, his love?

Today she'd find out.

Taking a deep breath, she pulled open the door to the club and went inside. Checking the room, she was surprised to find it looked like any other dive. A long bar spanned the back of the space, with a few middle-aged men sitting on bar stools and watching a basketball game on the television. The few tables sat unoccupied, half-drunk beers and wineglasses littering them. This didn't fit her idea of what a sex club would look like.

She casually glanced around the room again in an attempt to locate Sawyer, but she didn't see him. He'd walked in this place not ten minutes ago. Where had he gone? "You're new," said a husky voice behind her, a voice she'd only heard from across the gym.

How had he gotten behind her without her knowing?

She turned around slowly, tilting her head up to get her first good look at Sawyer Hayes. Her heart increased its tempo, and a soft gasp spilled from her lips.

After studying his photographs and seeing him from a distance, she'd thought she would be immune to his sexiness, but seeing him up close was like going outside on a sunny day after being in the dark. With his shoulder-length blond hair and twinkling brown eyes, he radiated an overwhelming sensuality and masculinity that she'd never before encountered, causing her nipples to bead and her pussy to clench. "Yes. How could you tell?"

"Well, for one," he said, stepping so close his chest brushed against her breasts, "I'm here enough, so I've met everyone already."

She shuddered from the contact. "And two?"

"All the regulars know that the good room is downstairs. You did come here for the sex club, right?"

The basement. So that's where he'd disappeared to earlier. She gave him a smile. "You're right. I've never been here before, but that's why I'm here."

"I've seen you before." His brow furrowed, the lines of his forehead grooved deep in concentration. "You work out at my gym."

She reared back. No one had ever recognized her before. How had he even known she was the same woman?

"I'm not sure. What gym do you go to?" she said, playing coy.

"You know exactly what gym, darlin'. You've been watching me, and now you just happened to show up here. I'm supposed to believe it's a coincidence?"

Shit. This was not going as planned. He didn't strike her as a man who would fall in love with a stalker. Improvising, she used a technique she'd learned long ago and forced herself to cry. Tears dripped down her cheeks as she brushed her face with the back of her hand. Hopefully, he wouldn't be able to resist a crying woman, and she could salvage the situation.

His arms circled around her waist, and he tugged her to his chest. "Shh. I'm flattered. Really. I just need you to tell me the truth."

Warm in his embrace, she inhaled his clean scent. "When I saw you at the gym, I was drawn to you, and when I followed you here and realized you were a Dom, I understood why." She peered up at him. "I'm a submissive. I don't have a lot of experience, but I trained under a professional Dominatrix. I know as the submissive I should wait for you to make the first move, but if you're willing, I'd like to do a scene with you tonight."

She held her breath in anticipation as he leisurely perused her from top to bottom and back again. Would he accept, or had she been too forward? Had she blown it?

His lips quirked up in a devious grin as his hand settled on her breast. He brushed his fingers lazily back and forth over her nipple until she gasped with pleasure. "So tell me. What's your kink?"

Heat spread through her core. "Being bound. Flogged. Whipped. Paddled. Fucked." She lowered her gaze demurely. "To name a few."

He paused. "You like pain. I think I can help you with that." He pinched her nipple. Hard. Harder. Harder. Until she cried out, and her cunt squeezed from the excitement. "And your limits?"

Her body buzzing from arousal, she blinked to clear her foggy head. When Mistress Kay had inflicted pain upon her, she'd enjoyed it, but this...this was bliss. As if she was drunk, she could barely think coherently. "No bodily fluids. No cutting. Nothing that would cause permanent damage like branding. No knives. No fire or electrical play."

"Any triggers?"

She wanted to lie. After all, what was one more? But she couldn't. Not when it came to this. "No triggers that I know of, but I was physically abused by a relative."

His jaw tightened, and his eyes narrowed. "Tell me the asshole went to jail."

She swallowed over the lump that had formed in her throat. "No. He didn't."

He held her tighter to him. "Well if I ever meet the son of a bitch, I'm going to introduce him to my fist and teach him a lesson he'll never forget."

She expelled her breath in a giant *whoosh*. He was angry on her behalf. "You don't even know me."

He pulled back and cradled her face in his hands. "You're right. I don't. But as long as we're being honest,

I should tell you you're not the only one who felt a connection at the gym. I asked around after you, but no one knew who you were or how to find you. And now you're here. I might not know you yet, but something tells me I'm going to. However, first I need to know your name."

She hesitated, a fake name on the tip of her tongue. But something stopped her. She wasn't sure why, but a vision of them in an alley, steam rising from the grates, her back pushed up against the brick wall of the club, flashed through her mind. "No names. I just want you to fuck me like I've never been fucked before. Do you think you can handle that?"

He gulped audibly. "Do you do this a lot? Anonymous sex?"

Laugher bubbled up in her throat, but she stopped it before it released. Nothing was anonymous in her world. She had files on every partner she'd ever had between her thighs. Names, dates, history. Hell, their favorite brand of ice cream.

But here, now, with Sawyer, the idea of pretending she had no clue that this man was worth billions made her heart race and her pussy wet. She was always pretending anyway. Why couldn't she pretend she was a normal girl looking for a man to screw her to an explosive climax before parting ways?

But according to her file on Sawyer, stranger sex wasn't something he did. Sure, he might whip a girl ten minutes after negotiating the scene, but he never fucked an anonymous woman. Would she miss her chance if she asked for what she wanted?

She toyed with the ends of her hair, forgetting momentarily that she had added extensions. Her dirty blonde hair careened down her back like a waterfall. Last week, it had been in a coal black bob.

"I've never had sex with someone I don't know," she answered honestly.

Surprise registered in his eyes. "No names, then. For now."

He scratched his head, his fingers messing up his blond locks, making him look even sexier than before. He reminded her of a pirate commanding his ship, the wind at the sails and a crew at his disposal.

As she stared at him, raking her eyes over the bulging biceps down to the hard length pressing against the front of his pants, she could almost imagine him in a billowy shirt and pantaloons, like on the cover of a romance novel. And she could wear one of those dresses that blew in the wind, passion in her eyes as he took what he wanted without permission.

Why was she having these thoughts? She didn't read historical romance novels. Hell, she didn't believe in romance or love.

Her hand seemed to have a will of its own as she clutched the fabric of his shirt in her palm. "Show me what it's like to be owned by you."

He blinked, his chest rising and falling harshly. "We should probably go downstairs, but I don't think I can wait that long."

He grabbed her wrist and dragged her down a hall that led to a bathroom. "The club safe word is 'red.'

Remember, you may be giving me control, but as the sub, you have the power to stop the scene at any time by using the safe word. The pain I give you should enhance your pleasure, not eclipse it. If it ever crosses that line for you, I want you to tell me."

She only knew Sawyer was a Dominant, but she had no idea of the kinds of BDSM activities he enjoyed. "Are you a sadist?"

He shook his head as he opened the bathroom door and pulled her inside. "No, I wouldn't consider myself a sadist. I don't get off on hurting people just for the sake of it. My pleasure derives from giving my sub pleasure." His arm reached behind her to turn the lock. "I learned during my time in the Army that I preferred to be the one in charge during sex. Maybe it was because I had no control in any other aspect of my life at the time." He shrugged, a hungry glimmer in his eyes. "Who the hell knows where our sexual preferences come from? After basic training, a buddy of mine took me to a BDSM club, and from that point on, I was hooked. I stayed away from relationships. Never considered having a permanent sub." He backed her up against the door, his hard cock pressing against her pussy. "Until ten minutes ago. I don't know who the fuck sent you and who I need to thank, but right now, I don't fucking care. All I need to know is if you taste as good as I think you will."

He fell to his knees and raised her skirt to her waist, and then he ran his nose up her slit, inhaling deeply. "You smell like a dream." He didn't give her any time to think before he tore the gusset of her panties, exposing her folds to him. "Fuck. Bare for me. You are a dream." His tongue swiped up one lip and down the other before plunging between them and tonguing the well of her pussy. He moaned, the deep rumble of it vibrating through her. "I could eat you all day. But I won't. I can't. Because if I don't get inside that tight little pussy in a minute I'm going to fucking explode." He spread her lips apart and blew warm air on her clitoris.

Arousal trickled down her inner thigh. She was so wet. Wetter than she'd ever been. And she hadn't even come yet.

"But first, I need to hear you scream," he said just before his lips descended over the pearl of her clit.

She couldn't figure out what he was doing with that sinful mouth of his, but it felt as though he was licking and sucking and fingering all at the same time, even though his fingers were nowhere near her clitoris.

When he scraped his teeth against it, she lost control, her pussy fluttering and pulsating with climax. "Oh, yes. Yes." She bit her lip and pulled on his hair, pushing him tight against her pussy.

Before she came down from the high of her orgasm, he spun her around and smacked her ass cheek, bending her over the sink. Ribbons of heat unfurled inside her core, and even though she'd just come and come hard, her arousal spiked, his rough treatment like an aphrodisiac. The more dominance he exhibited over her body, the more forceful he became, the deeper she fell into a space where nothing else in the world mattered. By handing over her power to Sawyer, she was free from thought. Free from responsibilities. Free from guilt.

She watched in the mirror as he tore open a condom wrapper with his teeth. He drove inside her without warning, his cock stretching her beyond what she would've believed possible.

Sawyer hissed. "Fuck, it's as though you were made for my cock. You're perfect."

He filled her completely, his length hitting places she'd heard existed but had never yet experienced. It wasn't as if she hadn't had adventurous sex. She had. She'd done things with both men and women that would shock most people.

Yet here she was, having a man who didn't even know her name plow into her from behind, his balls slapping against her ass, his length sliding in and out of her as wet sucking sounds filled the bathroom, and something inside of her felt happy. It was as if Sawyer had woken up a part of her that had been sleeping.

He took her chin in his hand. "Watch us in the mirror. Watch as a stranger fucks you. Do you like this? Like not knowing my name? I could be anyone. You could be anyone. Just two people using each other to get off."

Her heart hammered in her chest, her breasts bouncing with each forceful thrust. His jeans rubbed her skin, reminding her he hadn't even bothered to lower his pants. Just unzipped them and pulled his dick out before fucking her.

It was dirty as hell, and she fucking loved every minute of it.

"I wish I didn't have to wear a condom," he continued, murmuring into her neck. "I'd shoot my come in your cunt, so that when you left here, I'd still be deep inside you. Dripping out of you, down your legs because I tore your panties."

She whimpered. A goddamned whimper.

Who was this man?

He dropped his hand from her chin and curled it around her hip to cup her mound, pressing on her swollen bud. He pinched it, the pain driving up her arousal to another level. Unlike the pain she'd experienced from her father's abuse, this pain was in her power to stop.

He changed his angle, his hand splayed on the middle of her spine, pressing her lower, her ass higher, so that each thrust hit a place inside her that made her moan and tremble uncontrollably.

"You gonna come for me? You getting off by being fucked by a stranger? You'll leave here and never know if you'll see me again. I could be anyone. Anywhere. Anytime." He fisted her hair and yanked her head back, exposing the line of her throat in the mirror. "I want to feel that tight pussy get even tighter. I want you to come for me. Let me know what my cock does to you, my filthy stranger."

She wasn't sure if it was his command or the tone of his voice, but a tightening in her lower belly radiated outward until she exploded in a rainbow of colors, dizzy from the waves of pleasure permeating like lava throughout her body.

"That's it," he crooned in her ear, "come all over my cock. I can feel you spilling out. Fuck, you drenched me." His thrusting suddenly stopped, and he groaned, long and loud, as his chest covered her back and his dick pulsed inside of her with the force of his release. His teeth sunk into the soft spot between her neck and shoulder as a rumble tore from his throat. "Never come so hard in my life." He released the hold on her hair and slipped from her pussy, pulling off the condom and tying it before throwing it in the wastebasket.

The moment she straightened, he spun her around, and his lips covered hers, surprising her with their gentleness. He kissed her like a lover rather than a quick fuck in the dirty bathroom of a BDSM club. Like she mattered to him. Like she wasn't a stranger.

She was in so much trouble.

She wrapped her arms around his neck and held on for dear life as he stole everything she thought she knew away from her.

Just who was conning who?

She had to regain control of this situation or she'd never come out of this with her heart intact. A heart she hadn't known was possible to lose because she'd never known she had one.

Thinking back to his file, she recalled what she knew about him. He was twenty-four years old and had recently returned to the United States after serving in the Army. The man didn't need to serve his country, but when his parents had died in a car accident, he'd become the youngest billionaire in the world. The tabloids went wild, following him around like he was Prince Harry rather than a scared orphan and a sudden CEO of a multi-billion-dollar corporation. Before that, he'd been a regular teenager who had graduated high school as valedictorian and planned to go to Cal Tech and major in computer engineering.

The world as he'd known it had changed in a single night. Instead of going to college as he'd planned, the man disappeared from radar. Apparently, he had run off and joined the Army to avoid the scrutiny of the American public. When he returned four years later, he quietly immersed himself in Hayes Industries, learning the business inside and out before announcing his position as CEO and growing an already large corporation into a global empire.

From all reports, he'd never had a long-term relationship, preferring ménages and contracts with submissives. He wasn't a sadist, but he had no problem wielding a whip or flogging a woman. He was warm and personable, extremely flirtatious, but behind the act was a man who always stayed in control.

All too soon, his mouth left hers. She pressed her fingertips to her swollen lips and looked up at him, spellbound by the intensity reflected in his brown eyes.

He dragged his hand through his hair and held her captive with his stare. "Sawyer Hayes. That's my name."

His eyes dared her to recognize him, but she played it cool. She wouldn't lie, because he'd never believe she didn't know him. But she certainly wasn't going to fawn over him like a fan girl at a Justin Bieber meet-and-greet.

"Nice to meet you, Sawyer. Thanks for the orgasms." She smiled, flashing her teeth, and rolled her skirt down over her hips to cover herself. Her underwear remained on, despite the gaping hole in the gusset.

He zipped up his jeans and clenched his jaw, his arms crossing his chest. "Thanks for the orgasms? That's all I get?"

He pulled her away from the sink and spun her so that her back hit the door. Holding her wrists, he pinned her hands over her head and leaned into her, grinding his erection against her lower belly.

How the hell had he gotten so hard so quickly? Didn't he require any recovery time like normal guys?

Then again, nothing about Sawyer Hayes was normal.

His eyes locked with hers. "I want to see you again. I want to taste you again. I want to fuck you again." He paused, licking his lips as his chest rose and fell. "Just tell me your name."

Her breathing synchronized with his, a stirring between her thighs awakening once more. His eyes weren't an ordinary brown. They reminded her of pennies in a fountain, the sun gleaming off them. He held a world of secrets in those eyes. Secrets she'd harvest for her own gain.

She opened up her mouth to give him the name of Lisa Smith, the one she would use for this con. But as his eyes held hers in their grasp, everything else in the world disappeared. "Annaliese Hunt," she whispered. The danger of the words dawned on her the moment they escaped from her lips.

She had given him her real name

Chapter Four

Present Day

SAWYER HAYES FUCKING smelled the same. There were no words to describe it. Not musky or woodsy or spicy or anything else she could compare it to. It was just him. Her Master.

If she could've bottled that man's scent, she would have. As it was, she'd taken a couple of his shirts with her when she'd left. She slept with those shirts on her pillow for months, until his scent finally disappeared. But she'd never forgotten it.

He smelled like heaven.

And it was hell.

Her stomach pitched, nervous knots twisting inside of her. She couldn't decide whether she wanted to run away or run into his arms. But he was holding her hand, her small one in his large rough one, not giving her a choice.

"Where are you taking me?" Lisa asked as Sawyer dragged her toward the mansion that housed Benediction.

They'd left a speechless Logan and Rachel behind at the reception. And Rachel was never speechless. Lisa couldn't imagine the kinds of questions her reporter friend would have for her.

"To talk," he said flatly.

She tried to stop, but it was impossible in her four-inch heels. "I don't want to talk to you."

"Tough. You owe me at least a five-minute conversation. After all, you are still my wife."

Semantics.

They'd been separated for four years. Not a legal separation, but one caused by her packing a single suitcase in the middle of the day when he was at work and leaving him without a trace.

It was one of the worst days of her life, one that she didn't like to think about because the pain of it still caused her to fall to pieces. She hadn't wanted to leave him. But she'd had no choice.

If she hadn't left, he would be dead. And she would rather live her life miserably alone knowing he was safe than live with the knowledge she'd caused his death.

"How did you find me?" she said, stumbling into the den of the home. "Or is it just a coincidence that we've run into each other tonight?"

"Did you think I wouldn't recognize my own wife in a photograph? You should have been more careful if you didn't want to be found." He tugged her into a library of sorts, with books lining the walls, and he slammed the door, closing them in together. "Perhaps that's it. Perhaps you wanted me to find you."

His eyes were blank, like nothing she'd ever seen on him before. He didn't look at her as though he hated her, either. His eyes were empty. And she knew then she'd caused that. All those years ago, she'd helped heal the sorrow and emptiness that filled his life after his parents' deaths and had replaced them with love and hope. Now, none of those emotions reflected in his dark brown irises. Gone was the light that had shone through his copper eyes.

Without even knowing it, he'd taught her that she was worth more than being a puppet for her parents. She could be more. Do more. She didn't need to con people to make a living. He'd broken the walls around her heart and freed it. But he didn't know any of it. Because she could never tell him who she really was or why she'd left him without a good-bye.

"So you found me." She shrugged, not looking at him, but instead keeping her gaze on the books behind him, her hands clenched at her sides.

Looking at him was painful. He was the most beautiful man in the world to her, inside and out. To see him and not be able to touch him...to not be able to seal her lips over his and taste him, stung like a thousand wasp bites to her heart.

She missed the nights when, after they'd made love, they'd stayed up and talked for hours about everything and nothing. Her past had remained a secret, lies filling the void where the truth would ruin everything they'd forged between them. But with him she'd created hopes and dreams of a future she'd never thought possible.

"Yeah, I found you. Fucking knocked me off my ass when Logan and Rachel told me they knew you. I mean, what were the odds that you'd be in Detroit and end up helping to defend my best friend against murder charges."

"I hardly defended him. That was Kate's job. I just wrangled together the press conference." Because of her past, she'd avoided having her picture taken, but she'd slipped up when her photo recently appeared in newspapers across the country. At that time, her only thought had been of her friends. Working in public relations wasn't the best job for a woman trying to stay out of the way of a camera, but something about the career had called to her. It was what she'd imagined doing with her life when she'd been with Sawyer.

Unfortunately, after she left him, she'd had to lie low for a while, which was why she took the job as a secretary at a law firm and kept herself looking as nondescript as possible. Mousy is how she'd overheard a couple of female co-workers describing her in the bathroom when they hadn't known she was already in one of the stalls.

Settling in Detroit hadn't been random. She had remembered him talking about an Army buddy who had gone to law school after they'd left the military. Sawyer had been envious that Logan was able to follow his dreams, while he was responsible for thousands of employees and stockholders. He hadn't wanted to become CEO of Hayes Industries. He'd wanted to go into computer programming and create educational video games that children would enjoy so much that they wouldn't care they were also learning.

She hadn't remembered Logan's name, but a piece of her felt closer to Sawyer by living in the same city as his best friend. Who knows? Maybe a part of her had hoped she'd run into him again. But at what price?

If Sawyer had found her, how many others had recognized her? What if her family had seen the photo?

The panic that had held her in its grips earlier returned with a vengeance. "Were you watching me earlier?"

He frowned and ran his hand across the blond stubble lining his jaw. "No. I didn't get the chance to observe you in your natural habitat before running into you. Why?"

"No reason," she said quickly, not wanting to pull him into the mess of her life. "Just tell me what you want, so I can get back out there. I've got a wedding reception to run."

He stalked closer, bringing with him the scent of bergamot and orange. It was a scent she'd know anywhere and one she'd forever associate with Sawyer. He still used the same shampoo. It shouldn't surprise her. After all, it was one of Hayes Industries' most popular products.

"I want to know what you did with the money you took from our joint bank accounts. Someone worth millions wouldn't work as a secretary at a law firm or go into public relations. You shouldn't need to work. You should be living in a house rather than a small condo and own a car that doesn't have more than a hundred thousand miles on it. And you only have ten thousand in your checking account, three thousand in your savings account, and nothing else worth a dime."

She swallowed over the lump in her throat. "You did your homework on me, didn't you?"

"Didn't do it the first time with you, but I won't make the same mistake again." His lips curled into a cruel grin. "Nowadays, I always make sure I know exactly who I'm taking into my bed."

Her heart shattered into a million pieces. It shouldn't hurt her to hear that he had lovers. After all, she'd left him more than four years ago. She couldn't have expected him to stay celibate for that long.

It didn't matter that they were still legally married.

Or that she hadn't taken a lover in all that time.

"I don't have your money. And I can't tell you what I did with it." She peered up at him, flinching at the indifference on his face. "I'm sorry. I didn't mean to hurt you. But I did what I had to do. I was a con artist."

He went as still as a statue, his expression as stony. Then his chest convulsed with laugher, shocking her with its force. "Hurt me? I didn't give a shit about you leaving. Only my pride took a hit, because I hadn't realized what a lying bitch I'd married. And when you left, I realized what we had wasn't that great anyway. I mean, you were a great fuck, but I wasn't cut out for monogamy. You did me a favor by leaving." He gently pushed her up against the shelves, knocking a couple books to the carpet.

Her stomach clenched painfully. She shouldn't allow his words to hurt as much as they did. After all, he had a right to be angry.

The ten months she'd spent with Sawyer were the happiest she'd ever known. From the day they'd officially met, they'd been inseparable. Within weeks, she'd moved into his home, and it hadn't taken much longer for her to wear both his collar and his ring. It was a whirlwind romance intensified by their relationship as Master and slave.

They never seemed to run out of things to talk about. He considered her opinions and encouraged her dream of becoming a publicist, offering her a job within the Hayes Industries organization. He'd brought her sexual fantasies to life and never judged her for them. For the first time in her life, she'd been in love and loved in return.

For a while, she let herself forget that their relationship had been built on a lie. But her father had been all too eager to remind her. Once she became Sawyer's wife and he changed his will, leaving his entire estate to her in case of his death, her father had revealed his true plan: Murder Sawyer.

Seeing no other options, she had done the one thing she could do to save Sawyer's life.

She'd taken all the assets of Sawyer's she could quickly get her hands on and had given them to her father. Then she had stolen her father's black list—a journal documenting years of her family's cons—as an insurance policy and left her old life behind, Sawyer included. Within those pages were details about some very dangerous people. People who would kill her father slowly and painfully if they ever got the chance. Just as she had taken the black list as her insurance, it had provided the same to her father against those who wished him harm.

Her plan hadn't been foolproof, but she'd done what she thought was best at the time. She'd thought Sawyer would divorce her when she left him, but he hadn't.

As long as she had the ability to inherit Sawyer's estate, he was in danger. Now that he was back in her life, there was one more thing she could do to ensure his safety.

She squared her shoulders. "If I did you a favor by leaving, then you won't mind giving me a divorce."

He flinched, the first crack in his armor that she'd witnessed tonight. "That's what you want?"

Her breath stalled in her chest. "Y-yes."

A divorce was the last thing she wanted, but it was what they needed. She should have done it years ago, but she couldn't be the one to file, since she would be required by law to give her address.

A slow grin appeared on his face. "What will you give me for the divorce?"

She'd gotten butterflies every time he'd smiled at her in the past, but this time, a lead weight filled her belly. "Give you?"

He toyed with the ends of her short brown hair, his fingers restless. "You took that money from me. Even though you legally had every right to it, you played me to get it. You owe me. And I'm here to collect."

"I told you, I don't have the money. You saw it yourself. I own nothing. There's no way I can repay you." She took a deep breath, trying not to let his nearness affect her.

His hands framed her face. "I don't want money. There are other, more pleasurable ways to collect on the debt you owe me."

"What are you suggesting?" she asked, afraid of his answer.

"Seven nights. Same soft and hard limits as before."

Her heart sped up, making her breathless. Out of all the things she expected him to say, that wasn't one of them. "So if I make love to you for seven nights, you'll grant me a divorce and forgive the debt I owe you?"

He laughed. "What we'll do could never be classified as 'making love.' We'll fuck. I set the scenes. And you can do what you do best." His expression turned cold once more, while his eyes seared into her. "Pretend."

It shouldn't have hurt as much as it did. Like Sawyer had reached inside her chest cavity and squeezed her heart in his hand.

She could barely get the words off her tongue. "Role play. If you hate me so much, why do you want to fuck me again?" she asked. "I would think a divorce is exactly what you'd want. At Benediction, you have an entire sex club of women at your disposal."

The idea of him with another woman twisted her insides, but it would be much harder to take him inside her body again and not show him how much she loved him.

She wasn't that good of an actress.

"I already have an entire sex club of women at my disposal. Didn't Rachel and Logan tell you about their time at Paradise Found?"

Rachel had mentioned she and Logan had hid at Paradise Found, Logan's friend's club in Las Vegas, and Rachel had described to her at length the sinful things she'd seen there. "You own a sex club?"

"Why does that surprise you? You know better than anyone how much I enjoy a good fuck. Once you left, I considered myself a free agent." His lips tightened into a straight line, his eyes flat. "You didn't actually think I'd wait for you, did you?"

"No," she whispered. "Why would you? You were right. Our marriage vows meant nothing. You had every right to sleep with as many women as you wanted." She looked him straight in the eyes. "And I had the right to sleep with anyone I wanted, as well."

He didn't give her a warning before slamming her up against the bookshelf. If there had been any change in his eyes, anything other than the coldness still lingering, she would've believed he was jealous.

His scent and heat wrapped her in an embrace even as she tried to resist the spell he held over her.

She thought about what Rachel had told her about Paradise Found. She'd mentioned that Logan's friends were into ménage. Did that include Sawyer? While she had remained faithful, had he been indulging in wild sex parties and threesomes?

Sawyer braced a hand over her head, looming over her as he boxed her in. "For the next seven nights, you belong to me. You don't fuck anyone else. You don't even think about fucking someone else. Your nights are mine. Your body is mine. Do it, and I'll grant you a divorce and forgive your debt. You won't ever have to worry about me again."

Seven nights. It wouldn't be that easy to get him out of her system. Despite what he thought, she'd worry about him for the rest of her life. For the next week, the pleasure he'd bestow would be a living hell for her. It was punishment for her sins. It was no less than what she deserved.

She gave a sigh of resignation. "It's a deal."

A flash of heat banked in his eyes before it disappeared. "What's your name?"

Puzzled, she frowned. Why was he asking her name when he already knew it?

As she stared up at the man who haunted her dreams, the memory of their first night together slammed into her. Did he want to pretend they were strangers again?

She almost laughed. If only they could be.

"No names," she said, waiting for his response to see if she was correct.

He pressed himself against her, letting her feel his erection. Thank God he wasn't as immune to her as he appeared. She wouldn't be able to handle it if he was. Then again, it was just sex, wasn't it? And for a man who owned a sex club and had been with multiple women since she'd left him, sex meant nothing. She couldn't forget that. She couldn't allow herself to become confused about what this was.

This was Sawyer's revenge. Other than to remind her of all she'd lost, she didn't know exactly what he hoped to accomplish by bending her to his will for seven nights. But if it was the only way to save him, she'd do it.

"Have you ever fucked a stranger before?" he asked huskily.

She shook her head, her throat suddenly dry.

"You like that idea?" he continued. "Does it make you wet?"

The idea of fucking a stranger didn't make her wet. It was the idea of fucking Sawyer that had soaked her thighs.

He didn't wait for her to answer. "Show me. Lift up the hem of your dress and check."

Without thought, she clenched the fabric of her dress in her fists, raising it up her legs inch by inch and exposing her pussy.

"Dirty girl. You're not wearing any panties. You were waiting to be fucked, weren't you?"

Assuming it was a rhetorical question, she didn't bother answering, keeping the fantasy alive rather than explaining she had gone without because of fashion. Visible panty lines would've killed the look of the dress.

Keeping the fabric bunched up at the waist with one hand, she used the other to stroke over her folds. She was drenched.

It didn't surprise her. Not only had she gone without sex for more than four years, this was Sawyer. How many times had she brought herself to climax over the years by replaying their time together?

But her memories had nothing on the real thing.

He shocked her by dropping to his knees in front of her and holding her dress up so she could free her other hand. "Keep going. I want to see you touch yourself."

Her shyness took a backseat to the deep throbbing need that had her circling her clit with two fingers and gathering her wetness with two others. The sight of a strong man like Sawyer on his knees in front of her made her feel powerful in this powerless situation.

What was wrong with indulging in the fantasy that they were strangers? That they didn't have a past hanging over them like a storm cloud. Right now they were strangers, not a wife in love with a husband who despised her.

He grabbed her wrist and brought her soaked fingers to his closed mouth, smearing her arousal over his lips and making them glossy. Then, emitting a rumble of approval, he slowly and methodically glided his tongue along the plumpness of his lips, like her taste was a treat to be savored. The fingers on her clit were a pale comparison to the visual, and she shook from the heat that flooded her body.

Sawyer lowered his face between her curls and inhaled deeply, his eyes fluttering shut momentarily and strands of his blond hair tickling the inside of her thighs. She was desperate to feel his mouth on her, aching for his touch.

And then she didn't have to wait anymore.

He parted her labia, and his head descended, his hot tongue running up her slit before lapping at her clitoris with the precision of an expert.

She threw her head back against the books and covered her lips with her hand, muffling her cries of ecstasy.

He stopped his ministrations, lifting his face from her pussy to look up at her. "Take that hand away from your fuckable mouth. Those noises you're holding inside belong to me, and goddamn it, I want to hear them. Let me hear how much you like my tongue."

She gasped as he pushed a thick finger inside her and returned his tongue to the exact spot where she needed it.

"Oh God. Yes." Her muscles clenched as she approached climax. "I don't like your tongue. I fucking love it."

"So tight," he murmured against her folds. "If I didn't know better, I would think you haven't been fucked in a while."

"I haven't," she whispered, too far gone to think about what she had admitted.

He stilled. "How long? How long has it been since you've had anyone inside of you?"

Panic clouded her thoughts. "I don't—"

"How long?" he asked gruffly.

"Four years." She held his gaze, marveling at the intensity burning in them. "It's been four years since I've had anyone or anything inside of me. No fingers. No tongue. No vibrator. No cock. No one since my husband."

He blew out a breath. "You've stayed faithful."

His body slackened. The lines of tension on his face disappeared, replaced by a slight grin. There was something dangerous about the way he looked at her, a spark of light in his eyes as if he had hope.

Did he still love her? Or was he hoping to use her love for him against her?

Either way, she couldn't let him know how deeply she cared for him or what lengths she'd go to in order to keep him safe.

"I've stayed faithful only because the opportunity never presented itself."

A crease between his brows formed. "If that's what you tell yourself to sleep at night, go ahead and believe it. But you and I both know if you had wanted to get laid, you could've walked into any bar and picked someone up for the night."

She didn't know how to respond. He was right. Sex had never been something she had to work hard at getting. That's one of the reasons she had been successful as a con. She'd attracted both men and women since she first began using her sexuality as a tool at eighteen.

"You don't know me, and I don't know you. Tonight we're two strangers without a past." Unable to stop herself, she raked her fingers through his hair. "Please. Just let it go for one night."

He shuddered as if he was affected by her touch. "Just for tonight. But this conversation is far from over." Shooting to his feet, he snatched her wrist away from his head and turned her around to face to bookcase. He snaked an arm around her middle and pushed on her back with his other until she was bent over, her hands braced on the shelves.

A hard smack on her bare ass sent ripples of heat darting through her as she remembered the first time he'd spanked her. The way he'd bent her over the sink. The way he'd thrust into her from behind. He was truly recreating that night.

But for what purpose?

She trembled at the telltale sound of the condom wrapper ripping and waited impatiently for his next move.

"Sorry." Sawyer leaned over her, his cock nudging her opening. He still wore his clothes, the fabric of his dress shirt rubbing against her back. "This is going to be hard and fast."

He entered her, the burning invasion stretching her just beyond comfortable. But she didn't care. It had been so long since she'd had anyone filling her, and the fact that it was Sawyer almost brought tears to her eyes.

Sex had never been their problem. Even while engaging in role play, it had been the one honest thing between them. They'd silently bared their souls completely each and every time they'd made love. But as soon as they were done, the guilt over her lies had nearly shredded her.

And she was still lying.

Sawyer groaned as his cock slid deeper inside of her, eased by her slippery arousal. He curled his hand under her and played with her clit as he slammed into her over and over again, pushing her onto the balls of her feet with every thrust.

It was all too much—the sensation of him filling her, the scraping of his fingernail on her clit, the scratch of his slacks on her thighs—she couldn't hold back even if she wanted to.

What started out as a flutter in her lower belly grew into a full-out body quake. Her muscles tensed and her eyes flew shut as her pussy clenched and released relentlessly. Heat spread throughout her core, and the waves of bliss shattered her, leaving her breathless and broken.

Before she recovered, a silent Sawyer stilled behind her, the only movement that of his cock twitching inside her as his come jetted into the condom.

Reality of the situation crept its way into her consciousness like a fifty-pound weight sitting on her chest.

How could she handle six more nights with him when already a part of her clamored to tell him the truth about why she left?

But the truth could get him killed. She couldn't forget that for a second.

Sawyer's heat disappeared, leaving her chilled and confused. He slid her dress back over her thighs before issuing his gravelly command. "Clear your schedule for the week, Annaliese. Starting tomorrow, you're mine."

Chapter Five

KEYS IN HAND, Lisa climbed the stairs up to her condo. The night of Cole and Danielle's wedding turned out to be the longest night of Lisa's life.

After Sawyer had ordered her to be available to him for the week, he'd stormed out of the room. In a fog and questioning whether she'd really made love to her husband or imagined it, she found her way to the guest bathroom, where one look in the mirror gave her confirmation. Her hair was mussed, her cheeks flushed, her eyes glassy. Anyone who looked at her would know she'd just been fucked hard and good.

She'd spent a few minutes setting herself back to rights and returned to the reception, where she stayed busy, both to avoid Rachel's questions and to keep her mind off the deal she'd made with Sawyer. What she couldn't avoid was the sensation of Sawyer's gaze on her. Even as the night cooled the air, it had made her hot and kept her painfully aware of the delicious soreness between her legs.

At least he'd had the decency to leave the party right after dinner.

With sunrise on the horizon, all she wanted to do right now was slide into bed and sleep for the next eight hours. She needed a clear head to figure out how she could get out of her arrangement with Sawyer. There was no way in hell she could go through with it.

Her first instinct was to run. After having spent most of her life doing just that, the compunction about packing up her belongings and making a fresh start under a new identity pressed hard on her. As Sawyer's presence suggested, her past was catching up with her.

Who else might have recognized her from the photograph? If Sawyer found her, could the rest be far behind?

But if she ran now, she'd miss the life she'd built for herself these past few years. There was nothing like getting paid to manipulate and orchestrate. She'd been born for public relations. Or maybe if she'd had a different set of parents, she would've ended up as an attorney. As she'd observed working at the law firm, lawyers did plenty of manipulation and orchestration in their jobs.

Barely able to keep her eyes open, she leaned against the doorframe as she stuck the key into the lock. But before she turned it, the door moved inward as if it had already been unlocked and opened. She pinched the bridge of her nose and thought back to the prior day. She'd been in a rush to get to Benediction, carrying multiple bags with her as she left.

Was it possible she'd forgotten to shut the door?

She pushed it open, the porch lamp throwing a sliver of light into her condo's entryway. A streak of crimson on the carpet caught her eye.

Was that blood?

Her hands began to tremble, and her heart pounded.

Suddenly, she was wide awake.

She inched inside, leaving the door open, and flicked on the lights. Like she'd been punched in the chest, all the breath left her lungs as she took in the mess of her condo.

Splashes of blood-red paint stained the white walls and beige carpeting, its cloying scent obvious now that she stepped inside.

She continued farther into her home, stopping at the kitchen, where garbage had been strewn everywhere. Flies buzzed around the pile of rotten food covering her kitchen table. Gagging on the rancid smell, she covered her mouth and hurried out of the room.

Her couch cushions had been sliced, pieces of foam and cotton littering the room, and her television had been shattered as if hit with a baseball bat. Her bookshelves were now bare, her beloved books ripped apart and covered with the red paint.

Thank goodness she hadn't hidden her black list on those shelves. Perhaps it was time for her to put it in a safe deposit box at the bank.

But what if she had to leave suddenly?

No, she had to keep it accessible. For now, it was safe.

She briefly closed her eyes, terrified of what she'd find in her bedroom, but she had to see. Had to know.

Whatever had been done couldn't be any worse than the images playing through her mind right then, the worst of it being that the intruder was still in there.

This was no ordinary break-in. There was rage behind the chaos.

Since there was no sign of forced entry, whoever did it either knew how to pick her lock or had gotten her key.

Determined to stay calm, she held her breath and strode into her private sanctuary.

All her clothes were piled onto her bed and had been slashed and covered with paint. She inched closer, sensing something different about the mound of soiled fabric. It almost seemed alive, as if the fabric itself was stirring.

Breathing.

A piece of paper floated down onto the floor.

Although her instincts screamed for her to flee, she wouldn't crumble. Whatever this was, she would handle it. Alone. Just as she always did.

She commanded her feet to move and stretched out her arm, snatching the paper. The intruder left her a message written in block print.

Gotcha.

She'd been found.

But why had he or she gone through all this trouble, rather than call the police on her or kill her?

This felt like a dangerous game of cat and mouse. Whoever it was wanted to play with her before he finished her off.

Something caught her eye from the heap of clothes. Something black that appeared and disappeared before she could blink.

Clutching the letter in one hand, she gingerly lifted a couple pieces of fabric with the other, praying she wouldn't find anything. Her wrist tickling, she scratched it, but the irritation persisted. Not seeing anything on the bed, she continued to move her clothes. A black blob crawled and spread.

No, not a blob.

Ants.

Hundreds of them. Maybe thousands.

Her gaze fell upon her wrist.

Black ants crawled over it.

Slapping at her hand, she backed out of the room until she slammed into a solid form.

A person.

She screamed as she spun around and punched the intruder in the gut. She was raising her leg, preparing to knee him in the nuts, when she realized his identity.

Sawyer.

"What the hell are you doing here?" she asked, noticing he'd changed from his suit into jeans and a white button-down shirt with the sleeves rolled, exposing his forearms.

The timing of his arrival tonight and this break-in couldn't be a coincidence.

Was that why he'd left the wedding reception early? To ransack her condo and terrify her as a means of revenge?

Sawyer bent at his knees, and the next thing she knew, he had her airborne and hanging over his shoulder in a fireman hold as he stormed down the hallway. "I think the more important question is what the hell is going on? Who did this?"

The nerve of him! Who did he think he was coming in here and playing hero? It set her nerves on edge.

She tried wiggling off him, but he smacked her butt and held her tighter. "Why don't you tell me? I've lived here quietly for the past several years without incident, and in one night, I run into you and then come home to this." Her dress slid up her thighs. If he didn't put her down soon, she'd flash her neighbors.

He brought her outside and practically dropped her on her feet. "You think I had something to do with this?"

Slightly dizzy from hanging upside down, she leaned on the brick wall of her condo for support. "I don't believe in coincidences."

"Well, believe me when I tell you this." He tipped up her chin, forcing her to look at his face. "I had nothing to do with it. And to prove it to you, I'm going to call 911, like you should've done as soon as you realized someone had broken into your place." He stepped away from her and pulled a phone from his pocket.

Panic surging, she grabbed his wrist. "No, don't call the police."

"Are you serious?" He covered her hand with his own. "Annaliese—"

"Stop calling me that. My name is Lisa now." She couldn't handle the way her body reacted when he said her real name. As if it belonged in his arms. Preferably naked. She had to stay detached if she was going to save them both.

His jaw tightened. "You'll always be Annaliese to me, and right now, you're still my wife. So that makes you my responsibility."

His wife in name only. She'd never truly belonged to him, and she never would. "I'm no one's responsibility but my own. I'll deal with this mess. You can go now." She whipped her hand away from him and gestured to the parking lot.

He squinted at her arm. "What is up with the ants crawling on you?"

Smacking the ants off her, she shuddered. Even if she managed to kill all the bugs, she'd still feel them on her skin until she showered. "Check the bed. Someone left them as a present for me. I hate ants. Always have."

He paused, folding his arms across his chest, and glared, assessing her. "This isn't random, is it?"

In her view, nothing was random. Everything had its reason, and everyone had a motive. "No. Whoever did this wanted to scare me."

And it had worked, although she'd never admit it out loud, even to Sawyer. Especially to Sawyer. If she gave into her urge to turn to him for comfort, she wasn't sure if she could ever make herself leave again. But she wasn't the submissive Annaliese anymore, the girl who'd worshipped the ground Sawyer walked upon. She was Lisa. Cool. Collected. Capable. "It's someone from my past."

"How do you know?"

"Because he left a note." Damn, she'd left it inside on the floor of her room. "All it said was 'gotcha,' but I think I can safely assume this wasn't a random break-in."

"Pissed off a few people, have you?" He casually rubbed the blond scruff lining his jaw, but there was nothing casual about the fire in his eyes.

Good. At least it was something. She couldn't stand the dispassionate blankness his gaze had exuded at Benediction. If she was going to figure out how to get rid of him, she needed to be able to read him well, like she had all those years ago. She need him riled up. Angry at her. "Did you think you're the only one I conned in my lifetime? There's at least a half dozen people who would pay to kill me."

He stalked toward her and grabbed her shoulders, backing her up against the wall. "And how many of them did you marry?"

As he looked down at her, breathing heavily, his eyes full of lust, she couldn't lie. "Only one. Only you."

His eyelids fluttered shut, and he buried his nose into the side of her neck, inhaling deeply as if taking in her scent. "Guess that's something, huh? I'm special, then." She swore she felt his lips caress her skin before he lifted his head and gazed into her eyes. "So why don't you want to call the police?"

"What am I going to tell them? There's a handful of people who want me dead because I cleaned out their bank accounts? There's no reason to call them. I don't need them asking questions and looking into Lisa Smith's background. I've survived this long by keeping my head low and staying out of trouble. I'll hire a crew to clean up the place, and I'll change my locks." Or run far away where no one would ever find her again.

This time she wouldn't let her guard down. She'd go back to the persona of a mousy secretary and not think that she could have a semi-regular life with friends and a career. She hated the idea of leaving the friends who had become more like a family to her than her actual blood relatives.

He toyed with the ends of her hair. "Do you have any clothes to change into?"

"Yeah, I have a bag in the car with the clothes I wore as I set up the wedding. Why?"

"Because it looks like everything you own has been ruined, and as sexy as you look in that dress," he said, his gaze raking down the length of her body, "I doubt you want to wear it at the hotel."

No way could she stay in his hotel room.

It was hard enough to pretend she didn't still love him, but the more time she spent with him, the harder it would be to maintain the charade. "Hotel? I'm not going—"

"You are." He spoke as if she didn't have a choice, which if they were in a scene would really turn her on, but in the real world only managed to piss her off. "You're going to stay with me until we figure out who did this to your condo. It's not safe for you to be alone right now."

"I don't think that would work out too well. I can stay with a friend until my place is cleaned."

He snaked an arm around her waist and tugged her to him, bending to whisper in her ear. "Have you already forgotten your promise to me? I own you for seven days, and that means if I want you staying with me, you'll stay with me."

She shivered. It had nothing to do with the night air and everything to do with his display of dominance. "Six. Last night was the first, so we have six nights left."

He chuckled. "Last night didn't count. You hadn't agreed to my terms yet. So seven."

Intending to push him away, she placed a hand on his chest but instead found herself drawing closer. "Have you always been this bossy?"

"Yes. You never minded it before." He tipped up her chin, his thumb caressing her cheek. "In fact, I remember you loving my bossiness, especially that time when we played CEO and the secretary."

"In my defense, you made a hot secretary."

He bit her earlobe. "Maybe next time, I'll let you be the secretary."

She fought against the wave of pleasure rolling through her pussy. "So cliché."

"There's nothing cliché about you and me. Now are you coming with me, or do I have to pick you up and carry you again?"

She was losing control.

Control of her body.

Control of her mind.

Control of her emotions.

Grappling to regain some sense of restraint, she moved away from him and crossed her arms over her chest, as if that would give her some protection from him. "How do

I know this isn't all part of some wicked plan for revenge against me? You make me fear for my life, you swoop in as the hero, and then steal me away so you can cut me up into a million tiny pieces and feed me to the fish."

He shook his head and snorted. "I'm the owner of a multi-billion-dollar conglomerate, not a mafia enforcer. And if you still don't believe it wasn't me who did this to your condo, talk to the people working the front desk at the hotel last night. They can vouch for when I arrived and when I left." He clenched his jaw. "Is that what you need to trust me?"

Trust him? How could she trust him when she'd spent her entire life telling herself that everyone had a motive to lie?

But at this point, she didn't have a choice. She needed him to divorce her.

She had to see their agreement through.

Even if it destroyed her.

Chapter Six

"NICE ROOM," LISA quipped, standing right inside the door of Sawyer's penthouse suite. The suite came with two bedrooms, a living room with a long S-shaped couch, a large desk, and a full kitchen with stainless steel appliances.

Why did a single man need all this space? And how long had he planned on staying?

As if he couldn't get enough distance between them, he stomped past her, draping his jacket on the back of the couch before leaning on the wall across the room from her.

This hot and cold act from him was annoying her. One moment he couldn't take his hands off her, and the next he kept his distance.

Maybe she wasn't the only one who was confused.

He stuck his hands in his pockets. "Just because I lost billions of dollars doesn't mean I'm not rich."

She jolted. "I didn't take billions from you."

Just a few million dollars. It was still a crime, but it wasn't as if he didn't have money to spare. What did he mean that he'd lost billions?

"Didn't say you did." He rubbed his jaw distractedly and then gestured to the open door beside him. "Anyway, make yourself at home. You can take this room. Use the shower, and get some sleep."

Clearly, he wanted to change the subject. She filed it away for later, along with the dozens of other questions she had for him. The problem with asking him questions was it opened the door for him to ask *her* questions. Questions she couldn't answer, no matter how much she wanted to.

The sun had already risen high in the morning sky, its rays streaming through the wall of windows. Although she wanted to take a long hot shower to wash the creepy-crawly sensation of bugs from her skin, she couldn't afford to be alone with her thoughts.

She decided to take a play from his rule book, avoiding eye contact and remaining detached as she went into her temporary bedroom and dropped the bag with her clothes on the bed. "I don't have time to sleep. I have to get to work."

And away from him before she did anything stupid like confess everything.

He loomed in the doorway, gripping both sides of it as if the entire room would collapse if he let go. "It's Sunday. And I thought I told you to clear your schedule."

"Yes, well, despite your insistence otherwise, you don't own me. I need to go into the office and finish up some things if I'm going to take time off this week." She headed into the bathroom, expecting him to give her some privacy.

No such luck. He followed her in and turned on the shower. "Anything changing between now and this afternoon?"

Other than losing a bit more control over her life? She sighed, too exhausted anymore to fight. "No."

"Then you'll get a few hours of sleep before you go," he said decisively. "But first, let's take a shower."

He peeled off his shirt, gifting her with the first glance of what her husband hid underneath his clothes.

Her mouth grew dry even as the room filled with steam. When she'd known Sawyer before, he'd been toned and lean, but he looked completely different now. His chest was wider than she remembered, his arms thick with muscles. Her gaze followed the light trail of hair leading from his chest down his abdomen, where she could make out the sharp contours of those muscles. She wanted to lick a path down and see if she couldn't sate her thirst from the moisture collecting on his skin.

Frankly, his body intimidated the hell out of her. While she'd tried to stay in shape, her body had aged over the last few years. Her breasts were no longer as perky or her stomach as flat. It hadn't bothered her until now.

Would he still be attracted to her?

He must have sensed her apprehension. "It's important you know you can use your safe word if you don't want this."

She nodded. "I know."

But she did want it.

Wanted it more than anything.

Her pulse skyrocketed as he flicked open the fly of his jeans. "What safe word do you want to use?"

"Black list," she said automatically.

The words held more meaning than he would ever know.

"That's an odd choice. Care to share the meaning behind it?"

"No." She forced her gaze to his face. "That's a hard limit."

He paused, his eyes locked with hers as they tried to uncover her secrets. She used to joke that all he had to do was give her his "Dom eyes" and she couldn't refuse him anything. But today she held her ground, refusing to give into him. She almost expected him to walk out. Instead he resumed undressing, his nimble fingers doing the job she wanted to do. "Any of your other limits change?" His pants fell to the floor, and in a moment, his boxer-briefs joined them.

His cock was fully erect, long and curved, pre-come already dripping from the tip. He'd always kept himself so perfectly manscaped that she used to laugh.

She wasn't laughing now.

He'd kept up his habit of trimming the dark hair that nestled his cock. She didn't want to think about how many women in the preceding years had gotten to see that cock…touch that cock…taste that cock.

Before last night, it had been so long since she'd had sex, she hadn't bothered waxing herself bare, as he'd preferred her in the past.

What was the point when she was the only one who ever saw her naked?

"You remember my limits?" she asked breathlessly, her hands itching to wrap her hands around his cock.

Naked and unabashed, he walked behind her. His warm breath fanned her neck as he slowly unzipped her dress. "I remember everything."

Her dress slipped from her body. She leaned back, resting her head against Sawyer. "My limits haven't changed."

Not that she'd had many.

As her Master, Sawyer had ordered her to completely let go of her inhibitions and society's moral compass in order to experience a world she'd barely known existed. She'd lived for the nights he'd challenged her soft limits, pushing her further and further until she couldn't remember why she'd ever questioned them in the first place.

Bondage, submission, and beatings were only the tip of the iceberg. There were times he'd shown her such pleasure she could barely remember her own name. Times when they'd invited other men and women into their bedrooms and into their fantasies. Times when there were so many hands and tongues on her skin, she couldn't count them.

Sawyer pushed her forward until they both stood beneath the hot spray of the shower. "Good to know you're still the same kinky girl. It must have been hell to stay faithful." His hands worked magic on her scalp as he massaged shampoo into her damp hair. "Your best friends are all members of Benediction. Logan told me about that place. About the fantasy rooms. How did you stay away?"

He didn't allow her to answer, only chuckling when she shivered from the feel of his erection poking between the cheeks of her ass. She had no doubt its placement was intentional. He knew what got her excited.

She moaned, arching her back into him. Just an inch and he'd be inside her. She didn't care how or where he took her, as long as he did.

"I bet it killed you," he continued in a rough voice that sent tingles down her spine. He shamelessly ground his dick against her ass. "Do your friends know that underneath your conservative demeanor you're actually kinkier than them?"

No, they had no idea.

They couldn't, because she hadn't told them anything about herself, always managing to evade their personal questions. And as good friends do, they'd never pressed her for more. "I don't think anyone is kinkier than my friend Gracie."

He gently tipped her head forward, rinsing the soap from her hair. "Oh, I don't know about that. There was that time you left the patio door unlocked, and I came in while you were sleeping—"

"Is that what we're doing in here?" she asked, spinning around to face him. Enough foreplay. "Having a trip down memory lane? Or are you going to fuck me?"

His eyes darkened as his dominance reared to the surface. He sunk his fingers into her hair and pulled her toward him, lifting her to her toes. "Unless I say otherwise, you will refer to me as Master. Is that clear?"

Her pussy contracted, arousal spilling from her. The slight pain as he tugged on her hair coupled with the way he took control sent her into the submissive headspace. "Yes, Master."

"You want my cock in your greedy pussy, girl?" He pulled harder on her hair, eliciting a yelp from her. "You have to earn it first." With his hand on her head, he pushed her down. "Get on your knees and show me what you can do with that hot little mouth of yours. Make me believe you can't live without my cock."

She couldn't. She didn't know how she'd made it this long.

Haunted by the expiration date of their relationship, she'd have to savor each moment with him while it lasted. "This counts toward the seven nights, right, Master?"

The word "Master" tasted as good on her tongue as his cock would.

Missing the collar she used to wear in honor of his ownership of her, she rubbed her neck as she kneeled on the smooth surface of the shower.

"Yes, my girl. This counts." He grabbed the back of her neck and pushed her forward. "Now stop talking and fill your mouth with me."

She swallowed, preparing for his invasion. "Yes, Master." Opening her mouth as wide as it would go, she allowed him past her lips and took him inside. Sawyer wasn't gentle with her, giving her no time to acclimate before he began fucking her mouth, sliding his cock across her tongue until it bumped to the entrance of her throat before retreating.

She was helpless against the onslaught of his use of her mouth as his tool for getting himself off. In that moment, she truly belonged to him.

"Fuck," he swore, throwing his head back, the muscles of his neck protruding from his tension. His hands tightened on her head as he pushed her mouth farther onto his cock. "Swallow. Take me into your throat."

Breathing through her nose, she swallowed continuously until almost all of Sawyer's cock disappeared into her mouth. Her tears mingled with the water of the shower, soaking her face.

The more he made her feel as though she existed solely to satisfy his lusts, and the rougher his treatment of her, the more aroused she got. Her clit swelled and pulsed, demanding attention. All she had to do was touch it, and she'd go off like a lit firecracker.

But she didn't want to climax. She wanted to remain on this decadent pinnacle for a while longer.

A colorful variety of expletives continued to fall from Sawyer's lips as he increased his pace, fucking her mouth with reckless abandon. Adding vibration to increase his pleasure, she hummed.

He dropped his head forward and looked down at her, his fingers wrapping lightly around her throat, no doubt to feel his cock inside of it. Groaning, his pace increased, and his thrusts went deeper from his excitement.

She sensed the wild beast inside of him beginning to unleash, that part of him she both loved and feared at the same time. He'd never harm her.

But oh, how he loved to hurt her.

She used her eyes to give him permission. Not that he needed it.

He hesitated, the good man in him warring with the bad, bad boy who wanted to show her he could do anything to her.

His groans turned to a roar as he accepted what they both wanted.

He slapped her cheek. Not too forcefully, but just enough so she could feel the sting.

Her pussy spasmed from the pain, but she wouldn't give in that easily. He had to work harder.

More, she begged silently.

He didn't wait, slapping her other cheek, the sound of it echoing in the shower. Then another. And another. He alternated sides until the light tears she'd shed from him being inside her throat fell heavier. She had no doubt her mascara from earlier ran down her skin. Each tear was a release of bottled emotion that brought her closer and closer to complete surrender.

His hands tightened in her hair, her pain and her submission always an aphrodisiac for him. "You're going to drink your Master's come and not spill a drop of it, aren't you? Such a greedy girl."

He wiped under her eyes and showed her the black stain of her makeup on his fingers. Then, as his legs shook and his eyes widened, he pinched her nostrils with those fingers, sealing off her only present method for breathing.

Deep, wicked exhilaration coursed through her veins, heating her body. The beat of her heart thudded in her ears, her vision darkening along the edges and brightening with bursting stars within the center from the lack of oxygen.

Her clit pulsed in time with her heart. She clenched her pussy's muscles. Once, twice. And then she was coming, hot lava flowing outward from her core, her juices spilling with every hard spasm.

"Yes," her Master cried as he removed his fingers from her nostrils and followed her with his own release, shot after shot of his come gliding down her throat.

She swallowed continuously until there was nothing left to swallow, and his cock slipped from her mouth.

Bowing her head, she gloried in the first real taste of submission she'd had in over four years. When she'd left Sawyer, she'd also left her true nature behind, and as a symbol, she'd placed her wedding rings and platinum chain collar on his pillow. He hadn't just lost his wife when she'd run.

He'd lost his slave.

And she'd lost herself.

But now, buzzing on the high from her orgasm and her submission, she'd stolen back a piece of identity. She'd cherish and cling to it, until once more, fate and circumstance ripped it away from her.

Sawyer cradled her chin in his hand, caressing her cheek with his knuckles. "That was fucking amazing. I know you need your sleep, but I need to see you come."

She nuzzled his palm. "I just did, Master."

"Yes, but I was too far gone to appreciate it, so you'll have to do it one more time for me." Grabbing her under the arms, he lifted her onto her feet and nudged her forward until she was almost flush against the wall. "Hold onto the wall for support." He raised her left leg and rested it on the seat in the corner, spreading her open to him.

Without warning, he thrust his fingers inside her and twisted before retreating and repeating the process. "That's two. Since I just stretched you with my cock and you're nice and slippery from your orgasm, let's see how many fingers of mine you can take."

A whimper of need tore from her throat as he added the extra finger. The delicious anticipation for more nearly pushed her into another climax, but she breathed deep, holding it off. In her position, she was tighter than when he had her lie on her back with her legs spread wide. There was no way he'd fit another one inside her.

He stayed away from her clit, but as proven earlier, she didn't require clitoral stimulation to climax. When Sawyer dominated her, it brought her to a mental and emotional state in which she and her body lived to serve him.

In the months they'd been together, he'd taught her to come on demand. She couldn't do it anymore—it was like losing any other skill without practice—but she could come close.

"Come on, girl. Take one more for me." An additional finger poked at her entrance as the other three rubbed the walls inside.

She trembled from the pressure of it stretching her. "No, Master. There's no room."

Giving her the pain she required to become mindless, he smacked her ass hard then yanked on her hair. "Do you get to say no to your Master? There's only one way of stopping me. Are you going to use it?"

No, she wanted him to decide when she'd had enough.

She shook her head, and he slid his finger all the way inside. He gave her only a few moments to acclimate to the girth of his digits before he began wiggling the tips of his fingers over that perfect spot that made her eyes practically roll back in her head.

All he'd have to do at this point was give her a little pain to push her over the cliff. A bite on her shoulder. A pinch of her nipple. A squeeze of her windpipe. He knew the greatest torture of all was to keep her at the cliff's edge as long as possible without letting her drop.

The pleasure grew every second, so intense it bordered on painful. "Please, Master," she begged. "Help me."

"That's right, girl. All you had to do was ask." He grasped her face and turned it toward him. His jaw was rigid, and his eyes full of fire. "I want to see your face when I give you this gift. I want to hear my name on your lips. Stay like this."

His hand left her face, and in the next moment, he pushed his finger into her ass, the stretch and burn of it careening her into climax.

"Sawyer!" She shouted his name in thanks, even while she cursed him for making her remember how good it was between them.

It wasn't just her pussy that squeezed in blissful waves of climax. Every part of her, inside and out, celebrated the release.

Even her heart.

She stayed in position for several minutes, unable to find the energy to take herself to bed. Closing her eyes, she listened as Sawyer uncapped bottles of soap, cleaning himself and then her before shutting off the water.

He wrapped a warm fluffy towel around her torso and scooped her up into his arms. She tried to tell him she could walk, but she was too tired to speak.

He lowered her gently onto the crisp cool sheets of the bed and pulled the blanket up to her chin. As she began to drift off, she felt his weight depress the mattress and his lips brush her cheek.

"See?" he said softly from above her. "All you have to do is ask for help. Trust me."

Even half asleep she realized he wasn't talking about orgasms anymore.

He wanted answers. Why couldn't he be satisfied with what she had to give him?

A week. Nothing more.

"I'm sorry," she managed to whisper. "I can't."

She never would.

Not when asking him for help would be a death sentence.

Chapter Seven

THE LIGHTING WAS shit for such a delicate job, but desperate times called for desperate measures. Sitting in the back of his beat-up truck with the parts he'd purchased from the Home Depot store laid out in front of him, he fisted the wires and got to work.

Amazing what you could find on the Internet these days.

He rubbed his chest as a stab of regret hit him behind his sternum. If only she hadn't left him, he wouldn't have to go to such lengths. But she'd forced his hand.

She hadn't changed. Hadn't learned her lesson yet.

The woman was unyielding.

Unbreakable.

Why hadn't she fled?

At least the desecration of her space should have raised serious doubts about Sawyer Hayes. But rather than slam the door in the man's face, she had run into his arms.

Watching their little scene from a distance in his truck, he'd used his binoculars to see the way her eyes had softened at her old lover.

It was obvious that she still loved him.

And as long as she loved Hayes, she wouldn't be his.

He lowered the wires to rub his temples as the pounding in his head increased. Every time he thought about her, the pain inside him grew, and he became more and more confused. Why was she cheating on him with another man when he'd given her everything?

She was a greedy whore, and whores had to die.

He thought he'd already killed her. But here she was, alive and well, living it up as he struggled every day with his memories, her last words still ringing in his ears.

"Love? I never loved you. I hate you."

It didn't make sense. Once Sawyer had discovered her whereabouts, he had every reason to call the police. Yet instead, he had driven her to his hotel and allowed her to stay with him in his suite.

The fucking penthouse suite.

With no way to spy on her in there, he'd driven back to her condo and sat outside, holding her shirt up to his nose to take her scent into his lungs.

Barely an hour had passed before a cleaning crew had arrived. He watched as they came in and out of her condo, carrying bags of damaged clothes and books to the Dumpster.

Just as he'd expected, she hadn't called the cops about the break-in. But as hard as he tried, he still couldn't understand why Hayes hadn't. He had no reason to protect her.

What was his end game?

How easily she had allowed that man back into her life, a man she knew nothing about. She'd thought she was the liar in their relationship, but she wasn't the only one keeping secrets.

So many secrets.

Lights flashed behind his eyes, the pain intensifying. He banged his skull against the wall of his truck, trying to destroy the rampant voices in his head that wouldn't stop their chattering. He smashed it until a river of blood flowed down his face.

The blazing agony stopped.

The voices quieted to a dull murmur.

He resumed his work, twisting the wires according to the instructions.

He would make her love him again.

He had to.

And if she didn't, this time he'd make sure she'd never leave him again.

Even if it meant they both had to die.

Chapter Eight

LISA WOKE UP with a start, the heaviness of the blanket and the softness of the pillow foreign. She blinked a few times and rolled over, checking the clock on the nightstand as she remembered she was in Sawyer's suite.

Judging by the time, she'd probably gotten about four hours of sleep—enough to run to her office and function. She stretched, wonderfully sore in places she'd repressed since she'd become a born-again virgin.

Seriously, how could she have gone so long without it?

She hadn't lied about needing to work. There were several appointments on her calendar she'd need to reschedule and at least five press releases that needed to be written for the week. Once she finished those tasks, she'd free up some more time for Sawyer. She couldn't imagine why he wanted her available twenty-four hours a day, but she also couldn't imagine anywhere she'd rather be than with him.

It was dangerous.

Thrilling.

Wrong.

Wrong had never felt so right.

Sitting up, she smiled, noticing Sawyer had left her a fresh pair of jeans, panties, and blouse on the edge of the bed. He'd probably already ordered her an entire wardrobe.

She twirled the La Perla underwear on her pinkie. Money might not buy happiness, but apparently it did manage to buy designer clothes on a Sunday before the mall even opened.

Getting dressed, she thought about all the ways she could thank him for his generosity. Of course, none of them would result in her getting any work done this afternoon. She'd have to plan something for that evening.

Maybe she could pick up a costume from the sex shop and play the clumsy maid to his stern hotel guest. She'd flash him as she bent to pick something up, and then oops—she'd knock a bottle onto the floor, so he'd have to punish her.

He'd take her over his knee and spank her hard on her bottom until she learned her lesson. Until her skin was red and burning from his punishment. And then she'd retrieve the item she'd dropped earlier—a bottle of lube—and offer to let him fuck her ass. Or her tits. He loved to slide his cock between them and come all over her face.

Now soaking between her thighs from the fantasy, she buttoned up her blouse and bounced out of the room, eager to tell Sawyer of her plans.

Typing on his laptop, his tongue poking the inside of his cheek, he sat behind the desk, so deep in concentration he didn't seem to notice her presence. She took the opportunity to watch him in his element.

Her husband was a techie, computers and gadgets like food and water to him. When they'd been together, he'd told her stories about his friends from the Army, men like him who could hack into anything.

In fact, Sawyer and three of his friends had managed to use their skills to prove Logan and Rachel's innocence in the murder of a local mobster. That must have been when Sawyer saw her photo and figured out where to find her.

He'd never said the words out loud, but she'd gotten the sense that he'd resented having to take over as the CEO of his family's multi-billion-dollar corporation when his parents died. Not that he'd ever admit it. That role was his job. A responsibility. While computers were his passion. He'd rather be lost in cyberspace than at a board meeting. But never once had he complained in all the time they'd spent together.

She snuck up behind him and slid her arms down his chest, burying her nose into the side of his neck. "What are you working on?"

He slammed his laptop shut with a force that startled her. "You're up." He pushed away from the desk and stood, leaving her feeling a bit awkward, since he didn't seem as though he was pleased to see her.

What had changed between the shower and now?

She clasped her hands together to keep from touching him. "I have too much to do to stay in bed."

Although he faced her, he kept his gaze trained on the wall behind her. "It's Sunday. No one is waiting for you at the office."

Her stomach churned at Sawyer's icy demeanor. Why wouldn't he look at her? Had he changed his mind about their seven nights?

"True, but that doesn't mean I don't have tasks that I need to complete. Unless you're easing up on your orders for me to take the week off?" She gave him the opening to let her off the hook, hoping he wouldn't take it.

"That may have been presumptuous of me. I can't take all of your time. If you need to work, then work." He shrugged, his tone flat and lifeless. "Just leave the nights open for me."

Something was wrong. He hadn't broken their agreement, but he also didn't seem eager for it. What happened to wanting to spend the days as well as the nights with her? Had he not enjoyed their scene in the shower?

She took a step closer to him. "What were you doing on the computer that you didn't want me to see?"

He still wouldn't look at her. "Work. Just work."

And he'd given her a hard time about needing to go into her office? "Hmm. Seems like I'm not the only one who works on Sundays." She took another step toward him and placed her hand on his shoulder. "How is Hayes Industries doing?"

"Why?" His gaze shot to her face, the anger in his expression almost palpable. "Planning on taking more of my money?"

Screw him. She snatched her hand away as if he'd burned her and headed for the door. "Forget it. I'm leaving."

She didn't need this. He was the one who wanted her here, and now that she was, he was treating her as if she was dirt beneath his shoe.

Before she got to the front door, he caught her by the arm. "I'm sorry. That was uncalled for."

She twirled around. "I've given you no reason to trust me. But I thought after this morning…" She'd thought their connection was real. "If we're going to spend the next week together, I at least deserve your respect." She held her head high and squared her shoulders. "I may have been a thief and a liar, but I've spent the last few years atoning for my crimes and changing the direction of my life. I don't have much, and I live modestly. But I've earned everything I have, and I won't allow you or anyone else to shame me. The fact is I'm not the same woman you knew."

"No," he said quietly, turning away from her. "The fact is I never knew you at all."

Didn't he understand he knew her better than anyone? "What is your deal?"

He flinched. "I don't know what you mean."

"Yes, you do." She got into his face and angled his chin, forcing him to look at her. "Four hours ago, your dick was lodged in my throat, and now you won't even look me in the eye. What the hell happened between then and now?"

His eyes went liquid when she mentioned the blow job but then immediately froze again. "It's nothing. Don't worry about it."

She threw her arms up in exasperation. "I don't get it. You ask me to trust you and—"

"And you refused."

She studied him, noting the extra tightness in his jaw, the hardness of his eyes, and the rigidness of his shoulders. That was what this was about? Trust?

Why couldn't the trust she showed him through her submission be enough for him? She couldn't give him more. Besides, what did it matter when this whole thing between them was temporary?

"I was practically asleep," she said as explanation. "You can't blame me for something I uttered while I was crashing from our scene."

"You're right. I can't." He grabbed her shoulders and pushed her until she was flush with the wall. "So I'm asking you again while you're awake. Can you trust me enough to ask for help? Because I know there's a lot you haven't told me." He swept his thumb across her lips, and it took everything she had not to suck it into her mouth. "You loved me. I know you did. But when something or someone spooked you, you didn't love me enough to trust me." His voice cracked with emotion. "I would've helped you. I'll still help you, but you have to trust me first."

"It's not that easy." He couldn't save her with all the money in the world. If they stayed together, her father would find her. He'd go after the black list and kill them both. She couldn't afford to take that risk.

"It can be. Trust me, and I'll slay all your dragons," he said, cupping her face. "Tell me why you took that money from me and where it all went. Tell me why you're scared."

She covered his hands with her own. "I can't."

"You can, Annaliese. Just say the word, and I'll—"

"Black list," she whispered. If he kept pressing her, she was afraid she would crumble under the sweetness of his words and tell him everything.

He dropped his hands and stepped away from her. "Right." He cleared his throat, his gaze on the door. "Before I drop you at your office, I want you to make a list of people who might have done the damage to your condo. While you're at work, I'll see what I can find out about them. Maybe one of them recently flew into town."

"I'd ask how you're going to check the airline records, but I don't think I want to know."

He gave her a grin, but it looked forced. "It's probably better that way."

All business now, he strode over to the desk and handed her a notepad and pen.

She took it from him, nervous about what he'd think of her when she finished. Could she do this? She worried her lip with her teeth. As long as she didn't have to give him the details of her cons, she supposed she could handle it. "It's a long list, Sawyer. I've hurt a lot of people throughout the years." And without the list in front of her, she wouldn't be able to remember them all. Later, when she got the chance, she'd check the journal to see if she'd forgotten anyone.

He raised his brows. "How many years are we talking about? You're only twenty-five. Or did you lie to me about your age?"

"No. I didn't lie about that. But my age is irrelevant, because I've been conning people since the moment I was born."

He waited a beat, his eyes searching her face. "What's your real name?"

"Annaliese Hunt." She shook her head. That wasn't the name she wanted him to know her as. "Well, Annaliese Hayes. At least for a little while longer." Until their divorce.

His hands went into his pockets as he leaned against the desk. "Why did you give me your real name when we met?"

She'd spent countless hours pondering that very question, never coming to a concrete answer. But only one thing made sense. "Because from the moment I met you, I recognized you as my Master. I needed you to know the real me."

He frowned. "And yet I don't know the real you, because you haven't let me. Do *you* even know who you are?"

"I thought I did. Then you walked back into my life and have made me question everything I thought I knew about myself." Paper and pen in hand, she rested her backside against the desk, her shoulder brushing against Sawyer. "These last few years were the longest I've ever gone by the same name, did you know that? I've kept my hair short and brown, worn the same colored contacts under non-prescription glasses, and dressed conservatively. I don't have a hobby. I don't watch television. I don't date. With the exception of my weekly girls' night, I work and come home." Eighteen-hour days let her return home for a bath and a glass of wine before falling into bed exhausted.

Her friends were her lighthouse as she floated aimlessly on the endless sea. Without them, she would drown. They had no idea how their friendships had yanked her out of the deep, dark depression she'd lived with since losing Sawyer.

She waited all week for Thursday night, when they'd meet up at the bar for dinner and drinks. It was her chance to live vicariously through them as they shared stories about their adventures in kink.

Although she couldn't tell them the truth, she envied them for their ability to experience their sexuality freely. Kate, a masochist, got the pain she needed through whippings and floggings from her Dominant, Jaxon. Danielle was an exhibitionist, and she and her husband, Cole, loved to fuck in front of an audience. Logan and Rachel were into bondage. Gracie was into…well, everything, but she desperately sought a permanent full-time Master and loved to participate in threesomes.

Lisa longed for all of it and could have none of it. With the exception of Rachel, none of them even knew she was kinky. They thought she was uptight, conservative, no-nonsense Lisa Smith, the daughter of two teachers who had died in a car accident when she was eighteen. They didn't know she'd never gone to college. That every piece of ID she owned was fake. That even if she had wanted to go to the state and apply for a driver's license in her real name, she couldn't. According to the world, Annaliese

Hunt didn't exist. She had been born at home, so there was no birth certificate. Nothing to tie her to anyone. She was a ghost, a shell of a person walking around on this earth without any real substance.

Except with Sawyer. With Sawyer, she felt real. Tethered to this world. Whole.

He was right. She had no idea who she really was. "I mean, what kind of a person doesn't have a hobby?" She shook her head. "I'll tell you. Someone who doesn't know what the hell she enjoys."

He squeezed her hand. "Maybe it's time you find out."

"Maybe." She lifted a shoulder. "And what about you?"

"Me? I know what I enjoy."

She hummed in agreement. "Computers. So why are you still the CEO of Hayes Industries?"

He eyed her warily, his hackles coming up in his defense. "You know why. It was my parents' company, and I owe it to them."

"You owe it to yourself to be happy. Why not hire someone else to run the company, so that you can spend more time doing what you love?"

He released her hand to run his fingers through his hair. "You don't understand."

"No, you're right. I don't." She turned him toward her. "Because you've never explained it to me. All this talk about my inability to trust, and you're no better than me."

A million expressions flashed over his face until only sadness remained. "There are some sins we commit that are too dark to ever see the light."

"I get that. Boy, do I get that." She sighed. "But do you honestly think if you told me about your sins, it would change how I look at you? How I feel about you?"

Especially since she carried the heavy weight of her own sins on her tarnished soul.

"If I confess my sins, they become real. And I'm not ready to accept them yet. I'm not sure I'll ever be ready."

What terrible thing did Sawyer do to make him think he had to forgo his own happiness in honor of his parents?

And if he couldn't forgive himself for his sins, how could he ever forgive her?

Chapter Nine

BLOWING ON HER cup of hot coffee, Lisa stared at the computer screen in front of her, waiting for the feeling of normalcy to wrap her in its arms. Six hours in her office, and she hadn't accomplished a damn thing, still too shell-shocked over the last twenty-four hours. The soreness between her legs constantly reminded her of Sawyer. After she'd given him the list of people who had a reason to want her dead, he'd dropped her off at her office, telling her to call him when she was ready for him to pick her up.

She didn't like unpredictability. Her life was about staying in control and staying one step ahead of everyone else. She lived for the routine of the day and worked long hours so she didn't have time to think about all the horrible things she'd done in her past and all she'd lost.

She rubbed her temples, trying to focus on the numbers on the spreadsheets. She had to forget about any future with Sawyer. The sad truth was at the end of the week, she and Sawyer would go their separate ways. Permanently. There was no other option.

"Well, ain't you a sight for sore eyes," came a voice from the doorway.

She froze, her coffee halfway to her lips. That familiar southern drawl sent her heart beating double time. It couldn't be. And yet it was.

He'd found her.

She took a deep breath and got to her feet. Then, slowly, as if she could make it all go away if she just didn't look, she turned toward him.

Her brother.

"Where's my hug?" he asked, holding his arms open and smiling like four years hadn't passed.

And maybe they hadn't. He hadn't changed at all. Still her handsome big brother with his dark eyes and olive skin, hair as black as the night sky. So different from her light complexion and her almost Nordic appearance. It was something she'd questioned constantly as the only fair person in the family. Her mother had always said she'd taken after her maternal grandmother, that she was special because her grandma had been one of the most successful grifters in the country back in the thirties. While the Great Depression had ravaged the country, she'd prospered off people's hunger and had skillfully conned hundreds of men into giving her their last penny to buy foreign bonds that promised to quadruple in value in six months.

Resembling a criminal who took advantage of the weak was nothing to be proud of, and yet, when her mother recounted the tales of her grandma, she felt as though she belonged.

Her parents were cold and calculating people. There were no hugs. No bedtime stories. No cute notes in her lunchbox during the times they had allowed her to attend school. The only time she received any affection was when she made them money. But it was never enough for them. Every dollar they brought in somehow disappeared within a few short months. She hadn't understood it until she grew older and followed them one night to a casino.

They were compulsive gamblers. It wasn't the money they sought from the con. It was the rush. The high. They kept just enough so they didn't starve and always had a roof over their heads. Millions of dollars were stolen and lives ruined because her parents had a gambling addiction they had no intention of ever overcoming.

One of her brothers, Mitch, had been the same way. He loved the thrill of a con and felt no remorse for taking others' hard-earned money. He'd also been cruel, often beating her black and blue for fun.

But the brother standing in front of her waiting for his hug had been her lifeline. He'd bandaged her knee after she'd fallen off her bike. Had made her dinner when her parents had forgotten to feed her. Had comforted her when she had nightmares.

Asa was the only reason she hadn't left her family sooner. He'd always made it better. Until he no longer could.

She eyed him warily, but she couldn't stay away any longer. She hurled herself into him and wrapped her arms around him. "I can't believe you're here," she said shakily, suddenly realizing her entire body was trembling.

Her gaze jumped to her small bookshelf, where she kept her special copy of Charles Dickens's *A Tale of Two Cities*.

"I'm here. As soon as I saw your photo, I knew I had to see you. Let you know everything that's happened."

She pulled back, suddenly both curious and cautious. "What's happened? Is Dad finally in prison where he belongs?"

A slow smile broke out on his face. "No. Even better." He took her hand and squeezed. "He's dead. He ain't ever going to lay a hand on you again."

She stood there, unable to say or do anything.

Her father was dead.

The man had made her life a living hell after her mother had died, his abuse escalating to the point that she thought he would actually kill her one night. Intense relief flooded her, filling her with a light buzzing sensation. Not that there weren't several other people who wanted her dead or behind bars. But knowing her father could never manipulate her into doing his bidding again brought tears of joy to her eyes.

"What happened?" she asked, gesturing to a chair as an invitation for him to sit.

Along with her desk, she had a small round glass table where she occasionally sat with clients.

He plopped down in the chair, slouching to the side and kicking out his long legs. He did a quick perusal of the room, and then he nodded as if impressed by what he saw. "Heart attack. He and Mitch were casing a building, and dear old Pops just keeled over and died. Mitch didn't find no pulse or nothing when he checked. He couldn't carry him back to the car, so he left him. Sure he was bagged and tagged as a John Doe. County probably cremated his ass. Fitting, right?" His lips curled in disgust. "Don't worry. He's burning in hell for his sins right now."

She thought about Sawyer and his inability to forgive himself for his alleged sins. If there was no forgiveness for him, was she doomed as well?

"And what about us? Will we burn in hell for our sins?"

Her brother had the audacity to appear confused, as if he had no idea what she was talking about. "What sins do you think you've committed?"

"The same as all of us Hunts. Lying, stealing, cheating."

Her past weighed heavily on her shoulders. There was no absolution for her. No going to church to confess her sins to the priest. No forgiveness from those she had transgressed against. No way to escape the guilt that plagued her day in and day out.

Asa leaned across the table and held her hands. "Do you regret it?"

"Yes," she answered without hesitation. "That's not who I am anymore."

"You were never one of us, Annie," he said softly.

His old nickname for her brought back memories of all the times they'd snuck away from their parents to go fishing down by the creek or get ice cream cones in town. They'd spent days exploring every time they moved to a new city, riding their bikes through woods and taking long walks together. Unless they were given explicit permission from their parents to make friends, they only had each other for company. Usually the only friends they were allowed to have were the kids of the target, and it was difficult to let yourself become close with someone you'd eventually betray.

Until Sawyer, she'd always been able to stay detached from her marks. But she'd given him everything she had.

Except the truth.

And once again, it would tear them apart.

But was she truly different from her family? What differentiated them, when they'd all destroyed so many lives? Her guilt?

She leaned forward across the table. "Did you feel bad for lying to all those people?"

Asa's brows wrinkled, and his mouth pursed. "Not when we were kids. I thought it was a game. Without someone to teach me about right and wrong, I thought we were doing a job like everyone else. Rather than sitting behind a desk or saving lives as a doctor, this was how we made our money."

Yes, that's what it was like for her as well. "What changed?"

He took her hand. "I heard your argument with Dad over that Hayes guy. Heard the ultimatum Dad gave you. I realized then what we did had real consequences. I mean, stealing money is one thing...but killing someone is another."

Her throat tightened as she recalled that terrible day. "I didn't realize you were there."

He pulled back his hand and drummed his fingers on the table. "I thought there'd be time to tell you I supported your decision and would try to change Dad's mind, but you left without saying good-bye. Got to tell you, I was pretty pissed off at you for a while."

"I'm sorry. I shouldn't have—"

"Hell, yes you should have," he said, surprising her. "You didn't do anything wrong, and I understand why you had to go without any strings. But I would have gone with you, Annie. You were the most important person in my life. Until recently, you were the only person I ever loved."

"Until recently?"

He jutted his chin at the ring on his finger. "Married just over a year now. Got a daughter and one more kid on the way."

"I'm an aunt?" Joy warmed her heart, but she had to admit, she was envious.

Would she ever have that?

"You are. Here's a picture of my wife, Thea, with my daughter." He flipped open his wallet and retrieved a photograph of a perfect-looking family. A beautiful woman with long dark hair and a friendly smile sat on the steps of a house with a pudgy baby girl on her lap.

"She looks just like you. What's her name?"

His eyes twinkled. "Annie. I named her after you."

She swallowed the lump in her throat. "I'd really like to meet her and Thea one day."

"Yeah. You'll have to come out to our farm and stay with us."

Her jaw dropped. "I'm sorry. Did you just invite me to your farm?"

He nodded once, a huge smile on his face. "That's where I met Thea. I worked for her daddy. Knew the moment I saw her that I wanted to make her mine. That's why I stayed as far away from her as I could. Didn't think a man like me deserved a girl like her. Luckily, she did. Wore me down until I couldn't breathe without her. We've got our own house down the road from her parents."

The envy spread, invading her entire chest. But she was happy for him. "You've got a real family."

"I do. But that includes you. They've all heard all about you."

"Do they know that we were…?" *Con artists? Thieves? The children of psychopaths?*

He nodded. "They do. Didn't tell them right away, of course," he explained. "But before I married their daughter, I thought they deserved to know."

"And they accepted it?"

Sitting back in his chair, he stretched out his long legs. "Can't say they weren't worried, but I'd been working for them for three years at that point and had never caused them a day's trouble." He laughed. "I sing in the church choir, for Christ's sake. I told Thea before we"—he paused, gesturing with his hands—"you know. I put my faith in her hands and prayed that I'd find forgiveness in her arms. Shocked the hell out of her, but the love she had for me was stronger than the bonds of my past. Watching Thea with her parents and all her siblings, I learned that parents are supposed to love their children unconditionally."

Their parents hadn't loved them unconditionally. If fact, she wasn't sure if they'd loved their children at all; they'd only seemed to love what their children could do for them.

She hadn't really understood love until she'd met Sawyer. But when her father had given her the order to kill him, she'd chosen to sacrifice her own happiness so that he could live. Even if it meant he fell in love with someone else.

Did he love her enough to sacrifice himself for her?

Either way, she hoped to never find out.

"And what about everyone else?" she asked. "Do you expect Thea to love you unconditionally? What if something from your past comes back to ruin it all? Will she stand by you or kick you out?"

He leaned across the table and took her hands again. "I can't speak for Thea, but if our situations were reversed, I'd support her. We can't change our pasts. We can't predict the future. It's how we live our lives each day that matters."

"Well, isn't this cozy?" said Sawyer dryly, standing by the door.

What was he doing here? He wasn't supposed to pick her up until she called him.

She yanked her hands from Asa's and shot out of her chair. "Sawyer, this isn't what it looks like."

He crossed his arms, anger radiating off him. Was he jealous?

"Let me guess. He's a client." He continued, not giving her a chance to speak. "No? I'll try again. Brother." He shook his head. "Not it?"

"Actually, he is," she blurted. "My brother. This is Asa." She dipped her head, gesturing to her brother. "Asa, Sawyer Hayes."

Asa stood, his eyes narrowed into dark slits. "I know who he is."

Sawyer shocked her by continuing to appear angry. In fact, if anything, he seemed angrier. She would've thought that once he knew Asa was her brother, he would've relaxed. But his jaw was clenched so tightly, she wouldn't be surprised if he broke a tooth.

"At least one of us knows the other," Sawyer said. He shoved his hands in his pockets, something she suddenly realized he did whenever he felt vulnerable. "I thought you had no family. Of course, that was another one of your lies, wasn't it?"

She nodded. When they'd been together before, she had lied and told him she had no family. But once she left and until today, that lie had become her truth. "I have two older brothers. My mother died before I met you, and I just learned that my father died as well."

Sawyer winced. "I'm sorry for your loss."

"I'm not. He wasn't a good guy."

He nodded, his shoulders no longer around his ears and his jaw relaxing. He told her with his eyes that their conversation wasn't over. "The crew finished up with your condo. I made sure to pay in cash and paid them to lose the paperwork, so that there's nothing tying you to the vandalism."

Her brother's eyes widened. "Vandalism? What's going on, Annie?"

Sawyer snorted. "Annie? Cute."

She ignored him and turned to her brother. "Someone broke into my condo yesterday and trashed it. It's no big deal."

"No big deal?" Sawyer said from behind her. "They destroyed every piece of clothing and every book you owned. And don't forget about the ants."

Horror crossed Asa's face. "Ants? They knew you don't like ants?"

"No one likes ants."

But her especially. On her tenth birthday, her father had taken her and her brothers to a horse farm under the guise of giving them riding lessons. What she hadn't realized until later was that while she'd proudly ridden her first horse, he'd been conning the farm's owner out of ten thousand dollars. Unfortunately, when she finished her lesson, she found that her brothers had disappeared, and she'd run around the farm looking for them before stumbling face-first into a large sand hill. It didn't take more than thirty seconds before she was covered with ants.

Red ants that bit every part of her body until she was swollen and red.

To clean her off, her father had thrown her into a filthy pond, forgetting that she didn't know how to swim. She'd almost drowned before Asa had jumped in to save her.

Her brother moved closer to her, speaking low, as if he didn't want Sawyer to hear him. "You think it's one of your old marks?"

"You found me. Sawyer found me. It wouldn't be a stretch to assume someone else found me."

Sawyer joined their little tête-à-tête, puffing out his chest and pointing at Asa. "Or maybe he's the one behind it."

Asa clenched his hands into fists. "Do you really trust this guy?"

She threw up her hands in frustration. "I don't know who to trust right now. Maybe I shouldn't trust anyone."

Her brother gave her a look that could only be interpreted as disappointment. "I'm sorry you feel that way, sis. But when you remember I'm the one who loves you unconditionally, give me a call." He handed her a business card. "Here's my cell number. I'm staying at the hotel on Sheridan." After giving her a quick kiss on her cheek, he tossed Sawyer a scowl and strode out the door.

Tapping her foot in irritation, she folded her arms across her chest and glared at Sawyer. She hadn't seen her brother in years, and he'd managed to run him off within only minutes of his arrival.

Checking out her office, he made a complete 360 before mirroring her stance.

He might be her lover and Master, but it was time she reminded him of her power. Holding his gaze, she threw back her shoulders and slowly stalked toward him. He smiled as if expecting her to pounce on him.

She stopped in front of him.

Returned his smile.

And punched him.

Chapter Ten

Sawyer took her anger like a champ. Of course it helped that there was no real power behind her sock to his arm. "I hope you got it out of your system, because you're not getting a second chance."

Shame heated her cheeks. She shouldn't have taken her frustration out on him, even if he was acting like an ass. "I'm sorry. I shouldn't have done that."

The fear of becoming her parents had always hovered on the edge of her mind. There wasn't a day that went by during which she didn't remember what it was like to curl into a ball as the rain of fists came down on her. She swore she'd never raise her hands in anger, and she'd broken the promise to herself.

"I wouldn't have let you do it if I wasn't okay with it. You obviously needed to let off some steam."

She laughed, relieved he didn't hold her loss of composure against her. "You mind telling me why you acted like such a jerk in front of my brother?"

His expression turned serious. "Your brother is a reminder of how little I know about you."

"That's not true." She planted herself on the edge of her desk. "Believe it or not, you know me better than anyone else."

He pursed his lips, and frown lines etched his forehead. "Well, that's just sad."

She flashed him a sorry grin in agreement. "Sad but true."

He joined her on the desk, and they both sat with their legs dangling as if they were on the edge of a pier. "I want to know more. I'm not asking you to tell me why you took the money and ran or where the money went, but tell me something I don't know. Let me see a glimpse of the real Annaliese."

She paused, thinking long and hard about herself. What could she share with him?

There were no memories of Christmases spent opening presents under a tree decorated with twinkling lights. No memories of sleepovers at friends' houses or dates for the prom. No jobs working at the local fast food restaurant or spelling bees at school.

Her life had been about keeping her head down so no one noticed her and reported her to Child Protective Services. It had been about hiding food and change under her mattress so she didn't starve. When she'd gotten older, it had been about seducing men and women and making her father proud of her by pulling off a successful con.

Yeah, he didn't want to hear about that.

"My family moved around a lot when I was growing up," she heard herself say. "By the time I was eighteen, I'd lived in every state but Alaska, Hawaii, and Utah."

His eyes took on a playful glint. "I get Alaska and Hawaii, but why not Utah?"

She'd never asked, but only one reason made sense. "That's where my parents were from originally. I guess they didn't like it very much."

"Where was your favorite place?" He settled a hand on her knee, his thumb brushing back and forth. It was such an innocent touch. And yet it was as intimate as if he was touching her between her thighs.

"Arizona," she said automatically. It had nothing to do with the mountain views and the desert climate and everything to do with the fact she'd spent her time there with him. It was the only time in her life she'd ever known true happiness.

He stilled, it almost appearing as if he didn't even breathe. Then he squeezed her lower thigh, silently acknowledging the significance of her answer. "You and your brother seem close."

Close? Asa was someone she no longer recognized—the best version of himself. He'd become a family man, one who sang in a goddamned church and probably said grace before eating a meal consisting of fresh-off-the-farm chicken and milk direct from a cow. While she had been hiding behind the mousy Lisa Smith persona, he'd gone and found himself a real life. No, she and her brother weren't close. Not anymore.

"Before an hour ago, I hadn't seen him in more than four years," she said, her heart aching not only for everything she lost, but for every bit of pain she'd caused Asa.

Processing the information, he brushed his hand over his jaw. "Why not?"

She stared at the door, indecision warring within her. With her father dead, the threat to Sawyer's life decreased, but her brother Mitch was still a wild card. If he found her, would he try and carry out their father's original scheme so that she'd inherit Sawyer's fortune? Could he be responsible for trashing her condo? She itched to tell Sawyer why she'd left him. But once he learned about the terrible things she'd done, would he still look at her the same way? Or would he only see the criminal she'd been?

The black list wouldn't only condemn her father. In the wrong hands, the information written in that journal would land her and her brothers in prison—or even worse, in the hands of those who sought a different kind of revenge against them for the wrongs they'd committed. If it was only about her, she'd go to prison. But Asa had a family now. He'd changed. She'd already hurt him enough. She wouldn't be responsible for ruining what he'd worked so hard to build.

Her decision wasn't easy, but it was the only one she could make. "For the same reason I hadn't seen you in years. I can't talk about it."

He blew out a breath that sounded like frustration, but to give him credit, he didn't push her. "You said your father was a bad man. What did you mean by that?"

A chill went down her spine as if her father's ghost had floated into the room. Even dead, he terrified her. She turned to Sawyer and caught his gaze, needing him to say the words she couldn't. "What do you think I mean?"

His jaw ticked. "He's the one who hurt you. The one you told me about the night we met."

"Yes."

He actually looked pained, his skin pale and his hands trembling. "Did he…?"

"No," she reassured him. It had never gotten that far. Although after her mother died, she had been frightened by the way he stared at her sometimes. Not like a father looked at his daughter but like a man looked at a woman. "But when he had a bad day—which was often—he'd use me as his punching bag."

Sawyer swore softly under his breath. "And your mother?"

"You mean, did she come to my defense?" She shook her head, remembering. "When I was young, she'd dress me up and braid my hair. But by the time I turned seven, my mother grew bored of me like I was an old toy. She was never very motherly, but after that, the only time I got any attention from her was when she was hitting me."

"Jesus, why didn't anyone report it?"

She lifted one shoulder. "I'm sure people did, but we moved around so much, no one could find us." Noting the absolute horror written on Sawyer's face, she laid a reassuring hand on his arm. "It wasn't all bad. Asa and I were close. He took care of me when I didn't have anyone else."

He pivoted his body toward her to tenderly cup her cheek. "Then I'm sorry for the way I treated him. I came in here and saw you holding his hand...I sensed your closeness. I got jealous."

Her heart gave a painful squeeze. All Sawyer wanted was for her to let him in.

Why did he have to want the one thing she couldn't give him?

She seized the opportunity to change the subject. "Why did you come early? I told you I'd call you when I was ready to leave."

His thumb skimmed across her bottom lip. "Would you believe I missed you?"

"Should I believe you?"

His eyes filled with mischief. "I was curious. I wanted to see where you spend most of your days. Not that I got to see much of your condo, especially since everything was destroyed, but other than the books, there didn't seem to be anything of you in it. I thought maybe I'd get a better glimpse into Annaliese Hunt here."

She swept her gaze over her office, seeing it through his eyes. She'd purposely left the walls bare of artwork, telling herself she hadn't found the right ones yet. He was right. The space lacked any personal touches except for the shelf that held some of her most valuable books.

"But you're forgetting. Annaliese Hunt doesn't exist here," she reminded him...and herself. "This office belongs to Lisa Smith."

A tiny notch formed between his brows, and she ached to kiss it. "Is there a difference?"

Was there? If she chose a painting for her wall, would it reflect Lisa's taste or Annaliese's? Were they the same, or was Lisa merely a figment of everyone's imagination?

"I don't know," she answered truthfully. "I'm doing something I love. Something that I created and built from the ground up. That's all me, whoever I am."

"Your office is very neat and organized. But it's kind of sterile."

She nodded. So was Lisa. On the other hand, Annaliese was passionate and wild. There was none of her in here or anywhere else in her life. But her inability to choose artwork that reflected her tastes wasn't the only reason for the lack of personality in her office. "I've always got one foot out the door. I never saw any sense in decorating when I might have to leave everything behind."

At the reminder of her tendency to bolt, Sawyer's expression grew somber. His hands dropped away and he slipped off the desk, putting space she didn't want between them. "I started working my way down the list you gave me. Two of your old marks are dead from natural causes. A couple of them have been traveling on business by car, so it's not out of the realm of possibility that one of them made a detour to Michigan. I'll check their credit card statements to see if I can track their whereabouts."

"Do you really think you'll be able to figure out who trashed my condo?"

He shoved his hands into his pockets again. "I think I can at least eliminate some of the people on the long list of suspects."

She didn't miss the tightness of his voice. "Does it bother you that I've conned that many people?"

He paused, staring at her intently. "No," he finally said. "But it would be easier to understand if you just told me the truth."

"Why can't you accept that I was a con artist and I conned you? Why does there have to be more to the story?"

He leaned down and pressed his forehead to hers. "Because I know you loved me. I know you still love me. You want to be with me, but you're scared. And I'm going to put the pieces together, whether you tell me or not."

That's what she was afraid of.

She pushed against his chest so she could see his eyes. "You said earlier that some sins were too dark to ever see the light of day. Why can't you accept that mine should stay buried where they belong?"

He wrapped his arms around her, holding her close against his chest. "Because I can't bear to think of you suffering. I want to make everything better for you."

Circling her arms around his middle, she held him just as tightly. "Maybe I want to do the same for you. Are you willing to share with me why you're unwilling to walk away as CEO of Hayes Industries?"

He paused before his hands slipped away. "No."

She didn't know whether she was relieved or disappointed. "Then there's nothing else to discuss."

Sawyer lumbered to the door, and when he turned around, it was as if the last few minutes hadn't happened. "Are you hungry? We could go to dinner before we go back to the suite."

She stood. "If my condo is clean, I think it might be best if I went there tonight." Her eyes locked on his. "Alone."

He shook his head. "I disagree. The hotel is much safer for you right now."

"And it has nothing to do with our agreement?"

"I didn't say that."

She smiled. "You're infuriating, do you know that?"

"I do." He eyed her desk. "You realize I have to punish you for hitting me, right?"

Oh. Her jaw went slack, and her heart skipped a beat. *He wants to play.* "I thought you understood why I did it."

"I do understand. But as your Dominant, it's my role to make sure you never make that mistake again." He seemed to get taller as he stalked toward her. "Pull down your pants and bend over your desk."

Thank goodness. She might not be able to give him the truth, but this she could do for him. "Yes, Master."

As slowly as possible, she slid her pants down her thighs and laid herself out on her desk, pushing the papers out of the way.

He came up behind her and caressed her ass. "Don't bother counting."

Gripping the edge of the desk, she waited impatiently for him to begin. She had a feeling he wouldn't go easy on her.

When his hand finally landed, it came down with such force, it slid her forward on the desk. Again and again, he peppered her ass with hard smacks of his hand. He alternated sides, making certain to hit both cheeks as well as her thighs. She squirmed, the pain quickly morphing into pleasure that made her moan.

She threw him a glance over her shoulder, teasing him. "Is that the worst you can do?"

His expression grew feral, and his hands went to his belt. "Maybe a few strikes with this will help you learn your lesson."

She turned back around, a wide smile on her face. "Yes, Master."

He struck her hard, the sound of it and the bite of the leather belt hitting her flesh intensifying her arousal. If he kept this up, she'd come.

As if he knew what she was thinking, he stopped. She heard the crinkle of a condom wrapper, and a second later, he drove his cock into her pussy from behind. "Don't come until I tell you to."

With every stroke, her clitoris bumped the desk. Breathing through her nose, she tried not to come. But she knew it was a lost cause.

After a long groan and a single jerk of his body, he ceased his thrusting. When he slipped from her pussy, she realized he'd come.

"Get dressed," he said, moving away from her. She looked over her shoulder to witness him zipping up his pants.

"Wait," she got up from the desk and twirled around. "What are you doing? You're going to leave me like this?"

His lips tugged up in a grin that could only be described as sadistic. "You didn't think the spankings were your punishment, did you? That was just to make you horny, so that I could give you the real punishment—no orgasm."

She opened her mouth to speak, but no words came out.

Fully clothed, he strode to her and tweaked her nose. "Bet you'll never hit me again."

She growled as she pulled up her pants. "I'm thinking of hitting you right now."

"Think it all you want. I can't punish you for that." He laughed as he grabbed her purse off the floor and directed her out of her office. "Or could I?"

She hated him at that moment. Having a bit of a tantrum, she stomped all the way to his rental car parked in the lot across the street. "I really dislike this punishment."

"Good," he said as he slid into the driver's seat. "Then it's the right one."

She settled into the passenger side and put on her seat belt, wincing from the soreness of her backside. If he didn't take care of her soon, she was going to have to sneak in a self-induced orgasm when they returned to the hotel, consequences be damned.

Heavy metal blared from the radio. Ugh. They'd always disagreed about what to listen to in the car. She preferred good old country music to the raucous hair bands. This kind of music made her head hurt.

He drove out of the lot and headed down Main Street. Thank goodness it was Sunday, so there wasn't a lot of traffic. Only fifteen minutes of suffering left before she'd find a way to convince him to get her off or do the job the one-handed way.

Sawyer slammed his foot down repeatedly, the noise of it somehow cutting through the screaming on the radio.

"What's wrong?" she asked, noticing his skin turning pale.

"The brakes aren't working."

Ice cold fear gripped her, but she tried not to show it. She was surprised by how calm she sounded when she suggested, "Use the emergency brake."

He glanced at her, his face deadly serious. "It's not working either."

Just ahead, there were trucks in both lanes, giving them nowhere to go.

One way or another, they were going to crash.

As they got closer to the trucks and she screamed out Sawyer's name, she realized that everything she'd done to keep him safe was all for nothing.

Fate had caught up with them.

They were going to die.

Chapter Eleven

Lisa moaned, reaching out to turn off the alarm. It couldn't be morning already. She felt as though she'd just fallen asleep. And that didn't sound like her alarm. Her alarm buzzed. Loudly. This was a steady beeping.

Rather than hit her alarm, her hand smacked a warm solid body. Startled, she opened her eyes.

"You're okay," Sawyer said soothingly, taking her hand, his thumb sweeping across the soft spot between her thumb and finger. "It's just me."

He sat in the chair next to her, a long red scratch on his neck, but otherwise looking unharmed. Awareness crept back in. Lights. Sirens. A ride in an ambulance.

She was in the hospital because they'd hit a tree after their brakes went out. She'd complained about a headache, and the doctor had insisted she have a CT scan to make sure there was no bleeding in the brain as a result of the accident. An hour later, with a good report from the radiologist, the nurse had given her something for the pain. Whatever she'd taken had knocked her ass right out.

"I hate hospitals. Can we get out of here?" she begged Sawyer as she quickly sat up and swung her legs over the side of the bed.

She wondered how they'd get back to the hotel without a car. It was nearly impossible to find a taxi around these parts. Of course, Sawyer was wealthy. He'd probably have a limo pick them up and a nurse waiting back at his hotel suite to watch over her.

"You're not going anywhere until the doctor says you're ready to leave," he said firmly.

"Please. If there was anything wrong, they'd have me upstairs in a room rather than here in emergency. Let's face it, I'm not a priority. They'll make me wait here the rest of the night while they do my paperwork for my release. They've got my insurance. I'm sure they won't mind if we get out of here so they can use this room for someone who really needs it." She got to her feet and wobbled, woozy from the drugs they'd given her.

Sawyer shot out of his chair and steadied her, his hands on her hips. Staring intently at her mouth, he swallowed hard.

The curtain was pulled to the side, and the nurse walked in with a clipboard that hopefully had her paperwork attached to it. "How are you feeling, Ms. Smith?"

"Perfect," she said, stepping away from Sawyer to show him she could stand on her own two feet without his help. The room spun, but she kept her mouth shut about it. "Ready to go home."

"Not yet, young lady." The nurse shook her head as she led Lisa back into bed. "The doctor wants to observe you for at least another hour before he'll let you go." She wrapped the blood pressure monitor around Lisa's arm.

Observation? The man wasn't even in the room, and unless there was some video camera taping her unaware, no one was watching her other than Sawyer. And he could do the same thing at home.

Hospitals always reminded her of her father. He'd picked many of their marks in them, preying on people's vulnerability. He pretended to care about their well-being when all he cared about was what they could do to make him a buck. There were all different schemes. At one small-town animal hospital, he even sold a bogus cryogenics policy to a widowed elderly woman that would allow her and her dying dog to be frozen together, preserved for all eternity until doctors could bring them back to life.

The scams were bad enough. But he'd used Lisa and her brothers to help reel the marks in. She'd been the one to tell that poor woman in the animal hospital that her very own grandmother had been frozen with her poodle and that someday soon, she'd get to see them both again.

Lisa had been only six years old.

Who taught a six-year-old to lie?

"Blood pressure is normal. Any headache? Dizziness?" the nurse asked, reading off a list in front of her.

"She was dizzy when she got out of bed," Sawyer offered up just as she answered no.

Lisa glared at him and then smiled sweetly at the nurse. "A little bit, but it was from the drugs you gave me."

The nurse peered up at her from her clipboard. "Perhaps. But to be on the safer side, why don't you follow the doctor's orders and hang out here with us a little longer."

Between Sawyer and the nurse, she wasn't going to win this argument. When the nurse left her room, she turned to Sawyer. "Do you really think someone tampered with the brakes on the car?"

"Think?" He dropped into the chair. "I know someone tampered with it. Someone was trying to kill us."

Her thoughts went straight to her father. But he was dead. "Why do you assume they were trying to kill us both? It's me they want."

He kicked out his legs, playing it casual, even while his body radiated his tension. "And yet it was my rental car they messed with. Whoever it was had to have done it while I was at your office. Which means they not only know their way around cars, they did it without anyone seeing them."

"It's not exactly like there were people hanging out in the parking lot on a Sunday. No one was around except us."

He folded his arms across his chest. "And your brother. Don't you find it strange he shows up and this happens?"

Her chest tightened in anger. Asa would never hurt her. "Well if I did, I'd also have to find it strange that it happened after you showed up at my office, too. Should I also consider you a suspect?"

"Do you really think I'd harm you?"

She sighed. "No. I don't know what your plan is with me, but I do trust that you'd never harm me. At least not intentionally."

"You keep mentioning this plan of mine. There's no plan, Annaliese." He leaned forward, placing a hand on her thigh. "I wish you'd trust me."

It didn't make sense to her. What did he have to gain by spending a week with her other than sex? "Don't take it personally. When you spend your entire life lying, it's hard to believe in honesty."

"Then stop lying and start believing."

Her eyes burned from unshed tears. "I wish it was that simple."

He scooted his chair closer, the sound of metal grinding on the floor. "It can be. I—"

The curtain opened again, and the nurse peeked her head in. "Think you're up for some company? I have a couple of concerned friends outside who'd like to come back and visit."

Frowning, she racked her fuzzy brain to remember if she had made any calls to her friends about the accident. She turned to Sawyer and raised a brow in question.

"Logan and Rachel," he said, standing.

He'd called them? She loved Rachel, but the woman was a nosy journalist. If she got an inkling of a story, she'd want to track its scent like a bloodhound.

With a donut in her hand and a smear of chocolate to the left of her lips, her friend came rushing into the room, Logan right behind her. "Are you okay? I was so worried when Sawyer called and told us about the accident."

"I'm fine," Lisa said, surprised at how normal she sounded despite the fact that the room was now spinning.

Rachel lowered the guardrails on one side and plopped herself down beside Lisa. "What happened?"

"It was just a little accident," she said, waving her hand as if they'd gotten into a minor fender bender with a parked car.

She slid her gaze to Sawyer, begging him with her eyes to corroborate her lie. It's not that she didn't trust Rachel. She trusted her more than she trusted almost anyone—which unfortunately, wasn't that much.

Rachel wasn't malicious, and her need to uncover the truth of a story had more to do with her compulsion to help innocent people than to further her career. But that was the problem.

Lisa wasn't innocent.

Sawyer waited a beat, seemingly considering her silent request, and then spoke directly to Logan. "Someone cut the brakes."

She sighed. So much for keeping it secret.

"Guys, out," Rachel said, shooing the men with her hands like she was herding cattle. "Lisa and I need some girl time."

Surprisingly, Sawyer and Logan listened.

Logan slapped Sawyer on the back as they left. "Time to call the reinforcements?"

"They're already on it," Sawyer replied, sliding the curtains shut to give her and Rachel some privacy.

With Sawyer out of the room, Lisa decided she no longer needed to lie in bed like an invalid. Although she remained dizzy, she lifted her head from the pillow and swung her legs over the side to sit beside Rachel. "What reinforcements?"

Rachel looked pensive. "If I had to guess, it means your husband has Oz, Hunter, and Rowan putting their computer skills to work."

That meant three more people would know about her criminal history. Three more people had the power to use that information against her. Like this room, her life was spiraling out of control. "He should've spoken to me before getting them involved."

Her friend shook her head, a slight smile on her lips. "I'm still having a difficult time dealing with the news that you're not only married, but married to Sawyer Hayes."

"Surprise."

Rachel bumped her knee against Lisa's. "I only know what Logan told me, but he said Sawyer was pretty wrecked after you took off without a forwarding address."

She let out an unladylike snort. "Obviously not too wrecked about it. After all, he did have an entire sex club at his disposal."

"Yeah. Paradise Found is quite a club," Rachel said with a sigh, as if remembering it quite fondly. She hadn't given the girls all the details about what kinky experiences she'd partaken in at the club, but she'd told them enough that Lisa knew she'd enjoyed herself. Rachel's eyes widened as she realized Lisa wasn't exactly pleased about her husband's business. "Not Benediction, but it has its appeal."

She let her friend off the hook. It wasn't her fault that Lisa's husband had felt the need to fuck his wife out of his system with half of Vegas. "Right."

Rachel frowned, her head tipping to the side. "But you know what was odd? The time I spent there, I never once saw Sawyer participate in any of the offerings there. He was all business."

Lisa cursed the small burst of hope that bloomed in her chest. Because even if her husband didn't own a sex club, there was no chance that he had remained faithful to her all these years. "You were only there for a couple days, and he was busy helping you."

"Maybe," Rachel said slowly, as if not really believing that. "All I'm saying is I wouldn't assume anything until you hear it straight from his mouth. And their friends? You can trust them. They won't judge you, and neither will I." She gave her a quick pat on the leg. "So are you going to tell me why Sawyer called you Annaliese?"

It was so strange to hear her name come out of Rachel's mouth. Other than her family and Sawyer, no one had ever called her that.

She paused, contemplating how much she should tell Rachel. Could she trust her friend? Maybe it was finally time to find out.

"It's my real name," she admitted, her hands sweaty from nerves. "Annaliese Hunt." No, that wasn't right. She corrected herself. "I mean, Hayes." She angled her body toward Rachel, awaiting her friend's reaction. "But I've gone by at least a dozen others. Before I moved to Michigan, I made my living as a con artist."

Rachel shot up from the bed. "You're serious? So it is true? You stole millions of dollars from him?" Lines of worry formed on her forehead. "Did you even love him?"

She answered without hesitation. "Yes. I loved him. I still do."

When Rachel began pacing, Lisa could almost see the hamster spinning the wheel inside that mind of hers. "Then why? Why did you steal from him? If it was about the money, you could have stayed with him and had billions of dollars at your disposal."

Lisa stood, holding onto the chair in front of her so she didn't fall. "Please, Rachel. I know the reporter in you wants to sniff out the story, but I'm asking you to leave it alone."

"You're wrong." Rachel stopped her pacing. "Well, you're not entirely wrong. But I'm not asking you as the reporter. I want to know as your friend."

At that moment, Lisa knew she had made the right decision confiding in her. She blew out a breath, relieved. She didn't have to suffer in silence anymore. When Sawyer filed for divorce at the end of the seven nights with her, she'd have her friends to count on.

The room tilted, and her legs trembled as if they couldn't support her weight. Guess she was still too woozy to stand. She dropped into the chair and leaned forward, resting her elbows on her knees. "I'm sorry. I wish I could tell you, but I owe it to Sawyer to give him the truth before anyone else."

Rachel's lips pressed into a straight line. "Does it have something to do with the break-in at your condo and your brakes getting cut?"

She wished she knew. "Maybe? There's a lot of people who'd love to see me dead."

Rachel walked over and sat on the bed so that their knees touched. "Well, there's a lot more people who just plain old love you. Whatever you did in the past won't change how I and the other girls feel about you. If you need our help, don't hesitate to ask. In fact, I've got a suitcase of clothes out in the hallway for you."

Lisa took Rachel's hands. "Thank you."

The curtain slid open, and Sawyer stuck his head inside. "Is it safe to come back in?"

"It is," Rachel said, standing. "We're going to let her rest now, but there's a suitcase filled with clothes for her to take with her when you leave." She put her hands on her hips. "Sawyer, I'm only going to say this once. You're one of Logan's best friends and you saved my ass before, so I'm giving you the benefit of the doubt. But Lisa's one of *my* best friends, and I'll always choose her over you. So please don't do anything to fuck it up. Are we clear?"

Sawyer turned to Logan. "Is she taking Domme classes or something?"

Logan looked horrified. "Over my dead body."

Rachel threw her arms around his neck playfully. "Hey, I thought you liked when I—"

"Good-bye," Logan said, covering Rachel's lips with his fingers. He yanked her out of there before she could finish her sentence. "Feel better, Lisa."

An awkward silence filled the room. So many emotions poured through her right then, she didn't know which one to deal with first.

"Yeah," Sawyer finally said. "That was nice of them, right? Logan's letting us borrow his car—"

"You told your group of friends about me."

He nodded once. "I told my friends."

"You should have asked me first."

"This isn't only about you." He stuck his hands in his pockets and shifted his weight from foot to foot. "These guys had my back when you left me gutted. They were the ones who saved me when I thought I was beyond saving. Pulled me off the twisted and dangerous road I was on and got me back onto the straight and narrow."

Her heart clenched at hearing how much she'd hurt him. If only there had been another way to protect him, she would've taken it. She didn't regret her actions, because they had kept him alive, but she did regret how he'd suffered as a result. "What are you talking about? What happened after I left? Does this have anything to do with why you lost billions?"

"I tried to forget you," he admitted, staring at her so intently, she could almost feel the heat of it burn into her. "I practically drank myself into a coma those first few months you were gone. I went to the bars, to strip clubs, picked up women…" He stopped, as if realizing what he had said, and she tried not to let on how much it hurt her. "Nothing helped. Nothing until Vegas. I went there on business." A look of bliss entered his eyes. "The lights, the food, the free booze, the accessibility of drugs. It was intoxicating. A fantasy world. It started innocently enough. A few hands of blackjack here. An hour of poker there. Then it was craps. Roulette. It didn't matter whether I was winning or losing, because the potential to win was always there. That's all I thought about. That next hand and whether or not it would be the one to turn my luck around. Maybe then I could find you and bring you home."

A tear slid down her cheek. She didn't want to hear the rest. Didn't want to know that she'd caused the man she loved more than life itself such torment. She knew all too well about gambling and its consequences from watching her parents. People didn't understand that for some, gambling was like a drug.

Was there something about her that caused those around her to escape into the high that gambling afforded them? Or was it a coincidence that her husband shared the same addiction as her parents?

"How could you lose billions from a few days of gambling?" she asked.

"Because it took over my life. If I wasn't in Vegas, I was placing bets with bookies or playing poker on the Internet. At first, I won enough to make it seductive, as if it wasn't really harmful. Then, I told myself I was breaking even. But before long, the losses kept accumulating."

Even as the drug causing her dizziness left her system, Sawyer's disclosure caused the room to spin. "Surely you didn't gamble away billions."

"No. But I may as well have." He sat on the bed. "With my mind distracted constantly by the score of the football game or by the next poker tournament I had to get an invitation to, I neglected Hayes Industries. I lost huge contracts because I couldn't be bothered to sign them. It was all about the rush."

Hot tears filled her eyes. "I'm so sorry."

"No." He leaned forward and brushed his hands down her arms. "My gambling addiction isn't on you. That was all me. You can take responsibility for your own actions, but you cannot be responsible for mine."

She wasn't sure she believed that. If she hadn't left him... hell, if he'd never met her in the first place... would he still have turned to gambling to cope?

"How did your friends help?"

He smiled, the memories practically flickering in his eyes. "The kidnapped me and brought me out to what I later named the Paradise Lost Hotel. Spent a week basically detoxing from the addiction. No television, Internet, or phone privileges. They even brought out one of those shrinks to the stars from TV to get me to face my addiction and redirect my attention to healthier goals. My friend Oz pointed out the hotel was in a prime location for a sex club, being that it was outside the Las Vegas city limits, where it would be legal. I bought the place the next day and moved from Arizona to Vegas. I channeled all my energy into both Hayes Industries and the club. There was no time to think about you or gambling."

So she had Oz to blame for her husband's foray into the sex club business. She didn't like it, but at least she understood why now. "You're lucky you have such good friends."

"I would've done the same for them, but yeah, I'm damn lucky." His voice grew quiet. "What about you? Do you have anyone who picks you up when you fall?"

She thought about her friends. When she shattered into pieces at the end of her week with Sawyer, would they be there for her? And more importantly, would she let them?

Chapter Twelve

HE PACED ALONG the length of his trailer, pulling at his hair to get the voices to quiet. They wouldn't stop. One by one, the voices joined in a loud chorus of teasing.

Worthless.

Stupid.

Lazy.

Nothing was going according to plan. She wasn't supposed to be hurt. She was his. She couldn't die until the voices told him to kill her. This time he wouldn't mess it up. Timing was everything. Just one second too late, and they'd be separated for eternity.

Didn't she understand he couldn't survive without her? Her blood was on his hands, a stain that wouldn't go away no matter how many times he washed them. This would clean him, the voices chanted. This would give him forgiveness and place him in heaven with her, where they could frolic and make love once again.

This would make the voices *shut the fuck up!*

If he put little holes in his scalp, maybe they'd all fall out of his brain. He couldn't think when it got like this. Couldn't figure out what to do next. She wasn't supposed to stay here. She should've run. Why wouldn't she run?

Tufts of hair fell all around him, the holes in his scalp easing the noise buzzing through his brain.

Think, think, think.

He needed a new plan. He couldn't rely on the man he had entrusted. The voices must have gotten to him. Or maybe he was still as rotten and devious as the snake in the Garden of Eden, luring his wife to lie with him in sin. He had to die for his sins. Yes, the voices approved, their murmurs only a low constant hum of accord.

He'd tell him the deal was off.

Then he'd kill him. He'd kill both of them.

He'd take her to the oasis, where he could use his weapon to end their suffering.

He smiled, his hands bloody once again.

It was the perfect plan.

Chapter Thirteen

"You really didn't have to carry me all the way from the car," she said to Sawyer as he brought her into the hotel suite. "There's nothing wrong with my legs."

He cradled her in his arms as he crossed the room and went into his bedroom. Then he gently deposited her onto the bed. After pulling back the blanket, he sat beside her. "Let's take off your clothes and get you into bed."

She stared at him, wondering what was going through his mind. "No offense. I'm not sure I'm up to doing anything naughty with you tonight."

His lips tugged up into a slight smile. "As your doctor, I'll need to examine you fully. It's my job to take care of you and ensure your comfort. I'm sure there are lots of ways I can do that without you having to expend any energy."

All her breath expelled in one giant whoosh.

Doctor-patient role play.

He hadn't forgotten how much she enjoyed it, although in the past, she'd played the doctor to his patient. It would be fun to see how he'd do acting out the other part. And with everything that had happened, he owed her an orgasm or three after leaving her high and dry at her office earlier.

Her blood heated, the fantasy rolling through her mind like a dirty movie. "Yes, doctor. I'm quite sore. Do you think you could help me?"

The skin around his eyes crinkled in humor. "Of course. Anything to help."

His large hands settled on her hips, his fingers splayed wide, making her feel dainty and fragile. The dominance inside him quietly roared to life as he took over the scene, requiring her to relax and follow his lead. The tips of his knuckles brushed her bare skin as inch by inch, he slid her shirt up her rib cage. He did it as if she was a treasure he didn't want to damage. His gaze remained focused on her exposed skin, his eyes darkening and narrowing as he bared more and more of her pale skin. He looked hungry for her. Starved. And yet he remained gentle, his touch a mere whisper on her heated body.

He whipped her shirt over her head and slid his hand up and down the length of her spine, eliciting a trail of goose bumps in its wake. Her nipples beaded against her bra, the fabric suddenly tight and uncomfortable on the hardened flesh. His gaze dropped to them, his tongue slipping across his lower lip as he stared and stared without doing anything, driving her mad. She ached for his touch on her breasts. Ached for his hot mouth to suction around her nipple. The wait was agonizingly wonderful because it would make the contact that much more intense.

She thought he'd undo her bra next, but demonstrating he was on his own timetable, his hands drifted to her pants. "Lift up," he ordered, his voice raw and gritty.

Once she got to her knees, he eased her leggings down her thighs, exposing her soaking panties to his gaze. And there was no way to hide how incredibly wet she was for him. All he had to do was breathe, and her body prepared itself for his invasion. Welcomed him home, where it wanted to tighten around him and never let him go.

She'd thought him hungry for her before, but she saw the moment he realized how desperately she wanted him. Saw the way his hands clenched and his cock began swelling beneath his jeans, the huge outline of it like a present she couldn't wait to unwrap. He was as desperate for her as she was for him.

Which made their agreement even more dangerous. It was one thing if she was in love with him, but if he fell back in love with her, how would she ever walk away from him again? And yet she couldn't stop herself from taking everything he had to give her, too selfish to resist. She could play indifferent, maintain a controlled and detached manner even as they made love. And that's what this was for her. Making love. Not fucking. Never fucking. Not even when he beat her with a cane or shared her with another. It was always about him. Their connection. Their love.

But after she'd deceived him, lied to him, left him...how could he love her?

He couldn't. She was deluding herself. Forgetting that she wasn't worthy of his love. But right now and for the next several days, she'd pretend that nothing had changed and that she was still his Annaliese. Annaliese Hayes. The only name she ever wanted.

Yanking her from her thoughts, he rubbed a finger over her panty-covered slit. 'Seems to me this patient needs some relief. Or are you always this wet?" He pulled his fingers away and pressed them to his lips as if savoring her taste and smell.

"No," she said, barely able to speak. "I'm aching inside for something big and hard to fill me. Know any remedies?"

He smiled with a slight upward curve of his lips, a sign that had previously meant he was planning something she'd never expect. "I can think of a few things." He pushed her back onto the bed and removed both her pants and underwear before unsnapping her bra and exposing her breasts, leaving her naked while he remained completely dressed. "Lay back and put your head on the pillow. I need to get some items for your exam."

Her arousal increased as she pondered what he'd do to her next. Obviously, he didn't have any real medical tools here. Did he?

He went into the bathroom and returned a few minutes later carrying an armful of things.

"Let's begin with a sponge bath," he said as he sat on the bed. He dropped almost everything next to him, putting a cup of water on the nightstand and holding a white washcloth in his hand. "I want you nice and clean before I get you dirty."

He started at her neck, rubbing the warm, wet cloth across her collarbone with an almost detached demeanor. She could almost believe this wasn't arousing him, except for his rapid breathing and the fact his cock looked as though it was going to burst out of his pants.

He slowly worked his way up and down her arms before dragging the cloth over her nipples teasingly and then moving onto her upper abdomen. Unable to resist, she bowed on the bed, silently begging him to return to her nipples.

He arched a brow and tsked. "You're a greedy patient. But since this is about making you comfortable, all you have to do is ask for what you want and trust that I'll give it to you. Do you think you can do that?"

"Yes." She dug her fingers into the blankets to keep herself from forcing him to touch her. She had to ask. She could do that. "Please. I want you to clean my nipples some more. I need it."

He smiled. "Good girl."

She wanted to be a good girl. Wanted to be a good patient for him.

The headache that had lingered after the accident had disappeared and been replaced by an ache that only he could soothe. There had been plenty of memorable nights of erotic pain and wild sex that had left her sore for days. And she had loved those nights. But tonight wouldn't involve pain.

Tonight he would care for her as if she were a fragile china doll, and that's exactly what she needed. It had been so long since anyone had tended to her needs. Since Sawyer. It was a luxury to lie here.

One she couldn't afford to get used to.

He dragged the washcloth over a nipple with careful deliberation. She'd never noticed how rough the fabric felt across her skin. It was like a tongue, languidly licking over the bud, and as the air cooled her moist flesh, her nipple and areola pebbled even tighter, becoming almost painful.

His lips brushed across them, his short stubble scraping her skin in the most delicious way. She whimpered in expectation, her spine bowing to encourage him to take one of the buds into her mouth. And when he did, when those sinful lips of his sealed over her nipple and sucked it into the hot cavern of his mouth, she cried out his name, desperate for more.

More sucking.

Licking.

Nibbling.

Biting.

He gave it all to her and more, making sure he left that poor nipple sore and abused from his ministrations before moving onto the other one and mirroring his actions. Her arousal dripped from her pussy, her inner thighs slick with proof of her desire. She had a difficult time remaining still; her instinct to squirm and wrap her legs around his waist in hopes he'd fuck her hard.

But she was a good patient, and good patients waited for their doctor's instructions. She trusted he had a plan to get her off, and she didn't want to ruin it. Her Master had the most creative means of giving her pleasure, and judging by his earlier smile, she should buckle up for an orgasmic ride.

Although he'd worked her nipples for at least twenty minutes, it seemed as though no time at all had passed when he licked a path down her torso, abrading her flesh with his facial hair along the way. She couldn't wait to look in the mirror later, eager to see the marks he left behind on her body as evidence of his loving.

He wedged himself between her thighs, his hot breath blowing on the sensitive skin of her pussy. She held her breath, anticipating his tongue. Instead, she heard a hissing noise and jerked as a cool substance hit her labia. The scent of shaving cream reached her, and she lifted her head off the pillow, looking down at him.

"Relax," he crooned. "I need to shave you in order to really give you a thorough exam."

Right. It had nothing to do with the fact that he loved to keep her pussy smooth and free of hair, so that he could play with that sensitive skin. It was an act of dominance, a display of ownership that sent a chill racing down the length of her body. She had to trust him with a sharp blade and believe he wouldn't do anything to harm her.

The first scrape of the razor across her skin aroused her to the point of pain. Her clitoris swelled until it felt as though it had grown twice its size, and her juices trickled out of her, sliding down to lubricate between the cheeks of her ass. She practically vibrated from the tension of having him work so methodically and precisely on her mound.

His eyes narrowed in concentration as if he was performing surgery, his hands steady and sure as he stretched her skin to get the closest possible shave.

She grew more restless with each passing minute, the dampness between her thighs sticky and thick. And when he finished shaving and wiping off the excess shaving cream, she was rewarded with a quick swipe of his tongue up one side of her labia and down the other, his touch staying away from the spot where she needed it most. It was as if he was trying to kill her with unbridled lust.

"You taste so good I want to drink you all up," he murmured against her thigh. He moved away from her core and sat up. "But I won't. I need you good and wet for the next part of your exam."

Grasping the blanket in her hands to keep from touching her now hairless mound, she hoped the exam included probing her pussy with his cock. "I'm ready for you, doctor."

He snapped on a clear latex glove and held up a bottle of water-based lube.

Her heart went into a full-out sprint, and her breathing grew erratic as she realized why he required those two objects.

He'd only done it once before.

The night he'd first told her he loved her.

The night he'd collared her.

The night he'd asked her to marry him.

"Let your thighs fall to the side and relax," he said, and he poured a healthy amount of lube into the palm of his gloved hand.

She harrumphed. "Easy for you to say. You're not the one who's about to have an entire hand in her pussy."

Despite the name of the act, she knew he wouldn't put his entire fist in her. Well, not exactly. When he'd first told her what he wanted to do to her, she'd panicked, picturing him making a tight fist like a boxer and pushing it inside her. Then he'd explained that his hand would actually be in a shape that resembled a duck's beak, palm up with his fingers stuck close together.

"You have a safe word." His expression turned serious. "Do you want to use it?"

Holding his gaze, she recalled the last time he'd fisted her. He'd gone slow, easing her into it, a finger at a time, stretching her and lubricating her enough until all of him had fit inside of her. There had been some pain. An incredible fullness. A high from giving him her total submission. And the most amazing orgasm of her life up to that point.

After he'd cleaned her up, he'd gotten down on one knee, holding a jewelry box in his shaking hand, and declared his love for her. Without hesitation, she'd accepted both proposals, forgetting that it was all about a con, and cried happily as he'd slipped the diamond ring on her finger and fastened the chain collar around her neck.

Was this a test of her trust in him, or was he trying to re-create that night to remind her of what they had together? The act had brought them closer than she'd thought possible. For her to completely surrender to him like that had been a transcendental experience for them both.

It was the ultimate act of dominance over her.

Could she allow him to do it again and not lose herself to him?

She didn't know.

But she couldn't refuse.

God help her, she wanted to feel that incredible high where he showed her that even the seemingly impossible was possible. She wanted that staggering connection between them, if only for a few more days. If she was going to go the rest of her life without it, didn't she deserve to enjoy it when she could?

Her pulse thundered in her ears, her heart pumping so hard, she could feel it in the soles of her feet. When he flew back to Las Vegas and proceeded with the divorce, then she would deal with the repercussions of being in love with a man she could never have. But right now, she was going to pretend that their affair didn't have an expiration date.

She wasn't going to use her safe word. "No," she answered, her voice hoarse. "I want this."

"Do you remember the last time? You need to relax all your muscles and breathe deep. If there's any pain you can't accept, you can say either 'yellow' or 'red.' Yellow means I'll pause what I'm doing and we can talk about whether to continue. Say 'red' or 'black list,' and I'll stop everything and we'll end the scene. Do you consent, my little patient?"

"Yes, doctor. Whatever you feel you have to do to give me a thorough exam."

"This may feel a little cold."

She shivered as he spilled an obscene amount of lube over her spread pussy. He wasn't kidding about it being cold.

"Now I'm going to start with two fingers." He slowly inserted them inside, the glove and the lubrication helping them slide more easily. He thrust them in and out a couple times, giving her warm tingles that permeated through her belly.

His gaze was locked with hers, his eyes full of heat. He added a third finger, giving her a moment to acclimate before he slowly separated them in order to stretch her vaginal walls. He played with her inside, the pads of his fingers stroking various spots, some which made her jolt as if she'd been electrocuted and others that made her wince from discomfort. She continued to relax her muscles, knowing if she tensed, it would make it more difficult.

"I'm adding the fourth." He cupped his fingers close together, putting them in the shape of a duck's bill, and slipped them all inside of her, working them deep, past his knuckles and further still.

He filled her completely, the burning stretch from his fingers causing her to become even more aroused. It was pain, but it was the type she craved. An erotic pain caused by her lover and Master.

Her heart hammered wildly against her breastbone, the tightness in her core growing more and more pronounced as her climax neared. "Yellow," she said.

Sawyer stilled. "Am I hurting you?"

"Yes," she answered. "But it's the good kind of hurt. In fact, it's so good, I'm about to come. Just give me a moment to head it off."

His lips tilted up in a grin. "Take all the time you need."

She took a deep breath and closed her eyes, terminating the intense connection with Sawyer. About a minute later, she felt her arousal return to a mild simmer. "I'm good. Please continue."

His throat worked over a swallow. "Do you think you're ready for all five?"

"I don't know. You're the doctor. What do you think?"

"I think you can. I think you want it as badly as I do."

"What do you get out of this?" she asked, her gaze falling on the gigantic bulge in his jeans.

"Euphoria. How many other people have been inside of you like this?"

"None."

"Exactly. I own this pussy. It's mine to tease." He slid his hand out of her, and after adding more lube to his fingers, tucked his thumb in the middle of his palm and began to push back inside. "Mine to fuck. Mine to share."

A cry tore from her throat and her legs trembled as his entire hand began to disappear in her pussy. Her head whipped back and forth on the pillow, a chant of "oh my God" spilling from her lips. She'd thought she'd remembered what it had felt like, but she'd underestimated the intensity. The fullness. The surrender. It was like comparing a light rain to a category five hurricane.

"You should see how fucking sexy this looks. My entire hand up to my goddamned wrist inside of you. I wish I could take a picture of this, so I could jack off to it later. Good thing I've got one hell of a memory."

She felt the heat of his hand and every bump and ridge of his knuckles as they pressed against her inner walls. It was as if he was reaching so deep inside, he could actually touch her soul. When he gently wiggled his hand inside her in tiny circles, she gasped with the sensations swirling through every inch of her body.

For a long moment, she hovered on the precipice of something so large, there was no sound.

No smell.

No taste.

No sight.

Only *feeling.*

Her Master consumed her, taking her to new heights so frightening, she worried she'd never survive the fall.

The climax built and built and built, her muscles trembling and twitching out of control. Inhuman noises spilled from her throat, desperate moans that had she been in her right mind might have embarrassed her. A tension in her belly coiled tight as Sawyer's hand rubbed her G-spot. She was on fire, burning alive in heaven on earth. And when he finally used his other hand to pinch her clitoris and commanded her to come, her orgasm hit her with the force of a freight train, smashing her into a million tiny pieces. Liquid gushed from her pussy, soaking the bed, and wave after wave of intense contractions racked her body.

As she came down from the high, she heard him whispering endearments, calling her "good girl," and telling her how proud he was of her. She lay boneless on the bed, half asleep and half rejuvenated.

He lifted her off the mattress and cradled her to his chest. "You're sleeping with me tonight."

She snuggled into him. "Are you going to fuck me now?"

"No, my girl. You need your sleep."

"Okay, Master. Good night."

He placed her under the covers and then joined her, spooning her and tucking her head under his chin. A cool weight settled around her neck.

Her hand instinctively went to her throat, fingering the cool metal around it.

Dread washing over her, she opened her eyes to the darkness of the room.

He'd collared her.

Chapter Fourteen

Taking another bite of her crispy bacon, Lisa tried to pretend she wasn't eavesdropping on Sawyer's phone conversation with one of his techie friends who had been researching her old marks.

Things had been a little...uncomfortable for her this morning, in more ways than one. Her butt was still sore from the beating he'd given it yesterday, an examination in the mirror this morning confirming the belt he'd used had left red welts and bruises. Kinky freak that she was, she loved it. In fact, the more it ached, the wetter she got.

And she could still feel the stretch in her pussy, feel his entire hand inside her, filling her, rubbing her, completing her.

Sitting here, pretending she wasn't turned on, that her clit wasn't pulsing and her panties weren't soaked, was in itself a turn-on. She wanted him to hang up his call and order her to her knees so she could get him off and then push her backward onto the table, hook her legs around his neck, and eat his breakfast between her thighs.

She finished eating and touched the other reason for her discomfort.

Her collar.

Not because she didn't want it. But because she didn't know what it meant.

Was she supposed to wear it for the week and then return it? Or did he have expectations that what they shared would last beyond that?

When she'd opened her eyes this morning, it was the first thing on her mind. But he was already in the shower, and after he'd gotten dressed, there didn't seem to be a good way to approach the topic. Or maybe she just wasn't ready to hear his answer.

So instead she'd opted to wait for him to bring it up.

An hour later, and he still hadn't mentioned it. But his gaze continuously went to her neck, his eyes flashing hungrily each time. It was a sign of her commitment to him and a public display of his ownership to anyone who recognized the chain for what it represented.

She belonged to him.

Before, they'd considered themselves to have a 24-7 slave relationship. She was sure that others would have disagreed. After all, she hadn't walked around calling him "Master" and hadn't relied on him to choose her outfit for the day, nor had he expected her to eat a prescribed diet. Like all relationships, vanilla and otherwise, theirs was unique. They chose what they felt worked the best for them, and that was to maintain their roles outside of the bedroom. It had worked for them, and she'd never given a damn about anyone else's opinion.

She'd changed so much since then. Built a career and bought a home. She'd learned how to stand on her own two feet.

Even if somehow she and Sawyer stayed together, how would things work between them? Her business was here, and the main headquarters of Hayes Industries was out west. As long as he refused to give up his role as CEO, he was tied to that company.

There were still too many unknowns—lies and secrets between them on both their parts. If she questioned him about the significance of the collar and their future, she feared it would create a rift between them that would be impossible to fix.

As she placed her dirty dishes on the room service cart, she decided she'd rather not risk ruining their current agreement. If things ended at the end of the week, at least she would have a week full of memories. And she needed those memories. Because she'd never be with anyone else.

Sawyer was it for her. For now and for always. Time and distance wouldn't change that.

After saying good-bye, he put his phone into his pocket and strode over to her, his intent written all over his face. When he stood in front of her, he slid one finger under her collar, tugging her against him and kissing her deeply and unhurriedly, his lips somehow firm and yielding at the same time.

With a loud sigh, he pulled back, worry visible by the wrinkled lines around his eyes. "That was Oz. They haven't finished checking everyone out, but they narrowed down the list to three possible suspects, one in particular. Were you aware that one of your marks lives an hour from you?"

Her arousal died instantly. "No. Who?" What were the odds of someone she'd conned living so close?

Had they been keeping tabs on her? Or was it a coincidence?

Blue veins popped from his clenched fists. "His name is Chad Winters. The guys are checking his bank records to see if they can track his movement, but I think it's best if I go speak with him one on one."

The rage coming off Sawyer frightened her. What if he did something stupid that got him hurt or arrested? If Chad Winters was responsible for trying to kill Sawyer, she needed to be there to protect him.

She grabbed her purse off the couch. "I'm going with you."

If anything, he looked even angrier. "I don't think it's a good idea. If we're wrong, he could call the cops on you once you show up on his doorstep."

She hadn't thought of that possibility, but she'd risk it in order to ensure Sawyer's safety. "I'm willing to take that chance. Other than to you, I've never had the opportunity to apologize for what I did."

Although it wasn't the real reason she wanted to go with him, it was true. Maybe this would give her a bit of closure on her past.

He stared at her long and hard, and then he gave her a brief nod. "Let's go."

Their drive to the small town where Chad Winters lived was fraught with tension, each of them lost in their own thoughts. She nibbled on her thumbnail, growing more nervous with each passing mile and unable to shake the feeling that something terrible was about to happen. All these years she'd tried to protect Sawyer, and in less than an hour, they could be serving themselves up to the man who wanted them dead.

Several times she almost asked him to turn around, but she knew he would only drop her off and go back without her. She had no other choice but to see this through.

It shamed her that she couldn't remember much about Chad Winters other than the size of his bank account. Most of the men she'd swindled had blended into one faceless individual, their characteristics too similar to help differentiate them from the others. Most were wealthy, middle-aged, and lonely. Although they had money, they had little else in their lives, and their confidence was poor. So when she fell into their lives and worshipped the ground they walked on, they'd do anything to keep her…

Maybe she didn't want to remember them.

She knew she deserved to suffer for the way she'd treated them. While she never conned them out of enough money that they had become penniless, it certainly couldn't have helped their self-esteem to know that she'd never really worshipped them and that all the money in the world couldn't buy happiness.

They pulled into the trailer park. As she got a look at where Chad Winters now lived, pangs of guilt caused her stomach to cramp. She hadn't stolen much from him, but obviously, it had been enough for him to lose his house.

She'd lived in plenty of these neighborhoods throughout the country. A lot of them were beautifully maintained neighborhoods, where people looked out for each other and kids played outside.

This was not one of those.

That's why, as they parked the car outside of a dilapidated trailer with its rusted siding and multiple dents, she realized that her actions had consequences she hadn't foreseen.

Before taking Sawyer's millions, she'd never cheated anybody out of more than one hundred thousand dollars. That had been the arbitrary limit her parents had set based on their years of experience. It was enough to make the con worthwhile, but not enough to cause a millionaire to go to the cops. The marks were too embarrassed to file police reports or go to the FBI, and some were criminals who couldn't afford to get the authorities involved.

Chad Winters had obviously lost more than the money she'd tricked him out of. From what she could recall, she'd only managed to finagle fifty thousand dollars, after telling him she could get him a rare first-edition Superman comic book. At the time, he'd had a net worth of over ten million dollars.

Had her actions caused a chain reaction that had resulted in the man living in this trailer park?

Sawyer knew bits and pieces about her past, but she feared he would feel differently about her after meeting one of the other men she defrauded. The woman he thought he knew was not the woman Chad Winters would have known. She changed into whomever would most tempt the mark, whether that was a quiet kindergarten teacher, a bored college student, or the sexually adventurous submissive, as in Sawyer's case.

A loud bang tore through the car, the noise reverberating in her ears.

"Get down!" she shouted. On instinct, she ducked, expecting the glass of the windows to shatter, her entire body trembling and her heart racing as if she'd just finished a marathon.

Was someone shooting at them? Was Chad Winters trying to kill them?

Sawyer's hand came down on her shoulder, rubbing it reassuringly. "It's okay," he said in a soothing tone. "It was a car backfiring."

She covered her face with her hands. Realizing she'd been holding her breath, she exhaled.

He undid her seat belt and angled her knees toward him. "Hey. Are you sure you want to do this with me? I can take you back to the hotel. Talk to him on my own."

The coward in her wanted to do just that. To slink away and hide behind the locked door of the penthouse suite at the hotel. To never have to come face-to-face with her shameful past.

But she wouldn't. It was time to confront her past, and the only way to do it was to stand strong in the present. If Chad called the cops on her, she'd accept it. This was her chance to apologize for her crimes and to make reparations. Of course, if he was behind the break-in and the attempt on their lives, she'd make certain she wasn't the only one going to prison.

"I'm good," she said with a brisk nod. Even though her heart was still in her throat, she sat up, threw open the car door, and stuck one leg outside. "Let's go."

She could tell from the narrowing of his eyes that he didn't believe her. But to his credit, he didn't say anything. Merely got out of the car and strolled around it to take her hand, giving her a gentle squeeze that served as a reminder that they were in this together.

A dog barked from inside the trailer, and judging by the sound of it, the dog was a large one. She rubbed her sweaty palm on the side of her jeans and prayed that when Chad opened the door, she'd discover a poodle with a bark stronger than its bite, rather than the Doberman she was picturing in her mind.

They cut across the tall wild grass toward the front door and climbed the broken steps. Sawyer didn't let go of her hand as he knocked firmly with his other.

A man's voice from inside yelled at the dog, his footsteps approaching the door. The door creaked open, the chain lock still on. "If you're here to save my eternal soul, you might as well get your asses off my property now, 'cause I'm not in the mood to be saved and my dog's not the nicest of beasts."

She couldn't see all of him, but the voice was familiar, as was the visible ginger beard. Now she remembered him. Remembered him as a shy and extremely trusting man whose wife of thirty years, his high-school sweetheart, had left him for another man. A successful heart surgeon, he'd been a bit of a science-fiction geek, and they'd spent most of their time going to comic-book conventions. The other time was spent in bed, where she'd helped convince him his ex-wife definitely hadn't left him because of a lack of sexual prowess.

Staring at him now, she couldn't reconcile the man in the trailer with the man she knew. But when his gaze focused in on her and rage flashed within his eyes, she knew without a doubt he recognized her.

The door slammed shut only long enough for Chad to remove the chain from it, and then it opened wide, allowing the scary-looking pit bull to poke his head outside and snarl at them. She held her breath and froze in fear, waiting for him to attack.

"Chewy, sit," ordered Chad. Surprisingly, the spastic dog listened. Chad stepped out onto the porch and shut the door, leaving the well-behaved dog inside. "What are you doing here, Lana? Or should I call you Lisa Smith?" he spit out.

He'd definitely seen the photo from the newspaper.

She spoke quietly in an effort to calm him. "I know it doesn't mean much, but I'm sorry for what I did to you, Chad."

"Sorry isn't going to get my retirement savings back, now is it?" His lips twisted into a sneer. He was nothing like the man she remembered. Not that she blamed him. "What are you doing here?"

She glanced at Sawyer. He squeezed her hand, giving her the strength she needed. "Someone is trying to kill me."

"Really?" Chad asked, folding his arms across his chest and smiling. "Do tell. I love a good story."

"Our car's brakes were cut," she said, not offering any additional information.

Chad raised a brow. "And you immediately thought of me, huh? I'm honored."

"No," she admitted. "You're only one in a handful of possibilities."

His eyes narrowed as if he was angry that he wasn't unique. "Ah, of course." He turned to Sawyer. "So who's this? Your bodyguard?"

Sawyer dropped her hand and took a menacing step closer to Chad. "I'm her husband, and you're starting to piss me off. So answer a few questions for us. Do you know anything about those brakes?"

"I'm sure Lana—I mean *Lisa*—could tell you, I know nothing about cars. I'm more interested in taking apart a human, rather than a motor." He tapped a couple fingers on his forehead. "Although, I suppose I could have learned. I mean, I was one of the top heart surgeons in the country at one time. If I could carve into the chest of a living human and hold their beating heart in my hand, it wouldn't have been too difficult to study up on the mechanics of a vehicle, right?"

Sawyer grabbed the collar of Chad's shirt, yanking him forward. "Just answer the fucking question, Winters, before I pull out your heart and feed it to your psycho dog."

Worried Sawyer would push Chad to call the cops on them, she set a hand on his shoulder. "Sawyer," she said softly.

He turned his head, his hard gaze going soft as it landed on her. Stepping away from the other man, he released his grip, causing Chad to fall back into the wall of his trailer.

Using the back of his hand, Chad wiped the sweat that had formed above his brows. "I have no knowledge about your brakes."

"Where were you yesterday afternoon?" Sawyer asked.

Chad answered quickly. Too quickly. "Here."

Sawyer noticed. "Anyone who could confirm it?"

"Everybody who knows me," Chad said, spreading his arms out wide. "This is as far as I ever get from my home."

The meaning behind his statement slowly penetrated.

Sawyer cocked his head. "You're agoraphobic?"

"But you loved to travel," she said, remembering the train rides they'd spent laughing and kissing. "We went all over the country to those Comic-Cons."

"Everything turned to shit after you stole my savings," Chad said, the accusation in his voice. "I hired a prostitute who gave me the clap. I got sued after a patient died on my table. The hospital fired me. I discovered my ex-wife had been cheating on me throughout our entire relationship. And when I lost my temper at the New York Comic-Con and punched out the guy dressed up as Jar Jar Binks, I got banned from every major comic book convention in North America. I guess you could say I had a nervous breakdown. I bought this trailer and decided until my luck turned around, I wasn't leaving."

"How'd that work out for you?" Sawyer quipped.

Chad glared at Sawyer. "I'm still here, aren't I?"

"You do realize you can't blame her for all of that, don't you?" Sawyer pointed out.

Chad's shoulders sagged as he turned to her. "I was angry for a long time at both you and my ex-wife. Then when I saw you in the newspaper, it all boiled over. I went a little crazy for a couple of weeks." He put hands out in front of him. "But I'm better now. I still hate you. Don't get me wrong. And if I got word that you died, I can't say I wouldn't throw myself a party to celebrate. But I didn't cut your brakes."

No matter what Sawyer said, she was responsible for his breakdown. Or at least, she'd played a huge part in it. Her actions had consequences. She'd taken a broken man and had twisted the protruding knife left by his wife deeper into his back. If she had to spend the rest of her life doing it, she'd find a way to right the wrongs and make it up to all of them. Each and every person on that black list.

Sawyer reached into his pocket and handed Chad something that looked awfully similar to a check. "Here."

"What is this?" Chad asked as he took it.

Sawyer's arm banded around her waist. "It's a check for five million dollars. Cash it. Give it to charity. I don't give a fuck. But you forget you ever knew her, you got me?"

It was as if Sawyer had read her mind. His gesture overwhelmed her, tears of gratitude welling in her eyes. Yes, it was payment to buy Chad's silence, but for her, it was so much more. It freed her from the chains of guilt that burdened her. But although he had the money to do it, she wouldn't allow him to pay off everyone she'd hurt. Somehow, someway, it had to come from her.

"Yeah. Yeah," Chad said, nodding as he stared in wonder at his check. "I won't breathe a word. We're square."

"I hope someday you can forgive me," she said, relieved at the feeling of closure. Perhaps this would allow him to move on with his life, as well.

"Well, this check certainly helps," Chad said, waving it in front of his face. "Maybe my luck is finally turning around."

She gave him a small smile. "I hope so."

He rubbed his hand over his messy hair, his visible excitement over the check suddenly dimming. "Shit, now I feel really bad. I suppose I should come clean. I honestly didn't do anything to your brakes, but it's possible I know who did." Sighing, he folded the check and stuck it in his back pocket.

He looked directly at her. "I hired a hit man to kill you."

Chapter Fifteen

SAWYER'S FIST FLEW so fast, she had no chance of stopping him. Taking a hit to the jaw, Chad sailed backward, smacking his head on the trailer. Sawyer's eyes were murderous as he advanced with his fist raised, about to punch Chad again.

"Sawyer! Don't!" Even knowing it was dangerous, she placed herself between the men. Not because she cared about protecting Chad. No, he deserved everything Sawyer gave to him and more. She did it because she was afraid Sawyer would kill him.

Chad curled into himself, his arms protecting his head. "I'm sorry. It was a momentary lapse in judgment."

Still dark with the threat of violence in them, Sawyer's eyes lasered in on her. His chest rose and fell rapidly, his nostrils flared. Slowly, the anger bled out of him enough for him to regain control. Once he calmed down, she moved aside, allowing him to continue his questioning.

"How could you even afford to hire a hit man?" he asked.

Chad unfurled himself, his hand going to his swollen jaw. "Are you kidding? These days, you can find someone to off someone for a couple hundred bucks. It depends on the level of skill you want. I figured some gangbanger was as good as the next guy."

"Someone was going to kill me for two hundred dollars?" She wasn't sure if she was more mortified that he'd hired a hit man or that it had only cost him a couple of hundred dollars to do it.

He shrugged, appearing sheepish. "I got a special rate. Two for one. He was going to kill my ex-wife, too. I would have had him kill the bitch who gave me the STD, but I didn't get her name."

Nausea swept through her. Had he always been this demented? How could she have missed it?

"You don't leave this house," Sawyer said. "How'd you find the guy?

Chad swallowed hard. "On the web. I read about some site where you could place an ad for a hit man and name your price. I didn't really think it was real, you know? But there it was, out there in cyberspace, where anyone could find it. At first I thought it was some kind of entrapment set up by the Feds, but I figured, why not? What did I have to lose at that point? So I placed the ad, and wouldn't you know it, got three offers the first day."

"What's his name?" Sawyer asked.

"I never got it."

Sawyer shook his head. "You paid him?"

"Yeah. Anonymous wire transfer. I only got the routing number and bank account. Not his name."

"Give it to me."

Fear crept into Chad's eyes. "I don't have it anymore."

"E-mails? Anything?" Sawyer's jaw ticked.

"I got rid of any record I had when I changed my mind." Chad took a step toward his door, as if thinking about bolting. "I thought the cops could track that info, you know?"

She put a hand on Sawyer's chest. Maybe they could get more from Chad if she asked the questions. "How'd you terminate the agreement?"

"We communicated through the website. I wrote him and told him it was off. Asked him for my money back."

His money. That was his concern?

She suppressed her urge to punch the guy herself. "And what was his response?"

"I didn't get one. I figured he didn't write me back because he didn't want to return the money." Chad must have realized he was barking up the wrong tree and angled toward Sawyer. "Hey, it's not my fault if he didn't get it. I tried, you know? You're not going to stop payment on the check, are you?"

Sawyer remained calm, his burning anger having turned glacial. "If she dies, I'll not only stop payment, I'll make sure you die a slow, painful death. You get me?"

Chad swallowed hard. "I get you." He scurried into his house, engaging the locks on his doors.

Obviously, they didn't have to worry about Chad going to the cops. Not unless he wanted to go to prison for a long time.

She followed Sawyer as he stomped to the car. He didn't say anything, but the rage coming off him was palpable. As soon as she got her seat belt on, he gunned it out of the trailer park, a cloud of dirt kicking up behind them.

One of her biggest fears had been realized. Sawyer wouldn't even look at her. Seeing how she'd contributed to the ruin of Chad Winters's life had changed his feelings for her.

A gnawing ache settled in the middle of her chest. Trying to act as if she wasn't dying inside, she decided to talk about what they'd do next to find the person who'd attempted to kill them. "Do you think the guy he hired is behind my condo and the car?"

He gripped the steering wheel so tightly, his knuckles had turned white. "I'm not sure. My gut tells me it was personal for whoever destroyed your condo, and it's not the kind of thing a hit man would've done. The car is another story."

The ache spread, invading her stomach. "So you're saying there's a possibility that the things were unrelated?"

Still not looking at her, he lifted his cell from the center console, dialed, and put it to his ear. "We can't rule it out." He paused, waiting for the person on the other end to pick up. "Oz, did you get access to Winters's bank account?"

Wishing she could listen in on the conversation, she watched Sawyer's face, hoping the news on the other end would result in a smile.

His lips remained tight. "I need you to find a wire transfer that went to a hit man he hired in the amount of two hundred." He grimaced. "No, man, the fucker only paid two hundred dollars total. Trace the account, and call me with the name and address."

He hung up, not bothering to give her the details of what he had planned. Fury continued to emanate from him as they drove in silence.

Even though the ache had now infiltrated her entire body, she refused to cry. If he was done with her, then there was nothing she could do or say to change his mind. She'd known before their weeklong affair began that it would end. She was no worse off than she'd been before he walked back into her life.

She still had her friends. Her career. Her condo. And now that her brother had returned, she had a family again. So, she might never have children of her own. She was an aunt. She'd just spoil Asa's kids.

She'd survive without Sawyer.

She didn't have a choice.

Staring out the window to keep herself from crying, she noticed they were on the wrong highway. "Where are you going? This isn't the way to the hotel."

"No. It's not. We're going to Benediction." Finally, he looked at her. "You good with that?"

Hell yes, she was good with that. Maybe she'd been wrong, and his anger had nothing to do with her. Maybe he needed some time to cool off. The ache she'd been feeling receded, only to be replaced by a much more pleasurable one.

But could she go to Benediction knowing there was a good chance she'd run into her friends?

Except for certain events, Benediction was a members-only club, and from what she'd learned from Danielle, an application, health screening, training, and an interview were necessary to become a member.

"I'm not sure if you're aware, since it was open for the wedding the other night, but Benediction is a members-only club."

"Logan invited us," he said. "Apparently, your friend Gracie is in charge of the place while Cole is on his honeymoon, so he didn't think it would be a problem. I spoke with him this morning and set it up."

Gracie was probably ecstatic that she and Sawyer were coming to the club. But it also meant having to endure a horde of questions from her friend, questions she wasn't sure she even had an answer to.

Sawyer's gaze briefly fell to her lips before returning to the road. "You up for role play?

Her inner thighs tingled. "Yes."

A small smile tugged at his lips. "Good. Logan reserved a fantasy room for us. I'm not up for gentle tonight. Remember to use your safe word if you need it. Otherwise, expect rough and intense."

The tingles shot from her thighs to her pussy. "More intense than last night?"

"Last night doesn't even come close to what I've got planned for you," he said darkly.

She shifted in her seat to ease the budding arousal. What could be more intense than fisting?

The ride to Benediction seemed to take hours, even though only thirty minutes ticked by on the car's clock before they pulled up to the gate at the front of the club's driveway. After they identified themselves through an intercom, the gate opened, and they proceeded up to the house, passing the beautiful trees with leaves that were just beginning to change to a seasonal orange and yellow.

Although she'd spent a good deal of her life hanging around millionaires and even billionaires, she'd never become comfortable with blatant displays of wealth. Sure, mansions were nice, but she could never help thinking that if she misplaced her keys, she'd never find them again.

When she'd been with Sawyer, they'd lived in a spacious penthouse condo overlooking Arizona's Camelback Mountain. But according to what Rachel had said, Sawyer now owned mansions in both Las Vegas and Miami. To him, Benediction was probably just another large house. She couldn't imagine why her husband required not one, but two mansions.

The garden outside Benediction bloomed with gold and russet-toned flowers, the tall stems bent in welcome, and although not yet October, large round pumpkins decorated the porch. A valet took their car for them, and for the first time, she entered the mansion not as Danielle's friend and wedding coordinator, but as a guest of the sex club.

Wearing a neon pink latex dress, the petite Gracie tackled Lisa as soon as she walked through the door, throwing her arms around her and squealing at a pitch that couldn't be good for her vocal cords. Then she grabbed her hand and tugged her toward the closed door that led to the club. "We're staging an intervention," she informed Lisa, not explaining what she meant before tossing a "We'll have her ready in a half hour for you" to Sawyer over her shoulder.

What the hell was her friend up to? She really didn't want to have to answer her friend's questions. "I wish I could, but I need to go to—"

"Sawyer will be getting the fantasy room ready for your scene." She led Lisa down the hallway, past the library to the kitchen, and up the private stairs that led to the slave trainees' bedrooms. Gracie, although no longer officially Cole's slave, still lived in the mansion. "We've got a half hour with you, and we're going to make every second of it count."

"We?" she asked as Gracie flung open her door.

"The girls," Gracie said as if it was obvious.

And maybe it was.

When she went inside, she wasn't at all surprised to find Rachel and Kate sitting on Gracie's bed. She laughed to herself. The only reason Danielle wasn't there was because she was on her honeymoon. Of course, it also wouldn't surprise Lisa if Gracie patched her into the conversation via Skype.

What did surprise her was seeing Rachel and Kate together. "I thought you two didn't come to Benediction on the same nights?"

Since Logan was Kate's business partner, they both agreed it would be uncomfortable to see the other naked, so they'd worked out some schedule to avoid it.

Taking in the bright and colorful room, Lisa noted it definitely screamed "Gracie." Although she didn't have much furniture—a bed, a dresser, a nightstand, and of course, a vanity—she'd made sure every piece reflected her enthusiasm and lust for life.

Kate tucked a blonde strand of her hair behind her ear. "I made an exception after getting Rachel's phone call."

Lisa glared at Rachel. "You told them."

Rachel threw her hands up in front of her. "I only told them you were married to Sawyer. I didn't tell them anything else."

The relief was momentary. Rachel hadn't disclosed that she'd taken millions of dollars and then left Sawyer without a word. Apparently, she wanted Lisa to do the honors.

Gracie's almond eyes widened in excitement. "What else? There's more? All this time I thought you'd end up as a sexually repressed spinster with eight cats, and it turns out you were married to a gorgeous kinky billionaire." She covered her heart with her palm. "I think you're my hero."

"I don't understand. Why didn't you tell us you were married?" Kate asked. Lisa had been prepared for a cross-examination from her attorney friend, but she heard nothing in Kate's voice that suggested she was anything but curious.

She slid her eyes to Rachel, who nodded her encouragement. If she hadn't judged her, maybe the others wouldn't either.

Wringing her hands, she swallowed. "My name isn't Lisa Smith. It's Annaliese Hunt. Before I moved to Michigan, I was a con artist."

Gracie giggled. “Right. Good one,” she said smiling. When she realized Lisa wasn’t lying, the smile slid from her face.

“I married Sawyer to have access to his bank accounts and stole millions from him before running off one day, leaving behind my wedding ring and collar.”

Gracie’s gaze fell to Lisa’s bare wedding finger before jumping to her collared neck. She placed a hand on her cocked hip. “You lucky bitch. I can’t believe we’ve been friends this long and you didn’t tell us you were kinky.”

Lisa shook her head. Gracie never ceased to amaze her. “I just told you I was a thief, and that’s what you’re fixated on?”

“We’ve all done things we’re not proud of,” Kate said, getting up from the bed and crossing the room. “But you’re not a thief now, are you?”

“No, of course not,” she said vehemently. “But I lied to you.”

Kate tilted her head, a little smile playing on her lips. “You didn’t lie. You just didn’t share the truth. I think all of us have been guilty of that at some point.”

“Not me,” Gracie said. “I can’t lie. I’ve tried. I can keep a secret, but that’s not really lying, is it?” Without taking a breath, she continued. “Because I swear, I’d never tell a soul about you being a kinky ex-con-artist.” She made a motion as if she was crossing her heart and then threw her arms around Lisa in a hug, the force of it knocking Lisa backward. “I’ll go to the grave with that secret.”

She returned the hug, grateful to have her as a friend. “Thanks, Gracie.”

Rachel stood and strode to her side. "Don't forget the FBI owes Logan and me a favor. We'd be happy to use it for you." As if Lisa could forget that Rachel and Logan had foiled a terrorist plot that would have resulted in hundreds of thousands, if not millions, of deaths.

"And if you need legal representation, please don't call anyone else," Kate insisted. "We're all here for you. Don't ever forget it."

Gracie clapped her hands excitedly. "Wait until Danielle gets back from her honeymoon. I guarantee she's going to convince Cole to give you a free membership to Benediction."

"She doesn't need a free membership," Rachel pointed out. "Sawyer's rich as hell. Not to mention, he owns his own sex club in Vegas."

Gracie pouted. "Now that you're back with him, does that mean you're going to move away?"

Wasn't that the million-dollar question? She dropped onto the chair in front of Gracie's vanity. "We haven't discussed it. I think it's too soon to make any drastic changes to our lives. And we're still not sure who's behind the threats."

"Threats? What threats?" Kate asked, reminding Lisa a little too late that the girls didn't know about her recent hospital stay.

"Someone cut Sawyer's brakes and vandalized Lisa's condo," Rachel shared.

Gracie waved her hand. "Ah, there's always some danger happening around here. You'll get used to it."

"Sawyer and his guys are on it," Rachel said to Kate and Gracie. She turned to Lisa. "They'll figure it out for you. I swear, they should start their own security company or something. They've got mad computer skills."

Based on the fact that his friend Oz had already managed to access information on Chad's bank account, she believed it. She'd known that Sawyer had some experience with hacking. If the rest of his friends were as good as him, she had no doubt they'd trace the funds to find the hit man. And if it turned out to be a dead end, hopefully they would find another lead from the names she'd provided them.

Gracie's cell phone buzzed. Glancing at the screen, she smiled. "Sawyer's ready for you. I'm supposed to get you dressed."

A pulsing heat bloomed between her legs. "You are?"

Her friends all smiled at her.

Uh-oh.

Gracie went into her closet and returned with an outfit. "Here we are." Frowning, she cocked her head, assessing it. "I'm thinking innocent schoolgirl. What do guys think?" Piece by piece, she removed the items of clothing from the hanger and held them up.

There wasn't much to the outfit. An extremely short pleated red and black plaid skirt and a white half-blouse that tied below the breasts. White thigh highs.

No panties—of course.

"Oh! Don't forget the shoes." Gracie ran back into her closet and grabbed some patent leather flats.

What did Sawyer have planned for tonight? He'd told her to expect intense. She couldn't imagine that meant teacher-student role play. But why else would he have her wear these clothes?

While her friends talked to each other, she went into the bathroom and changed into the outfit. The skirt was even shorter than she'd thought. It only barely covered her ass. And the blouse was almost sheer, the pink of her nipples visible underneath it.

When she came back into the room, her friends were waiting by the open door.

Gracie looked at her appreciatively, making her blush. "I'll leave your clothes in the coat room at the entrance, so you can change back before you leave. It's time to take you over to the fantasy rooms. They're on the same level as the residences, but they're not accessible from here. If you're uncomfortable walking through the house like that, I can lend you a robe," she offered.

Did she care if other people saw her half-naked? Lisa Smith might be modest, but she wasn't. Besides, if her Master had wanted her to wear a robe, he would've provided her with one. He expected her to parade around the club this way. Even though he wouldn't be with her, he probably got off on the thought. And truth be told, so did she.

"I'm good," she said. "I'm ready."

Kate and Rachel went downstairs with her, but they parted ways at the stairs that led up to the fantasy rooms. Gracie hooked her arm in Lisa's and took her upstairs, using a keypad to allow them entrance into the hallway that led to the different rooms. The hallway was dim, only about four people wide, with doors to the room on the left and windows that allowed for a view inside.

She shivered, the idea of public sex both unnerving and arousing. For some reason, that had never been high on her list of kinks, which even she had to admit was strange, since she loved a small orgy. She'd long since stopped trying to figure out why certain sexual activities got her hot and others left her cold. Her Master had taught her she was just wired this way and that everyone had limits. Exhibitionism was a soft limit for her. She'd try it, but it wasn't something she preferred to do.

As Gracie led her down the long hallway, past each door that led to another fantasy, she couldn't help peeking through the windows to watch the scenes unfolding—her favorite being the two men getting each other off in a good old-fashioned sixty-nine—but Gracie was all business, keeping her eyes forward and walking in a brisk pace that didn't allow for Lisa to linger.

She realized this was Gracie the slave, a woman who didn't stop to play voyeur because she was ordered to bring Lisa to Sawyer. It was odd to see her so quiet when her friend typically didn't stop talking for a second. Although Lisa considered herself Sawyer's slave, Gracie served all the Dominants at Benediction. To her, it sounded awfully exhausting, but Gracie seemed to love it.

For Lisa, serving Sawyer allowed her to put all her fears and concerns out of her head and focus on him. She didn't have to worry about who was trying to kill them or what her friends thought about her now that they knew about her past. She only needed to focus on pleasing Sawyer and the sensations coursing through her body. Role play provided her with a new identity, one that wasn't for the purpose of conning a mark, but for pleasing her Master and herself.

Gracie stopped in front of a closed door and turned to her. Lisa noticed with relief that the window was covered by blinds and that no sound filtered into the hallway. Her heart banged against her chest as her anticipation peaked.

"Sawyer's inside." Gracie licked her lips nervously. "I'm supposed to give you this before I go."

Placing her dainty hands on Lisa's shoulders, Gracie leaned in, sealing her soft lips over hers. Surprised, Lisa squeaked, but she quickly surrendered, closing her eyes and falling into the headspace where all judgment disappeared and she could embrace her unique sexuality without criticizing herself for it.

She'd never been attracted to Gracie, but the girl knew how to kiss, her plump lips soft, her tongue unhurried. She tasted like strawberries and freedom. And if Gracie wasn't one of her best friends, she would've begged Sawyer to ask her to join them.

Her friend pulled away first, a shy smile lighting up her beautiful face. "Have fun tonight, and don't do anything I wouldn't do. Of course, I do everything." She tossed a laugh over her shoulder as she left.

Lisa didn't hesitate before opening the door to the fantasy room. She stepped inside, her eyes immediately falling on Sawyer dressed in a policeman's uniform. A cane rested along the wall, and next to the cane was a large cardboard box. Otherwise, the room was empty except for an ominous black leather spanking bench and a metal folding chair sitting in the middle of the space.

Goose bumps popped up on her arms. She didn't know what he had planned, but she did know one thing.

He made for one sexy cop.

His eyes heated as he raked his gaze from top to bottom and back again. Oh, he definitely liked what he saw, although she still had no idea who she was supposed to be. Then, without warning, he narrowed his eyes, his lips tightening with displeasure. Guess she was going to find out.

Their scene had begun.

Chapter Sixteen

SAWYER STALKED TOWARD her, his fingers hooked around his belt. With each step, he looked more dangerous, more formidable.

As a criminal, she'd never been particularly comfortable around the police. Her gut churned, a sense of unease drifting into her consciousness, and for a split second, she considered saying her safe word.

But this was Sawyer. He wanted this scene. So she wanted to give it to him.

She smiled sweetly at him, playing a role that fit her costume. "Can I help you, officer?"

He yanked her arm and flipped her around. Holding her tight, he walked her forward until she pressed against the wall. "You can help me by putting your hands behind your back and facing the wall, young lady. You're under arrest."

Her body shook from the intense arousal at seeing Sawyer dressed as a cop.

Maybe she was reading too much into it, but something seemed off with him. Yet at the same time, his powerful intimidation had already made her thighs dampen with her arousal.

She peered over her shoulder at him and batted her eyelashes. "What are you arresting me for, officer?"

He pushed his erection against her ass. "You know what you did. Are you ready to confess?"

"I can't confess to something I haven't done. I'm innocent."

He dropped his head forward to speak into her ear. "Innocent? Dressed like that? Your skirt's so short, I bet if you bent over I'd see your panties, girl, wouldn't I?"

Her nipples hardened painfully as she turned her head slightly, her lips grazing his whiskered chin. "No, sir. I'm not wearing any."

His arm snaked around her waist, and he flipped her around to face him. His eyes were wild, as if he was barely maintaining control. "Your sweet pussy isn't going to get you out of trouble this time. It's time for you to pay for your crimes. And it's going to hurt."

He marched her over to the bench and bent her face-down over it. Using the attached straps, he secured her so that she couldn't move.

A cane appeared in front of her face. "Kiss it," he ordered.

He'd warned her he'd get rough tonight, and to her, nothing said rough like a good caning. Her gaze flicked to his as she softly gave the cane a lover's kiss.

"Count out each one and ask for another until you get to six." He momentarily broke character, his stance softening. "You need to say anything before I start?" He was giving her the chance to use her safe word.

"Yes, officer." She smiled up at him. "Fuck you."

The skin around his lips twitched, as if he was suppressing his own smile. "Apparently you need to be taught a lesson." He blatantly adjusted his erection, tempting her with his covered dick. "And I'll be happy to give it to you."

Her mouth watered for a taste of him. But he didn't take out his cock.

Damn it.

He did, however, flip up her skirt and smooth his hand over her bare bottom.

She enjoyed the nice, knowing the naughty was soon to follow. He didn't make her wait long. His touch disappeared, and she heard him lumber backward, giving himself the room to really swing that cane.

The cane replaced his hand, the smooth wood gliding over her skin like a lover's caress, *down, down, down.* Sawyer slipped it under her, getting it slick with her arousal as he slid it back and forth over her pussy, the end of it brushing against her clitoris.

Air sawed in and out of her lungs at an alarming rate, her core tightening and her heart pounding. She was *this* close to climax when he ripped the cane away, leaving her unfulfilled. "Put it back," she ordered, forgetting her submissive role.

"You're not in charge here, girl. Just for that, I'm adding one more strike of the cane. Lucky number seven." He chuckled. "Well, lucky for me."

Sweet anticipation flowed through her limbs, the fear of the upcoming pain making her pussy dampen and her nipples peak into tight little points that poked against the shirt's fabric.

She processed the swish of the cane swinging through the air a second after the sharp pain surged through her left butt cheek like a flame to kindling. Heat sliced down her leg. She waited until the burn dulled to a manageable ache. "One. Please, officer, may I have another?"

His long silence kept her in suspense, the only sounds being her breathing and the beat of her heart.

Whoosh!

She jerked against the restraints, air trapped in her lungs as the cane hit again, not on her other cheek as she'd anticipated, but right above the first. "Two. Please, officer, another?" she asked through gritted teeth.

This time he didn't make her wait. The sting spread, warmth suffusing her pussy. Everything throbbed. Her ass. Her pussy. Her breasts. Hell, even the soles of her feet. But rather than fight against it, she wrapped her arms around it and invited it in. Welcomed it.

The world shrank until they were the only people who remained. Master and slave. Husband and wife.

Floating from the endorphins released into her bloodstream, she barely remembered begging for the next five strikes or the pain that followed. All that existed was the pulsing in her pussy and the need to please her Master.

At some point, she was vaguely aware that the beating had ended and Sawyer was rubbing cream on her sore ass. She sighed, enjoying the waves of bliss rolling over her.

"I don't think the caning did the trick," he said, coming around to stand in front of her. "You enjoyed it too much. This was about teaching you a lesson." He unzipped his pants and pulled out his cock, the thick head of it bobbing only inches from her mouth. "Maybe taking my dick in your throat will shut that back-talking mouth of yours."

Or maybe she'd talk back all the time so he'd have to administer this kind of punishment more often.

Still riding on the high of her caning, she parted her lips. He fucked her mouth with total abandon, reaching for his own pleasure rather than seeking hers. She sunk into that place where satisfying her Master became her whole reason for living, working hard to give him the climax he deserved.

In mere minutes, his come spurted into her mouth, hitting the back of her throat, leaving her spent and tired. She closed her eyes.

"Don't go to sleep on me, girl. We're not done. I still haven't gotten the truth out of you yet."

After tucking his cock back into his pants, he released her from the bench and helped her to her feet. His arm around her waist, he led her to the chair. "Sit and spread your legs."

She sat demurely, wincing at the ache of her ass as it made contact with the seat, and crossed her legs at the ankles. Her eyes widened in faux innocence. "But you'll see my pussy."

Leering like a dirty old man, he kept his gaze focused on her skirt. "Should have thought about that when you got dressed."

That almost got a laugh out of her, since he'd been the one to not only choose her outfit but to omit the panties. Instead, she played along and spread her legs, slowly, inch by inch, teasing him.

He rummaged through the cardboard box, pulling out a silver vibrator and a strap with a pink jelly-looking thing hanging on it. He kneeled in front of her. "Spread your legs."

She heard his sharp inhale of breath and felt his hands trembling as he slid the silver bullet vibrator inside of her. She tried to stay quiet, not giving the officer the satisfaction of a moan, but her body slid forward a bit, as if begging him for more.

He chuckled, low and dark, before reaching for the strap, which she could now see was a clitoral vibrator shaped like a butterfly. His thumb flicked at her clitoris, making it swell out from its hood, and he placed the butterfly directly on it before connecting the two ends of the strap to ensure it stayed on her.

After going back to the box, he returned with some sheer scarves. His eyes blazed as he crouched, tying her ankles to the legs of the chair. He wound another scarf around her wrists and secured her with her arms behind her back.

He had her just where he wanted her.

Now what was he going to do with her?

He whipped out his cell and jabbed at it. The vibrator inside of her began buzzing.

She smiled, impressed by his ingenuity. A vibrator controlled remotely by a cell phone. She wouldn't have expected any less from her techie husband.

Standing in front of her, he crossed his arms. "Tell me about Chad Winters."

The smile slid from her face. "What?"

Sawyer gave no reaction to her discomfort, his expression set into cold stone. "You conned him. How did you do it?"

Black list.

The words were on the tip of her tongue. She didn't want to talk about her past. Bad enough she had to write out the names for him. Was that what this scene was about? He was using it to truly interrogate her?

He'd honor her safe word. Would end the scene immediately if she uttered it or the club word, "red." It would be so easy. So why couldn't she get her mouth to speak them?

Because he was her Master.

And she loved him.

He'd built this scene not only for himself, but for her. To give her the choice, yet pretend she didn't have one. Somehow, dressed as an innocent girl, she found the courage to give him the truth.

"I..." She swallowed, the memory crashing into her. "He wanted a comic book, but he was cheap, even back then with all his millions. I told him I could get it for him for only fifty thousand. He gave me the money. I didn't get him the comic book."

Sawyer stared at her expectantly, as if encouraging her to continue. When she didn't, he fiddled with his phone again, setting off the butterfly vibrator.

A reward for her answer?

"And Corbin Draper of Colorado Springs," he said tersely. "Tell me about him."

She shook her head. "I don't remember."

He turned off the vibrators. "You mean you don't want to remember. If you want me to go easy on you, you'll try. Now what did you do to Draper?"

Just like with Chad, she couldn't remember much about him other than the con itself. "I pretended I was an event planner. He gave me twenty-five thousand dollars to organize his mother's ninetieth birthday party. I spent two and pocketed the rest."

The vibrators flipped on.

Despite her answering honestly, Sawyer's entire body tensed. "Did you fuck him?"

"No," she whispered, on the verge of tears.

The buzzing inside her grew stronger, a gift for her honesty.

She didn't want it. Her body was aroused, but her heart was breaking.

"Ronda Sykes of Baton Rouge."

Tears stained her cheeks. "Please, Sawyer. I don't want to do this."

He shrugged. "You've got your safe word. You remember it? Then if you want to use it, go ahead."

Hell yes, she wanted to use it. But he wanted to know about her past. So she was going to give it to him. "Ronda was my business partner. We were going to open a nail salon together. Once my name was on the account, I took the money and left town."

He arched a brow. "Business partners? Is that it?"

"No." Her gaze clung to his as she gave her honest answer. "We were lovers."

"There were more than fifty people on that list you gave me. Fifty people you duped with your lies. How many of those did you fuck? How many, Annaliese?"

"Please don't do this," she begged.

"How many?" he shouted.

"Eighteen." *Damn him.* "Forgive me. Eighteen, including you."

She sobbed now, the tears coming fast and heavy. He'd gutted her. Ripped her open and left her exposed. The caning, the humiliation, the forced blow job, none of that had hurt like this. Yet at the same time, she felt the heavy weight of her past lessen with each tear she shed. She didn't understand how he'd known what she carried inside of her when she herself hadn't known.

He kissed her tenderly on the brow. "I love you, Annaliese. You don't need my forgiveness. You need your own."

He loved her?

Cranking the vibrators to their highest level, he gave her the ultimate reward for her surrender to him.

The pleasure was brutal and unforgiving, the vibration on her exposed clit like a live wire, sending sparks dancing along her spine and causing her pussy to burst into flame. She screamed as the climax tore into her without forgiveness, her shuddering body no longer in her control.

Sawyer moved to stand between her legs, gently wiping away her tears with his thumb. "How many people have you called Master?"

"Only you," she whispered.

He dragged his wet thumb down her cheek and to her lips, painting them with her tears. "How many people have had their whole hand in you?"

She gasped from the memory. "Only you."

He tipped her head back by her chin. "How many people have you loved?"

There was no other answer but the truth. "You. Only you, Master."

His eyes darkened. "You. Are. Fucking. Mine." Claiming her, he kissed her with a ferocity she didn't understand.

But she didn't need to. She kissed him back, tangling her tongue with his until she became dizzy. And when he unknotted the scarf around her wrists, she drove her fingers into his hair, pulling him to her, greedy for him.

"I need to fuck you now," he said roughly. Crouching between her thighs, he quickly untied the scarves from her ankles and removed the vibrators. He released his beautiful cock, giving her no time to admire it before he rolled a condom down the length. He yanked her to her feet and lifted her off the ground. "Hold on."

She wrapped her legs around his waist, clinging to him for support. Kissing her as if there was no tomorrow, he marched forward, slamming her back into the wall. There was no warning before his cock thrust inside her eager pussy, hammering into her as if he hadn't had an orgasm in days, rather than mere minutes.

Her ass throbbed as it knocked against the wall, but it only served to heighten her arousal. His mouth was everywhere, biting and sucking at her neck, above her breasts, on her mouth. She was drowning in his love for her, and she couldn't think of a better way to go.

"I love you," he murmured into her neck. "I love you so fucking much. It's my collar on you. My ring that should be on your finger. I own you. You belong to me."

The words sent her soaring over the cliff and into a heart-pounding, mind-blowing, earth-shattering orgasm. Shortly after, Sawyer groaned and followed her into the abyss.

Still holding her, he slid to the floor and shifted her so that she sat on his lap. He rested his head on her shoulders as they sought to catch their breath.

He'd said she didn't need his forgiveness. But what if she wanted it?

Ever since leaving Chad's house, he'd been so angry, especially when interrogating her.

Did *he* have it in him to forgive her for her transgressions?

And if not, what would that mean for them?

Chapter Seventeen

RESTING AGAINST HIS chest, she tangled her fingers with his, ready for an honest conversation.

Sawyer's lips brushed her neck, his arms tightening around her waist as if he never wanted to let her go. But if that was true, what was the scene really about? If he couldn't accept her past, it was better to know that now, so she could prepare herself for the end.

"Tell me why you've been angry ever since we left Chad Winters's house," she said softly.

His growl against her neck sent a burst of heat to her belly. "I wanted to wrap my hands around that weasel's neck and squeeze the life out of him."

She raised her head, snagging his gaze. "I noticed. That's why I stepped in front of you. I didn't want you to do anything you'd regret."

His lips turned down in displeasure. "I wouldn't have regretted it."

"I understand you're angry at him for hiring a hit man—"

"That's not why I lost my cool. I mean, yeah, he's an asshole, and I'm obviously pissed, but it was more than that." He let out a shuddered breath. "You fucked him."

The disdain in his voice broke her into a thousand pieces. "Yes."

"You fucked seventeen people for money."

"Yes," she confirmed. How many had he fucked? How dare he judge her, especially after he'd just told her to forgive herself for it? "I knew if you met one of my marks, you'd look at me differently. You think I'm a whore."

He reared back as if she'd called him a whore instead. "You're not a whore, and trust me, I'm not judging you for sleeping with those people. I can't understand why you did it, but having sex with them doesn't make you a whore or a slut or whatever else you think I'm calling you. I'm angry because he's been inside you." His voice went low and growly. "I'm fucking jealous."

She shivered, goose bumps running across her collarbone. Jealous? In a million years, she wouldn't have guessed his behavior today had anything to do with jealousy. Sure, he was possessive, but at the same time, they were sexually adventurous and had participated in orgies together. Not once had he ever shown one iota of jealousy. Besides, she'd slept with those people before she'd met him. Before this week, she hadn't had sex since they separated. Unlike him.

She waved a finger in his face. "You have no right to be jealous. You own a sex club. Our marital vows didn't mean a damn thing to you once I left."

He snatched her hand and kissed it. "Our marital vows meant everything to me." He dropped the hand to trace her cheekbone. "I searched for you. I never stopped searching. I couldn't move on. I didn't want to move on. The sex club made me forget, kept me busy during the night so I didn't have to think about you and how much I missed you. A woman who took my money and stomped on my heart. My friends tried to tell me it was all about the money. That you never really loved me. But I never believed it. And as busy as I kept myself, I couldn't stop thinking about you." He rested his forehead against hers. "I didn't break my marital vows. There have been no other women since you."

She jerked back, searching his eyes for the truth. "How is that possible?"

"I won't say I haven't touched another woman. There were a few times I'd help my friends with a scene, hold a woman down, caress her breasts as my friends fucked her, and a few times I'd stay in the room and masturbate as I watched, but since you left, I haven't had my mouth on another woman. I haven't had a mouth on me or even a woman's hand wrapped around my cock." He captured her face in his hands. "The only times I've come were by my own hand, thinking of you."

A dam of tears burst wide open. Tears of relief. "You stayed faithful even when I hurt you?"

"Why are you crying?" he asked, wiping the tears away with his fingertips.

"I don't deserve you." She couldn't believe he'd been faithful after she'd taken his money and run. "It killed me to think of you with someone else." She laughed halfheartedly through the tears. "Which I know doesn't make sense, because I get off on watching you fuck other people."

He shrugged. "Don't question your kink. It is what it is. And it happens to match mine." He stroked his hand up and down her spine. "Do you know how jealous I was at the thought of you with another man or woman? It was unbearable. But once you told me that you hadn't broken our marriage vows, I knew that you still loved me. And nothing else mattered but breaking you down until you told me the real reason you left."

But he'd honored her limits and hadn't asked.

She wanted to tell him. Wanted to tell him so damn badly. She could hardly remember all the reasons to keep it a secret anymore.

Yet something held her back. That one string that tethered her to the past that wouldn't let her go and sowed the seed of doubt that had been planted by her father years ago.

"Trusting someone is like handing them a bomb. It might not go off right away, but eventually, it's gonna blow up in your face."

"I'm afraid," she admitted.

"You think I'm not?" He had as much to fear as she did. After all, he wasn't the one who'd walked out on their marriage. "We've all got our demons to bear. But you and I are stronger together than we are apart. That has to mean something."

"It means everything," she said, disturbed by the pain in his voice. She might not be ready to cut the ties to her past yet, but she could help him cut the ones to his. "Tell me your sins, Sawyer. Let me wash them away and purify your soul like you did for me tonight when you told me to forgive myself."

He shifted her on his lap and leaned his back against the wall. Sadness filled his eyes. "You know my parents died in a car accident. What the press never released was the fact that I had been driving that night."

Her heart ached for him. He'd only been eighteen at the time, and unlike her, he'd been close to his parents. But she was shocked that his presence during the accident had stayed out of the media. His parents' deaths had made Sawyer the youngest billionaire in the world. The press had treated him like royalty, following his every move and giving him no time to grieve. "You were there?"

"I wasn't just there." He didn't blink as his throat worked over a swallow. "I killed my parents."

She took his hand in hers to give him the strength to continue. "Tell me what happened."

Seemingly lost in the memory, he fixed his gaze on the wall across the room, avoiding eye contact. "We went to dinner to celebrate my graduation from high school. Everything was great. They were so proud of me. We talked about college and what I planned to study. They knew about my interest in computers, but when I told them I'd decided to go to Cal Tech to study computer engineering, rather than business at Yale, you could see the disappointment in my father's eyes. Three generations had graduated from Yale, and he'd always expected I'd be the fourth."

"But Cal Tech...They must have understood that you wanted to follow your passion."

He inclined his head. "Mom did. She tried to reason with my father, but he wasn't having it. When we left the restaurant, he was so angry. So disappointed. I'd shattered his dreams for me, and I was too stupid to care about anyone but myself at that point."

"Sawyer, there's nothing unusual about that. Most eighteen-year-olds are incapable of thinking about anything but their own needs. You didn't do anything wrong."

"I wouldn't let him drive, Annaliese." He clenched his jaw, rubbing his hand over it. "He'd had a couple of drinks with dinner, and he was so angry, I worried he'd give himself a coronary. I actually said that to him. Joked about him killing us all while he drove us home. So I took the car keys. And I drove us home. Or at least, that was the plan."

"What happened?" she asked softly.

He blinked a few times in succession, as if fighting back tears. "We were still fighting. Mom was in the passenger seat, Dad in the back yelling at me. He reminded me I was the sole heir to Hayes Industries. He expected me to run the entire company one day. I turned my head to say I'd no intention of ever working at Hayes Industries when an SUV coming from the opposite direction clipped our car. Dad wasn't wearing a seat belt. He was ejected from the car. Mom's head hit the dashboard. She died upon impact."

She laid her hand on his cheek. "How did you survive?"

"Sheer luck," he huffed. "I fucking walked out of the car on my own two legs. A couple of scratches. A broken arm. But otherwise, unharmed."

She held him tightly. "Poor baby."

Pushing her away, he looked at her, horrified. "Poor baby. Poor baby? I killed my parents."

That's what he believed? "You didn't kill them. It was an accident."

He lifted her off his lap and got to his feet, pulling up his pants and zipping them. "If I hadn't been driving, Dad would've been in the driver's seat. I would've been in the passenger's. Mom would've been in the back with her seat belt on. Don't you see? The accident wouldn't have happened, and even if it had, they would've lived. I would've been the only one to die that night."

She stood and placed her hand on his shoulder. "You can't know that. There's a thousand different scenarios of how that night could've played out, and in every one, the outcome might have been the same. We don't have control over who gets to live or die."

Sawyer tore away from her and paced the room. "I couldn't let them die in vain. My family's lawyers kept my part in the accident out of the press, but it's there in the official police report. But it didn't matter. The media became fixated on exposing the youngest billionaire in the world. They followed me everywhere." He turned to her and ran his fingers through his hair. "I couldn't escape the guilt. The attorneys suggested I go somewhere and lie low while I learned the business. I'm sure I shocked the hell out of them by joining the Army, rather than staying at my folks' vacation house in Aruba."

"Why the Army? Was that something you'd thought about doing before they died?"

His gaze fell to his feet. "I had a lot to atone for. I thought if I did some good, maybe then I wouldn't feel so fucking guilty."

"And did it work?"

His brows snapped together as he pondered it. "The Army gave me a new family. Logan, Oz, Hunter, and Rowan are my band of brothers. And there was always something to do. Someone to talk to." He shook his head. "But no, the guilt never left. So when I got out, I got my shit together and took over Hayes Industries as CEO. I owed it to my parents after killing them."

He didn't know how fortunate he'd been to have two parents who had genuinely loved him. She would've given anything to have had that herself.

Her parents should've never had kids. They'd had nothing to give to them but lessons on how to steal and cheat their way through life. At least Asa had gotten a bit of affection from their Mom. But it was as if once she'd given it, she'd run out of her limited supply and had been incapable of giving it to anyone else.

If Lisa had kids, she'd not only tell them every day how much she loved them, she'd show them.

"I think you're admirable for sacrificing your dreams for your father's," she said. "But he wouldn't have wanted that for you."

Proving she was starting to get to him, he shoved his hands in his pockets. "Didn't you hear what I told you?"

"Yes." She hooked her arms around his neck. "I heard you tell me about a terrible night when a young kid got into an argument with his father. I also heard the love in your voice. Sawyer, they loved you, too. The unconditional kind that children deserve from their parents. He would've come around because he loved you and wanted your happiness. Maybe you would've compromised. Or maybe your father would've realized that he didn't own your dreams. But I do know this. Your parents wouldn't want you running a company if it made you miserable. Because when you love someone unconditionally, you'll sacrifice your own happiness for theirs. He would've done that for you. And he would've been proud of whatever you did decide to do with your life."

He was quiet a long time, indecision warring in his eyes. When her words finally sunk into his stubborn mind, his hands left the safety of his pockets and his arms came around her.

She didn't say anything, waiting for him to speak.

"You certainly know a lot about unconditional love and sacrifice," he said, sensing she hadn't been solely referring to his parents. He took a step backward, grasping both her hands in his. "Now that I've told you my secrets, are you ready to share yours?"

Lisa looked up at her husband, a man with personal demons as dark as her own, and realized her father had been wrong.

Trusting Sawyer wouldn't blow up in her face.

Her father had controlled her with *fear.*

Well, fear was the opposite of trust, and it had ruled her life for far too long. Fear had kept her and Sawyer apart. It was time to fight back against it and embrace a world where she trusted those she loved. People like her friends and their husbands. People like her Master.

But her secrets didn't belong to her alone anymore. Maybe they never did. Her parents had made certain they entangled their children in their destructive web, never intending for them to free themselves. She and Asa had escaped, running as far as they could, only to discover they hadn't severed all the ties that bound them to the past and one another.

Would Asa help her cut that last remaining thread? If he didn't, if he asked her to keep it all a secret, she would have to make the impossible choice between her brother and her husband. She prayed that wouldn't happen.

She rested her head on his heart, letting his strong beat give her the power she needed to reveal the truth to him. "Before I tell you everything, I'd like to go see my brother at his hotel."

He caressed his hand down her back soothingly. "The reason you won't tell me. It has something to do with him, doesn't it?"

She sighed against him, not ready to leave his arms or Benediction. "Your secrets were tied to your family. Does it surprise you mine are as well?"

"No." He kissed the top of her head. "After what you told me about your parents, I'm not surprised. It's painted a picture of what it must have been like for you to survive all those years."

"So you understand why I need to go see Asa."

"I think I do. Text him and let him know we'll come by in the morning."

It wasn't something she could do with Sawyer by her side. He'd already gotten into a pissing match with her brother at her office. She didn't want to take the risk that Sawyer would somehow offend her brother again.

She moved out of his arms, hating to break their connection but knowing it was necessary to prove her independence. "No. I need to go without you."

His lips pressed together. "It's not safe."

No, it wasn't. But even if she and Sawyer wore bulletproof vests and stayed inside their locked hotel room, they weren't safe. And they wouldn't be until they found and stopped that person who was responsible for cutting their brakes. Still, she didn't bother saying that to Sawyer.

"Asa will protect me."

He narrowed his eyes. "I'm still not one hundred percent sold on his innocence."

She crossed her arms and glared at him. "Well, that's too bad then, because it doesn't matter. I'm going to see him whether you like it or not."

He took her by the arm. "I don't like it. But I won't stop you. I'll take you there and stay in the hotel lobby."

She squeezed her eyes closed, knowing what she was about to say would upset him and regretting that she had to say it. But she couldn't tell him she was planning on giving the black list to Asa.

"No. I want to go by myself. I need some space, Sawyer."

"Some space from me," he said harshly.

"I'm not running from you or trying to push you away, but I need time to think. I'm not used to having someone hovering day and night. And there are things I can't talk about with you that I can with my brother."

His eyes softened. "About your past."

"About my past. The present. My future." She couldn't talk about it with her friends or Sawyer. Going by what Asa had confided in her about Thea, she knew he'd understand and help her make the right decisions for all of them. At least, that's what she was hoping. "I want to share it with you, but until I work it all out in my head, I won't be able to."

"And you think your brother can help you do that?"

"I think if anyone can, it's him."

He sighed, nodding. "Fine. I'll take you to your car, and if everything on it checks out okay, you can drive yourself to see your brother. But I want you to text me when you get there and when you leave."

She swallowed nervously. Would he ask about the inevitable lapse between the time he dropped her at her car and the time she arrived at her brother's hotel? "I will. What are you going to do?"

His gaze sharpened on her as if he'd caught on to her anxiety, but he didn't mention it to her. "I'm going to call work and put out the dozen fires that are burning and then see if I can't track down the hit man Winters hired. I spoke with Oz tonight while you were with your friends getting ready. He got a lead on our hired assassin."

Irritated, she bit her lip to keep from saying something she'd regret. "And you waited to tell me about it until now?" *Of course he did. He's a man and wanted to get laid first.* "What did he find out?"

"Guy's name is Jeff Marshall. He's from Detroit. No bank account. The wire from Chad was actually a cash pickup, wired to a check-cashing store in Detroit. Rowan managed to hack into their records to get Marshall's information. Unfortunately, the address he gave was bogus. He's got priors for assault, armed robbery, and drug possession."

Sounded like Chad had picked a winner. She could only imagine what kind of person would kill for a couple hundred bucks. "Should we be glad he doesn't have any priors for murder?" she asked, trying to lighten the mood.

She hadn't fooled him. His expression grew somber as he gathered her back into his arms and held her tightly. "I think we're facing an unknown. Whether he's our guy or not, you cannot let your guard down until we find out. But I won't let him hurt you. I won't let *anyone* hurt you." He tipped her head back, his eyes dark with the solemnity of his vow. "Trust me."

Chapter Eighteen

He looked through the telescope poking out of the trailer's window and watched her walk out the front door of the mansion that housed a fucking sex club. He hadn't realized that's what it was the first night he'd spied on her at the wedding. But he'd scouted it out since then and seen all sorts of deviants coming in and out of there at all hours of the night.

He should have known that Hayes would sink his kinky claws into her. She was too easily manipulated.

She'd thought she'd beaten him, but no one got away with besting him. He'd teach her in the long run.

He always did.

His head pounded, the beat like a drum inside his brain, and the voices chanted their scheme. It was almost finished. She'd be so proud. He'd built it with his own two hands. She'd thought him *worthless. Stupid. Lazy.* She'd tried to con the master.

But he'd shown her.

And then she'd shown him.

Now he would get the last word.

His gaze traveled to the table in the middle of the trailer where his salvation waited. Soon.

Soon he would be with her.

Just a couple more steps to accomplish before she returned to his arms.

He lifted her shirt to his nose, remembering her sweet scent. Why had she forsaken him? She'd lain in the grass with her flesh, their limbs entangled in spent passion. And her lover had seen him watching. Had smiled at him knowingly but remained silent, getting hard against her leg as he'd suckled from the pig.

Filth.

Trash.

Sinners.

He'd loved her so much. Everything he'd done was for her. Money was inconsequential because he gave her something she couldn't get from *him*. Or maybe the little fucker had figured it out and had given her the ultimate rush.

The voices got louder, excited by the thoughts of blood and sex. They wouldn't lie together in this lifetime, but they'd find plenty of time for that in the next. Then he'd remind her of what it was like to have a real man between her legs.

His time on earth was growing short, shorter than the voices squeezing on his brain would give him. Soon all the pain and guilt would ease and his head would go silent. The voices didn't like that, they moaned and screamed in defiance. He didn't care. Let them throw their tantrum. There was nothing they could do to stop him. No one could.

If he had his way, Hayes wouldn't be a problem for much longer. The plan was in motion, and all he had to do was sit back and wait.

Wait for his world to go boom.

Chapter Nineteen

LISA WAVED AT Sawyer as she slid into the driver's seat of her car. He'd already checked her car out to make sure it was safe to drive. She'd take a guess that he'd be doing that to every car they drove for a long while, even after this mess was all over.

Assuming they'd be together.

Last night, he'd learned the worst of it. She'd seduced her way into more than a dozen beds during her grifter days. No, she wasn't a whore. At least a client got what he paid for with a whore. What she'd been was much, much worse.

Sawyer thankfully didn't see it that way. And once they'd returned to his hotel suite, he'd proven it to her again and again, making love to her throughout the night and again this morning. He'd been voracious for her, and extremely thorough, making sure there wasn't a spot on her body he didn't kiss, lick, suck, or fuck. Every move she made today reminded her of him in some way.

Her clitoris was raw, her mouth and lips bruised, her ass sore, and her pussy tender from all the attention he'd given them with his tongue, his teeth, his fingers, and his cock. He'd taken her in every room of that hotel suite and had shown her just how creative he could get in the kitchen. Who knew all those utensils could be used for purposes other than cooking? She'd never look at a spatula or a turkey baster in the same way again.

Giving her the ultimate pleasure and filling all her holes simultaneously, he'd plugged her ass and fucked her pussy while she sucked on a dildo, forcing her to climax over and over until she'd passed out cold from the pleasure. He'd allowed her a couple hours of sleep and then had woken her by putting her on her hands and knees, removing the plug, and replacing it with his cock. Her eyes had barely been open when he fingered her to an explosive orgasm and spent his release all over her back. Rather than clean it, he'd rubbed it into her skin, marking her.

For some reason, even knowing the truth, he still loved her. It gave her hope that she might find her happiness with him after all.

But before she could tell him the rest of it, she had to lie to him a little longer. She headed toward Asa's hotel, waiting until the highway split and Sawyer no longer had her in his sights before she got off and turned around to go to her office.

Guilt nagged at her conscience, but she had no choice. If she'd told him she had to stop by her office, he would've been suspicious or, even worse, would've come with her. There was only one way to convince Asa to trust Sawyer.

She had to give him the black list. Then *he* could decide whether to hang onto it or destroy it. Either way, it would be out of her hands. She was tired of the burden that went along with having it in her possession. The list had too much power. It was a curse. As long as she had it, she'd never be free of all it represented.

Lies.

Violence.

Fear.

Once she stopped by the office and retrieved it, she'd go straight to Asa's.

Soon, the past's hold on her would end, and she could move on with her life—a life that hopefully included Sawyer in it.

Her hands shook as she parked in the lot across from her office, half from nervousness and half from the excitement of beginning a new chapter in her life. Before they'd parted ways that morning, Sawyer had told her he had big plans for her when she returned back at the suite. While her body should've been sated by now, that announcement, along with the naughty glimmer in his eyes as he said it, had made her pussy wet and swollen all over again. It was as if she and Sawyer were making up for lost time and trying to cram several years into a single week.

She walked across the street to the small one-story building that held her office and two others, one leased by a psychologist who saw patients there a few times a week and the other by an accountant who seemed to only use it around tax season. It was the perfect spot for her, since both she and a handful of her clients preferred the privacy the residential location afforded.

Until two days ago, she'd never run into a single problem here, as the neighborhood was almost completely free of crime. That's why despite Sawyer's warning about not lowering her guard, she wasn't worried when she unlocked her office door and stepped inside, noticing immediately that the air felt hotter than normal.

The putrid smell tinged with sulphur was her second clue that something wasn't right. It smacked into her, making her gag and causing her eyes to water.

It smelled like she imagined hell would.

Her gaze took in the destruction of her office, her files torn, paper crumpled, her drawers left open as if someone had rifled through them. Her heart plummeted to her feet as she snapped her gaze to the shelf where her books should be.

Empty.

The panic was short-lived, as when she lowered her eyes, she saw that lying haphazardly upon the floor, seemingly undamaged, were her books—including her precious copy of *A Tale of Two Cities*. And thankfully, this time, there was no red paint on her walls, carpet, or books.

But splattered all over her desk was something much, much worse.

Something just as red as the paint.

Blood.

So much blood.

A dead animal lay in the middle, an arrow with a note attached sticking out from its furry dark body. She didn't want to move any closer, but she had to know. Had to read the note.

Covering her nose and mouth with her hand, she somehow managed to shuffle her feet forward until she reached her desk. Bile rose in her throat, choking her, as she saw the damage done to the poor squirrel. She only prayed that whoever had done this had found the animal dead on the side of the road first before he butchered it. The alternative was too horrific to imagine.

She wasn't surprised to see a trail of ants crawling all over the squirrel's rotting corpse. Snatching the note off the arrow, she made certain not to come in contact with the desk and shook the paper to ensure there were no bugs on it. The message was short and clear.

Next time it will be Sawyer.

Her stomach rolled and cramped, giving her almost no warning to get to the wastepaper basket before she lost her breakfast in it.

Sweat dripping down her neck, she realized the person who had broken into her office had cranked up the heat to high, most likely to increase the rancid smell.

Sure enough, when she checked the thermostat, she wasn't surprised to see it set to ninety degrees. She flicked on the air-conditioning and wiped her brow with the back of her hand.

What did they want?

There were no instructions. No demands.

The first note had taunted her with the knowledge that he'd found her. This one threatened Sawyer.

Was he the key to all of this?

Her life had been quiet until he'd shown up. And her photograph had appeared in the news weeks ago. Why had all of this only started after his arrival in Michigan?

Other than cutting the brakes on the car, whoever was behind all this hadn't made a move to hurt her physically.

What if she wasn't the target? What if Sawyer was? What if she wasn't supposed to have been in that car with him?

Clearly, they wanted her husband out of her life. But to what end?

She had no doubt her past was connected in some way, but she was confused. Why didn't they just call the police or kill her? Why toy with her like this?

So many questions with no answers in sight.

She folded the note and stuck it in her pocket, her eyes fixed on the books. The past refused to take its dirty hooks out of her. As much as she wanted to move on with her life, it still wasn't time. She couldn't turn over the black list to her brother until she figured out who wanted Sawyer out of the way. Not when there was even the slightest chance she might need it in the future.

She picked up her copy of *A Tale of Two Cities* and flipped through its pages, relieved to see the black list still intact. All these years, the cover had cloaked the journal from prying eyes and had kept it safe. But now, it wasn't enough.

She scanned the room for another option to hide it, her gaze falling on the perfect spot. Book in hand, she pulled out the air vent cover from the floor and slipped the black list inside. Hopefully, no one would bother to look there.

As she left her office, she considered calling Sawyer. He'd be even more worried about her when he learned about what she'd found.

Except, she wasn't supposed to have been there. How would she explain her detour?

Not to mention, she still needed to go see Asa.

She'd texted her brother this morning to let him know she was paying a visit to him later. He'd waited patiently for her these last few days, but he'd come all this way to see her, and she hadn't spent any time with him.

Here she'd been fucking her husband at a sex club while Asa was probably wanting to get back to Thea and Annie. She'd acted selfishly by leaving four years ago without giving Asa a proper good-bye, and she was acting just as selfishly now.

He deserved more from her. Even though she couldn't give him the black list yet, she could at least spend some time today reconnecting with him. Then he could return home to his family, instead of sitting around waiting to see his sister.

Remembering the name of the company Sawyer used to clean her condo, she called them as she drove to Asa's hotel and asked that they take care of her office, using her credit card to pay this time.

By the time she arrived at Asa's, her heart rate had returned to normal and she was certain the decision to keep the break-in at her office a secret from Sawyer was the right one. She'd barely knocked on Asa's door before he opened it.

Wearing sweats and a T-shirt, her brother grinned widely. "Come on in. I was starting to think I wouldn't hear from you. I'm glad you came."

Guilt gnawed at her as she gave him a hug. "I'm sorry I wasn't able to make it sooner. It's just the last couple of days have been..." How could she explain it to him so he wouldn't worry? She didn't want or need another overprotective man watching over her. She'd go positively insane. "I was in a car accident," she said, not elaborating.

Eyes wide with concern, he gripped her by the arms and turned her to him. "What? When? Are you okay?"

She patted him on the shoulder. "I got a mild concussion, but we were lucky since we weren't going fast when we hit the tree."

"We?"

"Sawyer and I."

With an unmistakable frown on his face, he led her to the couch, where they both sat. "I know you were married to him, but I don't like the guy, Annie."

She crossed her legs and leaned into him. "He doesn't have to like you, and you don't have to like him. But I sure wish you would, because it would make my life a whole lot easier."

His gaze narrowed on her as he gave her a curt nod of understanding. "You going to try again with him?"

Every time she got her hopes up, something would happen to rip them away. Someone wanted Sawyer gone, if not dead. When she'd walked out on him, she'd sacrificed her own happiness to keep him safe. If it came down to it, could she do it again?

"I don't know if it's possible," she said, shaking her head.

"Why? Dad's dead. He can't hurt you guys anymore."

No, her father couldn't hurt him. But someone else could.

"I haven't told him everything," she explained, falling back into the couch cushions. "He knows that I was a con artist, but I've kept the family out of it."

He angled his body, his knees brushing against hers. "Why? If he knew that Mom and Dad forced you into the life—that Dad threatened to kill him—he'd realize you leaving him was the best thing you could've done for him."

Was it? He'd been miserable without her. Just as miserable as she'd been without him.

She wanted Sawyer to know everything about her. Every dream, every nightmare, every hope, every fear. But Asa needed to understand the risk. "If I tell him, he'll know about you and Mitch. I'm worried he won't be able to accept that I'll never be able to stop looking over my shoulder, thinking the Feds or someone is going to find me. What if he decides to report you to the cops, thinking he could somehow get me a deal?"

His gaze burned into her. "If you're asking that, you don't trust him any more than I do."

She'd thought she trusted him, but her brother was right. Something prevented her from handing over her trust completely to him. Was she too fucked up to get past it?

"Do you trust Thea?"

"With my life," he said firmly.

"How? How did you realize that you could trust her and her family with your secrets?" Why had he been able to accomplish what she hadn't?

He lifted a shoulder and spread out his hands in front of him. "I don't know. I guess I realized I'd rather take that risk than live with the fear that one day, she'd discover the truth from someone else. But…" His lips pressed together in a straight line.

"But what?"

He paused, deep creases forming on his forehead. "That car accident. What happened?"

Her pulse kicked up a notch. She should've known her brother would ask. "Sawyer was driving us back to his hotel. The brakes didn't work, and we ended up hitting a tree."

He rubbed his hands on the knees of his sweats. "How do you know the brakes didn't work?"

"He told me."

His brow arched. "Did anyone confirm that? The police?"

"I don't know," she said, confused by his question. "He talked to them when the ambulance took me to the hospital. Why are you asking that?"

He placed his hand on her leg. "Because when you've lived the life of a con, you start to smell when one's being played on someone else."

Her body jolted at his accusation. "Me? You think Sawyer's conning me?"

"Think about it. He shows up, and then your place is trashed. Maybe he did it himself or hired someone to do it to scare you."

"Scare me? Why would he want to do that?" It didn't make sense to her.

She *was* scared.

But for *Sawyer.*

He grimaced, his face growing pinched, as if it hurt him to have to say these things to her. "To get closer to you. You're staying at his hotel, right?" At her nod, he continued. "I bet you wanted to stay somewhere else, but he insisted you stay with him. Am I right?" He shifted closer to her on the couch. "And then once you got there, he managed to charm you. Seduce you. Get you to rely on him and feel safe with him. And how do you know he didn't lie about the brakes and hit the tree on purpose to keep you thinking your life was in danger?" He set both his hands on her thighs, his thumbs brushing the inside of them. "I know it's been more than four years, Annie, but didn't all that ring any warning bells for you?"

A sinking sensation wreaked havoc on her empty belly. Isn't that what she'd originally thought at her condo? But she'd quickly dismissed the notion. "Yes, and I considered all that. You don't know Sawyer. I do. He's not like that. Besides, what would he have to gain from it?"

"Revenge. You fall back in love with him. Trust him. Tell him everything, including where that money you took from your joint account went and that there's a journal of all the cons our family has ever pulled. Then he goes straight to the Feds with it. Just like you feared."

Refusing to even consider it, she shot up from the couch. Sawyer wouldn't manipulate her like that. Sure, she'd worried he'd go to the Feds, but not for revenge but to save her. "No. He wouldn't do that to me. He loves me."

"You sure about that?"

She ignored the churning in her gut. "Yes. I am."

"I hope you're right." Her brother stood from the couch and gave her chin a little nudge. "Because if you're not, it's both our asses on the line."

Chapter Twenty

HANGING UP WITH the cleaning service, Lisa removed the key to Sawyer's suite from her purse, energized despite the late hour.

She'd spent the entire day with her brother chatting, eating pineapple pizza, and hanging out together like they used to when they were younger. He hadn't brought up his theory about Sawyer again, and she'd been careful not to mention anything that would renew their conversation, including what she'd found in her office.

There were some things she and Asa would have to agree to disagree on, her husband being one of them. Maybe someday they'd learn to tolerate each other, but even if they didn't, she refused to allow their petty behavior to bother her.

When she left Asa's, she'd called Sawyer to let him know she was on her way home. He hadn't mentioned finding anything more about the hit man, and she hadn't had the lady balls to tell him he'd likely been barking up the wrong crazy tree. Chad Winters and his hired gun weren't responsible for terrorizing her. She'd save that conversation for tomorrow, because tonight he had something planned for them, and she didn't want to do a single thing to jeopardize it.

Standing outside the door to the suite, she moistened her lips with her tongue and brushed her fingers through her hair, preparing herself for him. Her nipples peaked, pressing against her blouse as she breathed heavily. Just the thought of what might be waiting for her sent arousal shooting through her body.

Inside, she was surprised to discover the suite was pitch black, not even a sliver of light to help her find the switch that would turn on the lamps. The door shut behind her, the sound of it loud in the otherwise silent room.

"Sawyer?" she called out. Her pulse slammed into overdrive as her neck prickled. She swore she felt someone else in the room, but if it was Sawyer, why wasn't he answering?

She reached out her hand to flick on the lights, when someone came from behind her and shoved her face-front against the door. She cried out as the strong body pressed tightly against hers, a telltale bulge digging into her lower back, right above the crack of her ass. Panic assaulted her, and she was gripped with fear that something had happened to Sawyer.

Only a second or two passed before the familiar scent of him reached her nose. And although her heart continued to hammer wildly, this time it was from arousal. They'd played this game only once before, when, wearing a ski mask, he'd snuck into their home, pretending to be a stranger. It was a dance that stayed firmly behind the line of consent, but at the same time gave them the fantasy that it was otherwise.

"Don't scream and I won't hurt you," he said in a gritty voice, a tone that told her this scene turned him on as much as it did her. "Say your safe word and it all stops. Otherwise, I'm in control. You do as I say, you'll find it'll go much easier on you."

He wanted her to fight. To make him force her to submit. It was a wicked game and one she couldn't wait to play.

"Please don't hurt me. I'll do anything you say."

He flipped on the lights, his eyes stormy behind the mask he wore. He flipped her around and dragged a finger leisurely down her arm. "We're gonna have lots of fun tonight, aren't we?"

She nodded as if she was a good little girl who was going to let him have his way with her. The moment he took a step away from her, she shot off toward the guest bedroom, having no idea what she'd do when she got there but too excited to care. He chased her, his booming laugh bouncing on the walls as he dashed across the room in an effort to catch her.

She wanted it rough tonight, wanted him to stake his claim on her and tame her like a wild animal. It was a dark fantasy brought to life—with a set of parameters that would keep her safe.

Darting inside the bedroom, she slammed the door shut and turned the lock, trembling from the thrill and smiling to herself for getting away from him. By the time he figured out how to get inside, he'd be so angry he'd have to punish her severely for her actions. Her entire body quivered at the thought of all the ways he'd make it hurt.

"Hiding from someone?" asked a deep male voice from behind.

Her heart in her throat, she twirled around. Leaning against the wall as if he had every right to be there stood a man she knew immediately she'd never met before. Like Sawyer, he wore a black ski mask, but that's where the similarity ended. Dreadlocks poked out from the bottom of the mask, and on his shirt were the words *Byte me.*

She froze, unable to move or speak, her limbs weighted down by the heavy arousal coursing through her and her mouth dry as the Mohave Desert. The stranger stalked toward her with a predatory gleam in his brown eyes. "Cat got your tongue?" He chuckled as he reached behind her and unlocked the door. "I sure hope not, because you're going to need it tonight."

The door opened wide to a looming Sawyer, whose copper eyes had deepened to the color of a sunset. Right now, her Master exuded danger and wicked intent.

He wasn't going to go easy on her.

And she wouldn't have it any other way.

"Please," she begged, the tremor in her voice as real as the man standing in front of her. "I'm sorry I ran. I promise, I'll do whatever you say as long as you don't hurt me."

Sawyer took one threatening step forward and pulled off his mask. "Your promise is too late. You need to be punished."

Sandwiched between the two men, she exhaled all the air in her lungs, their combined dominance making for a heady aphrodisiac. Sweat beaded on the nape of her neck as her body heated from the inside out.

Sawyer's hands slid into her hair and tilted her head back until it rested on the stranger. "My men have been instructed on everything they need to know. Nothing happens without my direction."

His words assuaged her fear, assuring her Sawyer had informed them of her limits and her safe word.

Then it hit her.

Men? As in plural?

Her silent question was answered by the entrance of two more men. As a result, her panties dampened to a ridiculous proportion. Her desire for Sawyer to share her with others and to watch him with other women was a kink that had confused her in the past. In addition to his inclination toward dominance and sadism, his fetishes also included ménage and group sex. She'd thought the idea should repulse her, but instead, it had aroused her. She and Sawyer had discussed it at length before inviting a third person into their bed for the first time—a female Dominant he knew from the BDSM community.

And it hadn't been long before his kink had become her kink.

While Sawyer identified as 100 percent heterosexual, her sexual preferences had always been a bit more fluid.

Sawyer had loved to explore this aspect of her, pushing her boundaries to their limits. No matter how many hands and mouths touched her, they were all an extension of her Master, and rather than the experience causing any jealousy among them, they'd become closer as lovers and partners. It was all a matter of communication and trust.

She didn't have a chance to examine the additional strangers before Sawyer grabbed her waist with both of his hands. The man behind her moved aside, giving Sawyer the ability to shove her toward the bed. As the back of her knees hit the mattress, he whirled her around and, with a hand on her spine, pushed her facedown on the bed.

He replaced the hand with his knee, pinning her to the mattress. "Oz. Get over here and pull down these pants of hers. It's time we taught her a lesson she'll never forget."

She twisted her neck around to see the man with the dreads walk forward, a wicked grin visible even with the mask still on.

Oz.

The knowledge of who these men were popped into her head.

These must be his best friends—Oz, Hunter, and Rowan.

In one smooth motion, Oz yanked down her leggings and panties, baring her ass for all the men to see. A breeze that felt more like a warm breath wafted over her skin. Only a second later, a sharp sting on her right ass cheek drove her to her toes.

Son of a bitch. That *was* a warm breath. Oz had bitten her.

"Mm," Oz said. "I couldn't stop myself from taking a taste of that luscious ass. Just look how easily she bruises."

Sawyer tugged on her hair, jerking her head back. "Wait until we see it covered in red stripes. You got the crop, Rowan?"

"I do. Would you like to do the honors, or shall I get her warmed up for you?" Unlike the playful Oz, this man—Rowan—spoke in a clipped tone that conveyed his seriousness.

"You're the real sadist of the group," Sawyer said, climbing on the bed. He straddled her waist and restrained her shoulders with his hands. "I think you should go first. After all, this is a punishment."

"It would be my pleasure," Rowan responded. He didn't give her time to prepare before the first *whack* landed on the same spot where Oz had bitten her, the sting painful but not unmanageable. "Hmm. I was going to warm her up, but I'm in the mood to watch her squirm. Let's watch the little masochist dance."

Each blow stronger than the last, *whack* after *whack* lit up the nerves on her ass, a blazing heat spreading like wildfire across her sensitive skin. Tears pricked her eyes, the pain almost blistering as he made sure he didn't miss a single spot. She should've wanted to evade the stings, and yet she greeted every one of them with a subtle raise of her ass.

There was no escape from the onslaught.

Sawyer's weight on her body kept her from shifting, protecting her from harm if she made any sudden moves, the crop hitting a kidney a dangerous possibility.

There was no escape.

Not that she wanted to.

The arousal bloomed like a flower, colorful and vibrant. Her clitoris beat in sync with her heart, her body a live wire. She was sinking into a place she hadn't been in several years. A place where time had no meaning, love had no reason, and sex had no limits.

"I don't think the crop is much of a punishment for her," came a voice that was somehow rumbly and smooth at the same time. It must have been Hunter. He was the only one whose voice she hadn't heard before.

"You think you can do better?" asked a voice she recognized as Rowan's.

"Hell, yeah," said Hunter.

Sawyer lifted himself off her back. "Get her up, then. It's time to see how much she can take."

A moment later, she was hefted to her feet. Her limbs were liquid, her head heavy. One of the men maneuvered her toward an open area of the room. After he removed her shirt and bra, leaving her completely naked, her arms were raised above her head. A rope tied around her wrists. Her legs spread. More rope around her ankles. The ropes tightened. Her body stretched.

Wielding a black flogger in his hand, Sawyer stood in front of her, looking every bit the dangerous intruder he pretended to be. Fisting her hair in his other hand, he tipped her head back. "She's floating." He smiled, baring his teeth to her.

A sharp biting pain gripped her nipple. She cried out as her nipple began to throb. Then, before she could adjust, the same happened to her other nipple. Clamps. Sawyer had clamped her nipples, and if she had to guess, he'd used the clover ones that tightened when pulled.

"Let's take her higher, Oz."

She jolted as the falls from Sawyer's flogger hit her breast, the jostling causing the clamp to tighten.

Sadist.

The next blow landed on the back of her thigh, the sting of it spreading straight to her pussy.

How the hell had Sawyer hit her there?

Her confusion lasted only a few seconds as she realized Oz also had a flogger.

They were tag teaming her.

The dual floggers rained stinging kisses upon her body, sweeping her consciousness away as she closed her eyes and succumbed to the painful paradise. She'd never cared much for the thudding floggers, with their impact more like a massage. She preferred the kind that stung and made her feel alive. Her skin felt as though she'd fallen asleep in the sun and had gotten a wicked sunburn. Her breasts ached. Her pussy throbbed.

And if someone didn't fuck her soon, she was going to scream.

The flogging stopped. Hands, cool and rough, caressed her blazing skin. So many hands. Squeezing. Pinching. Slapping. Up her thighs. Over her ass. Down her spine.

Across her belly. Everywhere but where she needed them most.

She bowed her head, too into the sensations to care whose touch was where. It didn't matter anyway. They all belonged to Sawyer.

Agony, strong and swift, shot through her nipples as both the clamps were removed at once, allowing the blood to rush back into the pulsating buds. The pain hurtled her toward climax, and when two sets of lips descended onto her nipples, sucking them into hot mouths, she blasted apart, her pussy clenching and releasing over and over in pleasurable contractions.

A tongue slithered up her slit, lapping at her come. Another mouth nipped at her ass and then soothed with wicked licks. The cheeks were spread apart, and the tongue touched her *there*, the dark and forbidden spot that begged for more than a tongue. The mouth on her pussy moved higher, the coolness of a metal piercing joining the warm tongue in lavishing attention on her clitoris. She was sensitive from her recent orgasm, and the contact was too much for her to process. She tried to move away from it, but she was held hostage by rope and hands and mouths.

"Tastes good after she comes, doesn't she?" Sawyer asked, releasing one of her nipples to speak.

Approval in the form of a hum came from the one between her thighs, the vibration of it adding to the intense pleasure. She hurdled toward another climax, her legs shaking out of control, but before she could fall over the cliff, the men stopped, their hands and tongues disappearing from her body.

"No," she whined, pulling at the ropes to free her hands so she could force them to finish the job. When she opened her eyes, her gaze fell on Sawyer's beautiful face and the desire etched all over it.

He'd pleasured her with pain. Awarded her with an orgasm. And now it was time for her to return the favor.

The ropes were released from her wrists and ankles.

"We're not here for your enjoyment," he said, the lie almost sounding convincing. "It's time to put you and that pretty little mouth of yours to work." He pushed on the top of her head. "Get on your knees."

From the floor, she looked up at him expectantly. While she obviously loved the beating and the orgasm, she lived to serve him, the fulfillment it brought her more intoxicating than drinking a bottle of wine.

Belts unbuckled and fell onto the carpet. Pants were dropped, baring four men from the waist down. Sawyer and Hunter moved to stand in front of her, each with their legs slightly spread. Two thick cocks, one with a metal ball pierced through it, jutted out as if begging for her touch. Her hands itched to do just that, but she controlled her impulse, awaiting her Master's instructions.

She didn't have to wait long.

Sawyer kneeled beside her and pushed her toward Hunter's cock. "Open your mouth wide and take him in."

Her mouth opened as if she had no say in it. Which, short of using her safe word, she didn't.

Sawyer didn't give her a second to get acclimated. Just forced her down the length of Hunter's cock until she took every inch of him inside. His hairs tickled her nose.

She swore she could feel the piercing against the soft tissue of her throat, but just as she got used to him, Sawyer tugged her back by her hair. He pushed and tugged, pushed and tugged, controlling the blow job she was giving his friend.

Then Sawyer ripped her away from Hunter, and another cock entered her mouth, this one longer. She wasn't sure who it belonged to, and she didn't care. She became a vessel for the men's pleasure, the gift her Master bestowed upon his friends.

Closing her eyes again, she sunk into the rhythm that Sawyer played with her, letting him use her mouth to please his friends as they each took turns inside her mouth.

She wasn't sure how much time had passed when her mouth was no longer filled. Sawyer lifted her soaking pussy onto his waiting cock. He didn't move. Just held her tightly to him, breathing heavily into the crook of her neck, as if they were the only two in the room.

"Can you handle more?" he whispered, breaking character.

"I can handle as much as you give me, Master," she replied, kissing the top of his head. "Give it all to me."

He continued holding her to him as one of the men worked a lubed finger into her ass and began fucking her with it. She squirmed on Sawyer's lap, eager to be filled with two cocks.

"Stop moving," he ordered roughly.

Breathing deep, she somehow stifled the urge to move up and down on Sawyer's hard cock, instead concentrating on pleasing her Master.

She rested her head on Sawyer's shoulder as one finger became two and then three. Sawyer tilted himself backward, rolling her with him then resting the upper part of his back against the wall.

Lube poured down her crack and a hand pressed against her spine right before she felt the stretch and burn of a cock entering her ass. Minutes ticked by as the stranger worked his thickness as far as he could go.

The man behind her groaned loudly, his body quaking. "Yeah, give it to me. Fill me up."

Startled, she opened her eyes. Sawyer's lips turned up in a little grin. "You're not the only middle in this sandwich. Look over your shoulder."

Following his suggestion, she saw Oz behind her and another man behind him. The idea of the dominant Oz being topped by another man sent a wave of heat flowing over her. When a pierced cock appeared in front of her face and she took it in her mouth, she realized Rowan was the one in Oz's ass.

Slowly, the men began to move, pushing her pussy onto Sawyer then her ass back onto Oz while Hunter fucked her mouth.

It was dirty.

Naughty.

Depraved.

And she loved every fucking second of it.

The men moved like a unit, their experience with ménage apparent from their silent communication and the ease with which they thrust and retreated in perfect harmony. It was a sinful dance she never wanted to end.

Her nipples, still aching from the clamps, brushed against Sawyer's sweaty chest, and each time she was thrust forward, her clitoris grazed his pubic bone. She held onto him like he was her anchor in a windstorm and if she let go, she'd blow away, never to be found again. Her body was on fire, as if hot lava coursed through her veins.

She could feel Sawyer's heart beating against her chest. They breathed in sync. Together, they were one.

One heart.

One mind.

One soul.

He'd trusted her with his deepest, darkest pain and proven that she could trust him with the same. He loved her enough to give her this fantasy, to share her with his friends without judgment or jealousy.

It was time to trust him with more than her body. He deserved to know the truth. She had to have faith that once he learned that truth, he'd still love her and love her enough to keep her secret.

Her belly quivered as the muscles underneath it tightened, the climax gathering at the base of her spine. Her fingernails dug into Sawyer's arms as bands of heat wrapped around her middle and squeezed. She was helpless to the sensation growing sharper and more acute by the second, mindless from the carnal pleasure of having these men inside of her.

They were Sawyer's closest friends...his band of brothers. He was giving them to her as a gift, as a sign of his never-ending devotion and his desire to include her in the family he'd created. Their use of her body signified their acceptance of her into their fold and tethered them in a way only those with this particular kink would understand. They loved her because Sawyer loved her. They would protect her as one of their own.

She belonged to them all now.

The climax crashed into her, her body jerking uncontrollably and white lights exploding behind her eyelids. For a moment, they all stilled, allowing her a brief respite before chasing their own orgasms. Hunter came hard, ropes of his come shooting down her throat as he groaned her name. Only seconds later, Oz and Rowan shook with their own releases, although she wasn't sure which of them achieved it first. Then, staring into her eyes with more love than she would've believed possible, Sawyer reached his own climax.

The fantasy was over, but the reality was only beginning.

After cleaning her up and getting her into bed, Sawyer slipped under the covers beside her and took her into his arms.

One by one, her new friends kissed her cheek and thanked her. She rested her head on Sawyer's chest, listening to the steady beat of his heart.

She'd asked her brother how he'd known when to trust Thea, and he'd answered that he'd just known. She hadn't understood what he'd meant, but now, she finally did. There wasn't an ounce of doubt left in her. Sawyer loved her enough to share her with his friends. To other people, that wouldn't mean anything, but to her, it had meant everything.

When the front door of their hotel suite closed and only they remained, she propped herself up on her elbow, ready to trust him with the truth. She had nothing to fear.

Chapter Twenty-One

LISA'S VOICE PIERCED the darkness. "I'm ready to tell you everything. Asa wasn't thrilled with my decision, but I can't hold it inside me anymore, and you deserve to know the whole truth."

Sawyer rolled over and turned on the lamp. He sat up and settled against the headboard. "Whatever you say, I promise not to judge you."

She believed him.

She trusted him.

Shifting to rest her head on his chest, she exhaled a shaky breath as she recalled the terror of her childhood. "My first memory is from when I was three years old. I was with my family, and we were at some county fair. Everything was so exciting. The rides that whirled around and around. Laughing families. Scents of the fried foods coming from the stands. I was barefoot, wearing a pretty blue dress and a matching ribbon in my hair. My parents had me sit at a picnic table and told me they'd be back in a few minutes. They took Asa and Mitch with them. I sat there all day in the hot sun. Thirsty. Hungry. My skin burning. I watched as kids ate hot dogs and drank lemonade and went on the rides. Everyone was happy. I didn't leave that table, even when I had to pee so badly that I ended up soiling my underwear. I worried if I left, they'd never find me again. When they finally came back at dusk, my brothers were all sticky with ice cream stains on their shirts and my parents' pockets were stuffed with cash they'd managed to pickpocket. That was the first time I realized we weren't like other families. Most of the time, we lived in the back of a truck, because we could park it in different lots and no one thought too much about it."

Fat tears rolled down her cheeks, the pain in her heart excruciating. For years, she'd refused to think about those early memories of abuse and neglect. She'd filed them in a locked drawer somewhere in her mind. Now that she had unlocked that drawer, the memories crashed into her consciousness, making her body tremble and her heart race as if she was watching a slasher film. But unlike watching a scary movie, she couldn't escape the images when she closed her eyes.

Sawyer brushed his hand up and down her arm. "It's okay, baby. You can keep going. I'm here."

She tilted her head up to look into his eyes. "My family perfected the art of grifting. According to my Dad, I come from a long line of con artists on both sides. He made it seem like a privilege." She frowned, realizing how silly that was. "It was a long time before I understood that what we did was wrong. It was my normal. By the time I was six, I got to help them with their cons, and by junior high, I had my own swindles going."

Nothing that would get her into too much trouble. She mostly sold candy bars at a premium under the guise of the money going to charity—only she was the charity.

Continuing, she sat up and reclined next to him, putting her head on his shoulder. "Obviously, we had to move around a lot to evade the authorities. You'd think we'd have lived well, but turns out, my parents had a bit of a gambling problem. The money we earned from our cons was usually in the bookies' hands by the end of the football games on Sunday night."

So much money gone in the blink of an eye because of their greed and selfishness. The high they got from gambling was more important than feeding their children. Most Sundays would end with her hiding under the trailer to escape the beating that would follow the games.

There were hundreds of stories to tell, and someday, she'd share them all with him. But right now, she needed him to know the worst of it. "After my mom died, my dad told me it was time to perform the same sort of cons she did. I was only fifteen at the time, so Asa convinced him to let me wait until I turned eighteen." She swallowed, her throat growing thick and tight. "That's when I started using sex as a weapon."

She hadn't been a virgin by then, but all the same, the first time she'd slept with a mark, she'd gotten physically ill afterward. That's when she learned to dissociate her mind from her body. When she was with her marks, she was no longer Annaliese Hunt. She was whoever they wanted her to be. Somehow that had made it easier.

"I didn't become attached," she explained on a whisper. "It was a job. Nothing more." She captured his gaze, holding it hostage. "Not until you. When my father gave me your file and I saw your picture for the first time, I became obsessed. I read everything I could about you. I dreamed of you. I stalked you for weeks. I went above and beyond my normal preparation. Something about you called out to me, and it wasn't your money." She reached out and cupped his cheek. "It was the pain in your eyes. I wanted to ease it in any way I could. As your lover. As your slave. As your wife."

His throat worked over a swallow. "So I was more than your mark?"

She sat up and laid her hands on the sides of his face, needing him to understand. "You were my everything."

He nodded, his eyes closing as if in pain before they opened again, shining with relief. If she had to spend the rest of her life proving it, she would; she never wanted him to doubt how much she loved him again.

As if she was outside naked in a blizzard, her entire body shook violently, her teeth chattering. "At first, my instructions were to marry you, divorce you, and take you for as much money as I could without getting any attorneys involved. But my dad got greedier. He decided he wanted all of it. If you died, you would have been worth a lot more to me than you would as my ex-husband."

Her throat constricted, preventing her from speaking. It took her three tries before she could say it. The words were like razor blades, cutting her from the inside. "I was ordered to kill you."

He didn't seem surprised.

Pulling on the blanket, he wrapped it and his arms around her, enveloping her in warmth. "You should have told me."

Relief swept through her as she cried into his chest. The truth had never tasted so sweet. "I wanted to. Believe me, I wanted to. But if I didn't do it, he would have. There was only one way to save you. He kept a book—he called it his black list—that logged every con he'd ever done. I stole it from him. I left a note telling him if anything happened to you I'd give it to the FBI. And then I ran." She couldn't stop crying, her tears soaking his skin.

"Why didn't you go to the FBI in the first place?" he asked softly. "I would've helped you. We could've stayed together."

"We would've been torn apart." At least that's what she'd thought then. Now, she wasn't as certain. "Even if you forgave me, my father wasn't the only one who had committed a crime. My brothers—Asa and Mitch—and I would have been sent to prison, as well. I couldn't do that to them. And I was scared. Scared once you knew the real me, you'd hate me. Scared to spend the next twenty years in prison. Scared my father would find a way to kill you in retaliation. I didn't see any other way."

He ran his hand over the stubble lining his rigid jaw. "I would've had my attorneys negotiate a plea deal for you so you'd do as little time as possible, if any at all. You didn't trust me enough, you didn't trust in our love enough, to take that risk."

He was right.

But she'd given him all she had at the time. "I loved you as much as I knew how to love anyone."

A notch formed between his eyebrows. "If you had to do it all over again, would you make that same decision?"

She'd asked herself that same question several times this week, and she still didn't have an answer.

She blew out a breath. "I don't know. All I do know is I can't change the past."

His eyes blazed with heat as he dragged his finger down her throat and hooked his finger in her silver collar. "Your father is dead. There's nothing standing in our way anymore. Let's break our damned agreement."

Her heart thundered as he stood from the bed and, in all his naked glory, strode across the room to where his pants were draped over a chair. He dug through his pockets, coming back with a closed fist. After shifting her so that her legs hung over the side of the bed, he kneeled on the carpet and opened his palm, revealing their wedding bands. "I don't want a divorce. I just want you. My wife. My submissive. Forever and ever, until death do us part."

Her hand itched to snatch the ring and place it on her finger. But he needed to know the risks in being with her. "Someone wants you dead because of me."

He shrugged as if it was nothing. "Let me worry about that."

"I went to my office earlier today, before I went to Asa's," she said quickly, so she wouldn't chicken out. "Someone had broken in and left me another note."

His face went stony. "You lied to me?"

"I didn't want you to follow me there." She slid off the mattress onto her knees in front of him. "I was going to get the black list and give it to Asa so that I could move on with my life. With you."

His expression softened. "What did the note say?"

"*Next time it will be Sawyer.* The note was attached to a dead squirrel. Whoever is doing this isn't going to hurt me." She placed her hand over his heart. "But he will hurt you."

"I'm not going to let anyone keep me from you ever again," he vowed, as if he could stop death from claiming him.

"If we stay together, we'll be risking your life."

His heart began to beat a bit faster underneath her palm. "Love is always a risk. But we'll find out who's behind the threats. And then it will just be you and me with no more lies between us."

She wanted to believe it was possible more than anything. "If you died because of me, I would never forgive myself."

He covered her hand with his, trapping it against his chest. "I understand what that feels like. I've blamed myself for my parents' deaths for years. But you were the one who allowed me to see that I could have done everything differently and the outcome would have been the same. We can't predict when I'm going to die. There are some things even a Dominant like me can't control. If it's my time, then I'm going to go—whether it's because some nutcase cuts the brakes on my car or I get hit by a bus walking across the street. I choose to live each day to the fullest. And that means living it with you. I choose you. What are you going to choose?"

She realized then there had never been any choice to make. She'd known from the moment he'd breezed back into her life that she belonged to him.

She unfolded his fingers from his closed hand and took the rings from his palm. With shaky but eager hands, she slipped his ring onto his fourth finger and then happily adorned her own finger with the symbol of their eternal love. "I choose a life where I finally get to be the real Annaliese. I choose you."

Chapter Twenty-Two

EVEN THOUGH SHE was asleep, she sensed that someone was watching her. The last thing she remembered was falling asleep in Sawyer's arms after consummating their vow to remain married. The details of where they'd live and how they'd keep her picture out of the press hadn't been discussed, but it didn't matter. She trusted they'd figure it out.

Warm breath that smelled of oranges and vodka blew across her face. "Rise and shine, sleepyhead."

She shot up, holding the sheet against her chest to cover herself.

Crouching by her side of the bed was a pleased-looking Oz. "No need to be modest. We're all friends here. If you want, I'd be happy to lose my clothes, too."

"Get out, Oz, and let us sleep," mumbled Sawyer, not opening his eyes.

Oz chuckled as he stood. "No can do. We need to have a chat. I wouldn't have broken into your suite if it wasn't important. The guys are waiting in the other room."

Sawyer rolled over, opening his eyes. "Fuck. Give us five minutes."

Oz was still chuckling as he closed the door behind him.

She got out of bed and started to dress. "He broke in? Why didn't he just call?"

Sawyer shook his head, his lips slightly tipped up in amusement. "That's Oz. Hell, that's all three of them. They have their own way of doing things. I've gotten used to it over the years."

He was lucky to have them.

Envy warmed her heart. "They really care about you."

He stepped into his boxers, sadly covering up that part of him she was hoping to see again soon. "We care about each other. And that includes you now. Are you good with that?"

"What does that mean exactly?"

He stopped dressing and faced her. "It means that if anything happened to me, they'd take care of you."

"How?" she asked, not wanting to think of a world in which he wasn't with her.

"Financially, emotionally, physically—"

"Sexually?"

He tilted his head to the side, his eyes sparkling. "If you required some sexual healing, I'm sure they'd be happy to help. But it's not about the sex. There's a bond between us, something unique that can never be broken." He strode to her and snaked his arms around her waist. "You're part of that bond now. That's one of the reasons I flew them out here yesterday."

"What if I didn't want to be part of that bond? What if I didn't want you to share me with them?"

He lifted a shoulder. "Then I wouldn't."

"Would you...have sex with their women?"

"Currently, none of them are seeing anyone, so it's a moot point, but if they were, I wouldn't do anything you weren't comfortable with."

Comfortable? That wasn't the word she'd use right now, since the last thing she felt was comfortable. All this talk about sex with other people had made her slick between her legs. And she'd bet anything that Sawyer knew it. "You didn't tell me all this five years ago."

"I wasn't sure you'd accept that part of me." He stepped in closer to her, letting her feel the erection he was sporting. Good to know this conversation was affecting them both. "Now, I know how important it is for us to be honest with one another. Role play, BDSM, group sex, it's all just icing on that delicious cake, but I can live without all of it. What I can't live without is you."

"You're never going to have to worry about that, because I'm not going anywhere. But for the record, I liked last night and I wouldn't mind it happening again someday." She kissed him gently on the lips, quickly pulling away before she forgot they had people waiting for them in the next room.

Not that those men were easily forgettable. She had a feeling they'd star in her midnight fantasies for years to come.

She brushed her thumb over the cool metal of his wedding ring. "Are Rowan and Oz a thing?"

The arch of his brow and the tug of his lips told her he knew exactly why she was asking. "Unless something has changed without my knowledge, I don't think so. They're both bisexual and pretty sexually adventurous. It's just sex to them. Nothing more than scratching an itch. I've never seen them kiss each other or anything."

She let go of his hands and trailed a finger down his chest, lower and lower. "It was pretty hot when Rowan fucked Oz. Have you ever...?"

He snatched her hand before she could get to her destination. "Not my thing. But I wouldn't say no if you wanted to fuck my ass with a strap-on one day." He winked and pulled her toward the door, leaving her breathless with that sinful image in her mind. "Come on, let's go see what they want, so we can go back to bed."

He led her to the suite's main room, where she found the three men having breakfast. She waited for the embarrassment over last night to wash over her, but it never came. If anything, she was having a difficult time not picturing what they all looked like naked and how she could still feel them on and in her body.

Hunter reclined on the couch, the huge man looking completely at home drinking a cup of coffee. She hadn't gotten a good look at him or the others last night, even after they'd removed their black ski masks. She'd been too punch-drunk on sex. But today, with the hotel lights on and the sunlight filtering in through the blinds, she took her chance.

Among the group of self-professed techies, the bald Hunter appeared most out of place, with a full sleeve of tattoos decorating both his arms and tongue, lip, and eyebrow piercings. He was so broad and muscular, she couldn't help thinking of the Incredible Hulk.

Then again, as her gaze bounced to the dreadlocked Oz, who was eating a chocolate chip cookie while sitting next to Hunter, she realized she wouldn't exactly have pictured him as a computer genius either. Of course, like last night's *Byte me* T-shirt, his *There's no place like 127.0.0.1* T-shirt today proved how looks could be deceiving.

Rowan's appearance surprised her the most. He could have been a model, with his wavy black hair and perfect bone structure. When his intense gray eyes fixed on her, she felt as though he could see straight into her soul.

"About time," he said, his tone admonishing. "I thought you two would never get up."

Sawyer stole a couple of pieces of buttered toast off the plate in front of Hunter and handed her one. "Why the hell are you guys up so early? It's like five in the morning out west."

"Never went to sleep," Hunter said in his rough voice. "We found something that needed to be discussed with both of you."

Her pulse kicked up a notch.

Sawyer stopped mid-bite. "Did you locate Jeff Marshall?"

"Yeah. He's in jail for armed robbery," Rowan said. "Been there for more than a week."

Sawyer nodded as if not surprised. "Then he's not our guy. So what did you find?"

The guys shared a look between them.

Oz's gaze went to her. "Maybe we should talk to Annaliese first—"

"No," she said firmly. "Whatever you have to say to me can be said in front of Sawyer."

After exchanging another ominous look with his friends, Oz scratched his head. "When Sawyer first had us check you out, we must have missed it. How many bank accounts do you have?"

She frowned, surprised by his question. "Two. A checking account and a savings account with about three grand. Why?"

Hunter got up from the couch and walked over to her and Sawyer. "We found another savings account in the name of Annaliese Hunt."

Never in her life had she opened an account in her real name. "Couldn't it be another Annaliese?"

Hunter shook his head. "Your social security number is listed."

She'd never used it. "Maybe my parents set it up in my name to hide money and forgot to close it."

"I don't think they would've forgotten about this account," Oz said. "It's got more than a million dollars in it."

The room went silent.

Panic surged through her as she spun to Sawyer. What if he believed the money was hers? What if he thought she'd lied to him?

She couldn't lose him. Not now. Not ever. "It's not mine. I swear. You believe me, don't you?"

She waited for him to say something. Do something.

But he kept his gaze on the floor as if he hadn't even heard her.

It felt as if someone was crushing her heart. She couldn't breathe, the ache in her chest making it too painful to inhale.

All that talk about trust.

Well, last night she'd proven she trusted him.

Now it was his turn.

"Sawyer?" she whispered, taking his hand and placing it over her throat and to her collar. "You believe me, right?"

His gaze flew to hers, and he cupped her face in his hands. "I believe you."

Relieved, she sucked in a breath and threw her arms around her husband, the heavy weight on her chest gone.

Still eating his cookie, Oz joined their side. "Good thing you do, because someone only wanted it to look like it was her account. It was only opened a couple weeks ago. Unless you hid your money under the mattress, there's no way it could belong to you. We were very thorough in our investigation of you."

"I never thought I'd be saying I'm glad you checked me out before you came to see me," she said to Sawyer. She turned to Oz. "So who opened the account?"

"We're working on figuring that out," Oz said. "It's through one of those online banks, and so far, I haven't been able to hack my way into their system to retrieve anything other than the account names and amounts."

"Can you do it?" she asked.

"Of course. I'm Oz," he said, as if that explained everything. "My computer is currently running a program to find the match for the password. That will be quicker than accessing the system's back door and shouldn't leave any trail, so we won't have the Feds knocking down our door in the middle of the night."

Unlike the other two men, Rowan stayed across the room from them. "Any ideas as to why someone would put a million in an account in your real name?"

There was only one thing that made sense.

"Yes," she said. "To break up my marriage to Sawyer." She lowered her voice as she spoke to her husband. "If you believed I'd kept the money and that I'd been lying to you these past few days, you'd leave me."

His eyes grew sad. Sad for *her.* "There are only a few people who know who you really are, Annaliese. And since I know no one in this room is responsible, that only leaves—"

"My brothers, Mitch and Asa."

Sawyer scowled. "I told you I didn't trust Asa."

"It's not him. He would never do this to me. He wants to see me happy," she said, even though she was plagued with doubt. She wasn't ready to accept that Asa might be lying to her. "But the apple doesn't fall far from the tree when it comes to Mitch. He was evil even as a child. He's got to be behind everything."

"Why target me?" Sawyer asked.

She didn't know, but she had a guess. "You're the one thing that means the most to me. He's punishing me for leaving the family."

Still, it didn't feel right to her. Why would he have vandalized her condo and left the squirrel for her? Why not just kill Sawyer?

Sawyer smoothed his hand over her hair. "What are you thinking?"

She was thinking Mitch was far more dangerous than she'd ever given him credit for. "The clothes, the papers, the books...He searched through my condo and office. What if he was looking for the black list?"

Without it, she'd have nothing to hold over him, freeing him to take everything she loved away from her.

Sawyer's gaze snapped to Oz. "We need to find him. Now."

Oz didn't appear in a rush as he nibbled on the last bite of his cookie. "Name?"

"Mitch Hunt, but he's got a couple of dozen aliases," she said.

Hunter plucked the cookie from Oz's hands and tossed it in his mouth, leaving poor Oz looking devastated. "Right now, we've got to figure out where that million came from. Maybe that will help us narrow down what name he's currently using."

She took a step toward the bedroom. "I should call Asa and tell him."

"No," Sawyer said, grabbing her by the arm. "Not until we know for certain that he's not involved."

She waved a finger in his face. "Someday you're going to regret not trusting him. He's got a wife and a family now. Even if he was capable of being behind this, he's not going to blow what he's built. I know it's got to be Mitch. I feel it in my gut."

Sawyer's cell buzzed in his pocket. "Damn it." He yanked it out and jabbed at the screen. "Hayes." He paused, listening. "Can't I fax it to you?" A growl tore from his throat. "Fine. I'll be there within the hour."

He slipped the phone back into his pocket. "For some reason, the airport is requiring my signature on the flight plan for the guys' return flight, and they won't accept a fax." He jutted his chin at Hunter and Oz. "I'm going to go down to the airport and then come right back."

She yawned as she followed the guys to the door. "I'll be fine. I'm still pretty tired, so I'm sure I'll fall asleep five minutes after you leave anyway."

The guys said their good-byes, Hunter giving her a hug, Rowan giving her a curt nod, and Oz kissing her on the mouth, trying to slip in his tongue before Sawyer punched him in the arm.

When they left, Sawyer kissed her thoroughly, as if he'd never see her again. "Do not open this door for anyone, do you hear me?"

"I won't," she promised, smiling against his lips. "I love you."

She watched him as he got onto the elevator before shutting the door. Then, after taking a bite of another piece of toast, she got into bed and slipped beneath the sheets.

The moment she closed her eyes, her phone chimed, signaling a text had come through. She snatched it off the nightstand and read it. Although the phone number was listed as unknown, she knew from the message it was Sawyer.

I forgot my wallet, and the key to the room is in it. Can you let me in? I'm in the hallway.

She laughed as she rolled out of bed and crossed the suite to the front door. He should've just had Oz break in again.

When she got to the door, she swung it open, expecting to see her husband's face.

Her laugh was suddenly cut short as her eyes fell on the last man she wanted to see.

"Mitch."

Chapter Twenty-Three

HER BROTHER HADN'T improved with age. Although he was only in his thirties, he looked as if he was much, much older. His olive skin had an unhealthy grayish tint to it, and his eyes were bloodshot.

The scent of alcohol slapped her in her face. It was only nine in the morning, and he was already drinking. She remembered him always having a beer in his hand, but she'd never considered that he might have a drinking problem.

She went to shut the door, but he wedged his foot inside. "Moving up in the world, aren't you, sis?"

"Hello, Mitch." Her heart was beating so quickly she felt as if it was going to jump out of her chest.

His face contorted into a half smile, half sneer. "Aren't you going to invite your oldest brother in?"

Could she say no?

One way or another, she needed to find out why he was here and what he wanted from her. With the exception of causing her car accident, he hadn't hurt her. She had to believe he wouldn't harm her now.

She held the door wide open for him and swept out her hand in welcome. "Come in. What are you doing here? Did Asa tell you where to find me?"

His eyes turned dark, fury emanating from him. "Asa? You've been in contact with him all this time?"

"No," she said, trying to keep him calm. "He found me from the newspaper. Just like you did, I'm assuming."

Trapping her inside, he leaned against the door, his back up against it and his arms folded in front of him. "I got tired of waiting for Hayes to find you. Kept track of him for years, thinking maybe you'd think it was safe to go back to him or his investigators would find you. Never thought you'd be stupid enough to get your photo taken. You've gotten lazy in the past few years. But that's all going to change now that I've found you."

"What are you talking about?" she asked in a shaky voice, unable to conceal her fear.

His smile broadened, displaying yellowed teeth. "You're going to give me that black list, and then you're coming with me."

She shook her head, wondering if there was another way out of here. "I'm not going anywhere with you."

He pushed off the door and stalked to her. "Where is it, Annaliese? You got it here with you? Couldn't find it in your condo or your office."

She took a giant step backward. "You're the one who trashed them?"

"Trashed them?" He laughed. "Looked good as new when I was there. Busted through your locks, though. You really should invest in better ones."

She pointed at the door. "Get out."

His brow shot up in amusement. "Tell me where it is."

"Somewhere you'll never find it." She squared her shoulders and spoke with a confidence she didn't feel. "And don't think for a second I don't have a contingency plan in case something should happen to me. If I die or disappear, the black list goes straight to the Feds."

He loomed over her, his whiskey stench overwhelming. "I'm not going to kill you. You and me, we're going to work as a team again. We'll be the new Bonnie and Clyde."

"Bonnie and Clyde were killed by the cops," she pointed out.

He shrugged. "Then we'll be better than them."

He was crazy if he thought she'd go anywhere with him.

"I have no desire to go back to the life of a criminal. I've got a good life now. Why can't you just let me be?"

"You ain't living. You're biding your time until your life begins again." He grabbed her by her shoulders, his fingers digging into her flesh. "Conning is in your blood. You don't turn your back on it. You can pretend all you want, but it's who you are, and one day, you won't be able to control yourself. It will start with a little lie. Nothing too fancy, but just to see if you can get away with it. And when you do, that high will surge through your blood, and you'll crave a stronger hit. I'm saving you the trouble and all that wasted time you'll spend being someone you're not. Don't you remember the rush you got when you pulled off a successful con? Don't you miss it?"

Miss it? Most days, she felt as though she hadn't stopped. Pretending to be Lisa Smith was just another long con. Only this time she hadn't been conning a mark. She'd been conning herself.

"No," she said vehemently. "Because I never got any satisfaction out of swindling people. Only you and Mom and Dad did. I did it because I had no choice. Because I didn't have any other options. But now I do, and I choose to work a legitimate job for my money." She shook off his hold on her and stormed to the door, opening it. "So I'm going to tell you again, get the hell out of this hotel and out of my life. For good."

For a moment, she thought he wouldn't leave. But with a swagger a man who looked like him shouldn't have, he walked out into the hallway and turned to her. "You will give me that black list, Annaliese. If you don't, the people you love will eat one of my bullets, starting with your husband and ending with your friend the reporter. That's what happens when someone like you cares about people. You put their lives in danger. I'll give you twenty-four hours, and then I'm going to blow your lover's brains out right in front of you." With an evil glint in his eyes that told her he meant every word, he got onto the elevator and left.

She slammed the door and locked it with trembling hands. It felt as if the air in the suite had dropped to arctic temperatures. Her teeth chattered, and her body shook uncontrollably.

Cold. So cold.

She felt as if she'd never be warm again.

She couldn't call the police. Not unless she wanted to spend the next twenty years behind bars. She couldn't call her friends. Mitch had obviously done his homework on her, as he'd proven when he'd mentioned Rachel.

Sawyer. She needed Sawyer.

She tried dialing, but her fingers were shaking so badly, she kept messing up his number. It took her three tries before she managed to get it right. It rang and rang and rang until she finally got his voice mail. She hung up and tried again, but the phone slipped from her hands onto the carpet.

She left it there.

Stumbling into the bathroom, she flipped on the shower, making it as hot as possible without burning her skin. She waited until the room filled with steam before she removed her clothing, stepped under the spray of the shower, and slid to the tile floor.

It would never end. No matter how much she wanted to forget the past, it refused to let her go. Would there ever come a day when she didn't have to look over her shoulder? When people like Chad Winters wouldn't hire an assassin to kill her? When she wouldn't have her family threatening to take everyone she loved?

Her mind turned to Sawyer. Always Sawyer.

Was it fair to bring him into this kind of life?

What if they had children?

As her body was racked by harsh sobs, she saw them in her mind's eye, a little boy with golden hair and eyes as copper as a penny, holding his daddy's hand, while his sister, a girl with curls, blue eyes, and chubby cheeks, sat on her daddy's shoulders eating cotton candy and laughing at all the carnival's sights.

With Sawyer, she had the opportunity to have a real life with a real family. Could she throw that all away? Allow her life to continue being controlled by fear?

She wasn't sure how long she rocked back and forth under the water. It could've been minutes or hours. Time had no meaning. Not until Sawyer pulled open the shower's glass door and stepped inside, fully clothed.

He crouched down beside her. "Annaliese? Honey? What is it?"

"I can't do this," she whispered, her throat raspy from crying.

He brushed her hair off her face. "Do what, baby?"

"This. My life as Lisa Smith. All of it. It's not me."

He turned off the water and helped her to her feet. "I agree. You're not Lisa Smith." He peeled off his shirt, dropping the soaked garment onto the floor of the shower. "You're Annaliese Hunt. My wife. My submissive."

Every word was like a dagger to her heart. "You don't understand. I can't be with you right now. Everything is happening too fast."

"You're running again. Don't do it. Most people don't get a second chance like us. Don't throw it all away." He grabbed a towel for himself and quickly dried off before hauling her off her feet and carrying her to the bed. "Tell me what's got you scared."

She waited until they lay side by side. "Mitch was here."

His eyes widened as he propped himself up on his palm. "Your brother? Did he hurt you?"

"No, not physically." Sometimes the emotional harm was much worse than the physical. She hoped that Sawyer could repair the damage her brother inflicted. "He didn't admit to being behind the threats and the car, but he has to be." She paused, searching his face. "He wants the black list."

"So give it to him," he said, without hesitation.

She sat up. "Give it to him? Are you crazy?"

His hand settled on the inside of her thigh. "You don't need to protect me anymore. So what does it matter if he takes it?"

"He wants me to go with him, Sawyer. He wants me to leave you. Leave everything behind. He says this isn't who I'm meant to be. What if he's right? What if I wake up one day and decide I've been denying my true nature? That I can't outrun the blood that flows through my veins?"

Sawyer caressed her skin, calming her. "Your blood doesn't define you, and sharing DNA doesn't make your brother your family. Love. Trust. Support. Those are the things that make a family. Just like I have with Oz, Hunter, and Rowan, you have that with your friends. You have it with me. Trust me this time. You are not your mother. You are not your father." His eyes shone with love for her. "You are Annaliese Hayes. The strongest, most loyal, talented, and loving woman I've ever known. That's who you are. Don't let your brother screw with your head. You've got my love. You've got my trust. You've got my support." He took her hand and tugged her onto him. "And I'm not going to fucking let you walk out of my life ever again."

"Make love to me, Sawyer," she whispered, her fingers brushing the hard planes of his chest. "I need my Master, my husband inside of me right now. I don't want to think. Please, love me."

He cupped her cheek. "I do. So much. I always have, and I always will."

His words warmed her even more effectively than the hot shower. "I love you, too. I promise, I won't repeat my mistakes. I'll do it right this time. I promise." She kissed him, letting her mouth seal her vow. "I promise."

He bent and took her nipple into his mouth.

She tossed her head back, her hands delving into his hair to hold him hostage against her breast. Every part of her ached and throbbed, her desire so potent she could smell it radiating from her skin. She loved this man so much she couldn't breathe at the thought of losing him.

As she cried his name, he sucked on her, using his tongue and teeth to drive her out of her skin.

It didn't matter how he touched her, whether it was whisper soft or strong and painful. She craved it all. Needed it like she needed oxygen. He was her drug, and she was never going to kick the habit.

"Hurry, Sawyer," she begged.

He moved over her, his gaze holding hers, before descending to take the other nipple into his mouth, giving it the same rough treatment as the other. She melted into the mattress, becoming liquid, boneless, surrendering to his innate dominance. Her nails raked down and up his spine, leaving behind her mark on his skin.

She scissored her legs, the pressure between them growing to a powerful tempest of need. Every worry disappeared, nothing and no one existing in the world except for them and their love.

Arching her back, she managed to roll him over and lie on top of him. She kissed her way down his body, paying special attention to that spot on his collarbone that always drove him crazy.

He moaned, its vibration sending shards of pleasure to her pussy. There was nothing better than pleasing him, and she'd spend the rest of her life proving that to him. She'd make up for lost time, rediscover his body and his preferences, show him how much she loved him.

He linked his hands together under his head, watching her with hooded eyes as she settled between his legs. Pre-come beaded on the head of his cock, the pearly liquid waiting to be devoured.

Wrapping her hand around the base of his shaft, she licked it up, the taste of him better than a glass of her favorite wine. Salt. Musk. Man. It was his passion on her tongue. And she couldn't imagine anything sweeter.

She played with him for a while, enjoying his moans and the tremble in his hand as it skimmed her cheek. She wanted him to burn as bright for her as she did for him. Brighter than the sun.

She took him to the back of her throat, hollowing her cheeks and sliding her tongue along his sensitive underside, savoring the saltiness of his skin. She rolled his balls in her hand, squeezing.

Feeling experimental, she walked her fingers lower, brushing them over his sensitive perineum for a minute before dipping them between his cheeks. He froze momentarily before spreading his legs apart to give her better access. Sliding herself lower, she switched hands, wrapping one around his cock and licking the fingers of the other. Deciding to go easy, she started by sticking the tip of her pinky into him.

When his body relaxed around the invasion, she began to gently thrust it back and forth, pushing it further inside each time until he took the whole finger. Her intention was to massage his prostate while she blew him, but apparently it would have to be another time, because on a groan, Sawyer rolled her under him once again.

"I love it when you play with me, but I need to get my cock inside that pussy of yours," he said gruffly.

"Yes."

He reached over to the nightstand and groaned. "Fuck. We're out of condoms."

She flashed back to her earlier vision of their children. She laid her hand on his cheek. "I trust you, and I'm clean. No one has ever been inside of me without one."

"Are you sure?" His fingers danced along her collar. "There are other things condoms protect against."

She blew out a breath. "Would it be so bad if I did get pregnant?"

He blinked, a smile lighting up his face. "No. It wouldn't be so bad. In fact, I hope you do."

Maybe it was selfish to bring children into her world, but she had to believe that together, she and Sawyer would prevail. He'd been right. She wasn't Lisa Smith or Annaliese Hunt.

She was Annaliese Hayes.

His wife.

His submissive.

His world.

And he was hers.

She took his cock into her hand, wrapping her fingers around the silky skin that covered his hard length, and brought it to her opening. Her thighs parted, her ankles hooking around his legs as she arched up to meet him. She took his bare cock inside her slick channel, indulging in the sensations awakening in her.

"It feels different somehow," she said as he slowly began to move inside of her. "What's it like for you?"

"Like being enveloped by a warm, wet cloud." On that, he slammed fully inside her. "It's too good. I'm not going to last long."

She grasped him at the nape of his neck and pulled his face down to her. "Then you better make it count."

He made love to her then, slow and steady, his gaze locked with hers as his cock thrust in and out of her and his hips pressed tiny circles against her clit. Their limbs entwined in a passionate embrace, they were no longer two, but one.

And when she came in a torrent of pleasure, her pussy milking the come from his pulsing cock, she knew she'd do whatever it took to keep Sawyer safe.

So when his eyes closed and his breathing slowed, she took her cell into the bathroom and made a phone call to ensure that happened.

"Pick me up at the hotel," she said when the person on the other end answered. "I'm giving you the black list."

Chapter Twenty-Four

LISA LEFT A lightly snoring Sawyer in bed and waited in front of the hotel for her brother. Hopefully, she'd return before he even knew she was gone. If not, he was going to spank her ass so hard, she wouldn't be able to sit for a week.

She agreed that she had to get rid of that black list, but there was no way she was going to hand it over to Mitch.

She'd considered waking Sawyer and having him go with her to her office, but honestly, she didn't want him and Asa around each other. One or the other or both were likely to say something that could mess up her plan. And she couldn't allow that to happen. Not if she wanted to move on with her life.

Yes, there was always that risk that someone would recognize her or the authorities would catch up with her, but with Sawyer by her side, she'd live each day to the fullest, without regret. Thinking about having his baby, she covered her lower belly with her hand.

Ten minutes later, she headed to her office, sitting in her brother's rental car and drinking the iced coffee he'd brought her.

"Are you sure you want to give me the journal?" Asa asked, drumming his fingers on the steering wheel. "If you gave it to the Feds, Mr. Moneybags could probably use his millions to get you a reduced sentence in exchange for throwing the rest of us under the bus."

She ignored Asa's criticism of her husband. They were both under a lot of stress now that they knew Mitch was responsible for the threats and was after the black list. It was just as important to Asa that the journal not fall into their brother's hands.

"I wouldn't do that to you. Not when you've worked so hard to build a better life and become a better man. Thea and your children need you."

He slid her a glance and smiled. "That's what I love about you, Annie. You always take good care of me. Except, of course, when you left."

The accusation in his voice stung. "I regret leaving you behind, but I don't regret leaving. I did what I had to do to keep my husband safe, and I'll continue doing whatever I have to. I love him, Asa. Just like you'd do anything for Thea, I'd do anything for Sawyer. I won't let Mitch hurt him."

He parked in the empty lot across from her office and unsnapped his seat belt. When he turned his gaze onto her, she was surprised to see the anger in it. "It's always about Sawyer. What did he do for you that I didn't? I was the one who held you when you had nightmares. I'm the one who bandaged you after one of Dad's beatings. I would have done anything for you." He took her hand and kissed the top of it. "I love you, Annie."

She smiled at him. "I love you too, Asa."

He shook his head, squeezing her hand a little too tightly. "No, Annie. You don't understand. I'm *in* love with you. I want to spend the rest of my life with you."

Her world started spinning.

She must have misunderstood.

Asa couldn't be in love with her.

He was her brother.

Asa continued, not noticing her abject horror. "Before you say no, just think about it. You and me together on the road, traveling wherever we want, pulling off the kind of con that would even make Dad proud. You'd never have to worry about anything ever again. I'd take care of you, and you'd take care of me. Like we used to."

The spinning increased, making her feel as if she was in a rowboat on a tumultuous sea. She wiped her sweaty forehead and unfastened her seat belt. "Asa, you're my brother. I love you, but not like that. I love Sawyer. And you love Thea."

He rolled his eyes. "There's no Thea."

Her breath stalled in her chest. "What?"

He chuckled, shaking his head in disbelief. "You really have been out of the game too long. Couldn't even tell when your own brother was pulling a con on you."

She couldn't focus anymore, her head feeling heavy on her shoulders. The dizziness wasn't normal. She looked down at the coffee, realizing he'd drugged her. "I don't understand. Why would you lie?"

He shrugged. "You understand how the game goes. Got to get the mark to trust you before you can make your move. What better way to get you to trust me than to let you think I'd changed my ways?"

Her tongue felt thick, and her stomach churned. "So there's no farm? No Thea?"

"Oh, there is. I fleeced her parents good." Laughing, he slapped his knee. "Get it? Fleeced? Like sheep?" His eyes grew hooded, a sleepy look in them. "She was a sweet thing. Real trusting. All I had to do was convince her I loved her, and she gave me everything I needed to steal her parents' nest egg. Really was stupid of them to put all their eggs in one basket." He laughed at his dumb joke. "I'm killing it today!"

He was crazy. How could she have been so blind? Sawyer had seen straight through Asa's act. He'd tried to warn her. And she'd dismissed it.

She put her hand on the door handle, not surprised to discover it locked. But when she pressed the button to unlock it, nothing happened. Her hand clenched into a fist.

How could she have forgotten that her brothers and her father all knew their way around cars? If they were different men, they would have ended up as mechanics or engineers, rather than criminals. "You're not as funny as you think. Now let me out of this car."

"Sorry, Annie. Can't do that. Someone's meeting us here. Oh, and give me your phone. I don't need you calling your lover boy to come get you."

She reluctantly handed over her cell and shivered with revulsion, his nickname for her tainted by his abnormal affection for her. "Someone's meeting us here? You're working with Mitch?"

His expression grew cold, a darkness she would've never expected radiating from him. "I was before he changed our plan. Mitch will never touch you again. I made sure of it."

"What did you do?" she asked, her speech now slurred.

"He wanted to teach you a lesson, and I couldn't let him hurt you. So I put a few bullets into him. If you don't believe me, you can see for yourself. I left the proof in your office."

She hated Mitch, but she never would've wished him dead. She had just wanted him out of her life for good.

All this time she'd believed she and Asa had been two peas in a pod. She'd lived with the guilt of having left him behind.

What would've happened if she had never left or had taken him with her? Would he have snapped then, or had the years turned him into this person she didn't recognize?

Sawyer had told her she wasn't her family. That she could make her own choices and live her life her own way.

Had Asa chosen to continue his lying and cheating ways, or had it been written in stone?

She would never know, and at this point, she no longer cared. She couldn't save the brother she'd once considered her best friend. He was gone. Or he may not have ever really existed.

Right then, her only consideration was getting out of this alive and returning to Sawyer. As her head hung to her chest and her eyes fluttered shut, she fought against the drug, knowing she couldn't afford to pass out.

She inhaled a huge breath and lifted her head, lasering her stare onto Asa. "You killed your own brother?"

He scratched the back of his neck, not an ounce of remorse on his face. "What did Dad always say? Eat or be eaten. It's survival of the fittest, and only the strong survive." He pointed his finger at her. "That's you and me. We're survivors. We always have been. And now that we're back together, nothing can stop us."

If he believed that, he was crazier than she'd thought. Did he really think she would leave everything behind and become his lover? Her body shuddered from her disgust.

"I don't want to see Mitch's body. I want to go back to Sawyer."

He ignored her, rambling. "We had this plan, see. Scare you into thinking one of your old marks was after you, so you'd come home with us, where we could keep you safe. But then Sawyer showed up and got in the way. So I had to get rid of him. I was ordered not to kill him, but it's not like I had a lot of options. I never intended on you getting hurt. You weren't supposed to get in that car with him."

Sawyer had been right. Hopefully, he'd get the opportunity to tell her so. "You trashed my condo and office and tampered with the car's brakes."

At that, a flash of regret entered his eyes. "I did. But I did everything because I love you. I've waited for you to be old enough for me for years." He licked his lips. "And now, look at you. You've turned into a beautiful woman, Annie."

If she never heard that name again, it would be too soon. She wasn't Annie. "My name is Annaliese Hayes," she said with a strength she didn't feel. But she wasn't going to be a victim. He thought he knew her. Thought she was a girl who wouldn't fight back against her family. Fear years, she'd done everything they'd asked of her and had allowed herself to be used as their punching bag. Well, she wasn't that person anymore. She would fight and fight hard.

She wouldn't make this easy for him. "I don't think you love me. You don't terrorize someone you love. Besides, you're my brother."

"No, I'm not." He tried grabbing her hand, but she shook him off, flattening herself against the passenger-side door in an effort to get as far away from him as possible. "It's time you saw me in a different light. Once you do, I swear to you, I'll make you forget you ever considered me your brother."

His gaze darted toward her office, his nostrils flaring. "Get out of the car. He's waiting for us." He pulled a gun from under his seat and unlocked the doors. "And even though I love you, if you try anything, I will shoot you."

She stumbled out of the car, the drugs still making everything spin despite her trying her damn hardest to fight against it. Her legs buckled underneath her weight, but before she hit the ground, Asa caught her, his arm around her back. His gun was sideways, trained on her in case she made a wrong move.

At this point, her best bet was to play along with him and not run. Especially since she wouldn't get very far drugged like that.

She allowed him to lead her to her office, hanging on him as he opened the door. "If you're not working with Mitch, who are you working with?"

He brought her inside and locked the door behind her.

Mitch's bullet-ridden body lay on the floor underneath her bookshelf, his chest and head bloody. She stared at him, waiting for him to show any sign of life, but he never blinked. His chest didn't rise or fall. The blood didn't flow from the bullet wounds.

He was dead by his brother's hand.

And according to him, he'd done it for her.

Her attention jumped to her desk. Someone was sitting in her chair, the back of it facing her, obscuring the person's identity.

The chair slowly spun around. "Good to see you, Annaliese."

She blinked, her eyes trying to make sense of what she saw.

It had to be a mirage.

Or a ghost.

He couldn't be here.

He was supposed to be dead. Asa had said that he'd died.

Of course he had. He'd conned her. Made her believe she was safe.

After years of hearing and telling lies, she should've known better than to accept the death at face value.

A single word escaped her mouth as she slid to her knees in shock.

"Dad."

Chapter Twenty-Five

How COULD SHE have been so trusting?

Asa stood with his back up against the door, blocking the exit. "Okay, so I got her here," he said to their father. "As you see, I made sure Mitch didn't get the black list or her, so I've done my part." He turned and waved the gun at her. "You give Dad back his black list, and we can leave together. That's the plan."

Her father looked so much smaller, his muscles having wasted away and the extra weight he'd carried gone from his frame. He'd never been a tall or particularly big man, but now he was a shell of the man she'd known and feared. Somehow, he didn't seem as intimidating. With all his wrinkles and his gray hair, he just looked old.

But she wouldn't make the mistake of believing the image he projected. That was one of his greatest skills. He was a chameleon who could change his skin as easily as a person could change his clothes. He'd always claimed she was just like him, comparing her to a chameleon and saying she had a reptilian sense of preservation about her.

Pretending to be weak and frail would give him an advantage over her. She wouldn't expect him to have the strength to overpower her. Underestimating him could get her killed.

By the way Asa was speaking to him, she wondered if Asa believed their father's act. She had a feeling that Asa's plan and her father's plan were not one and the same.

She stared up at her dad. "I thought you were dead."

His smile made her skin crawl. "Aren't you going to give your old man a kiss?"

"No," she said, standing with her arms crossed.

"Where's the black list, Annie?" Asa asked. "Just give it to him, and he'll let us go. That's all he wants. I searched everywhere for it." When she didn't answer, he began to shout. "Where'd you hide it? You said it was here."

Her father pushed back from the desk and stood, holding a gun by his side. He turned toward Asa. "Fool. I don't give a shit about that black list. It's useless to me now. Just like you've been useless your entire life. You thought you were so cunning, manipulating your mother into loving you best. You stole her from me, and now you want to steal her again." He pointed his gun at Asa. "I've been waiting years to do this."

Her brother didn't have time to react before the bullet pierced his brain right between his eyes.

She screamed, her ears ringing.

As he fell forward, the gun went off again, the bullet hitting him in the throat this time. But she doubted he'd felt it, the first bullet having been a kill shot. By the time he landed face first on the floor, he was dead.

Still, that didn't keep her from racing over to him. "Asa!"

"Don't touch that boy, you hear?" She froze to her spot, her father's voice too powerful to resist. "He's gone. Roasting in hell with his brother. He'll never get his paws on you again. That I promise. I did all this to protect you. To be with you."

Protect her? When had he ever protected her?

There was only one man who'd ever protected her, and she'd left him sleeping back in their hotel room.

By now, he would've gotten up from his nap. He would've realized she was gone.

Would he look for her? Or would he believe she'd run from him again? She had to believe he'd find her.

What did her father want with her? Both his sons were dead at his feet. Was she about to join them?

Her heart was racing, her ears were still ringing, and an unknown drug was making her sluggish, but she refused to give up, refused to give into the bone-chilling fear of her situation. Instead, she chose to trust that Sawyer would find her and she'd make it out of here alive.

She ambled closer to her father, stopping on the other side of the desk from him and holding onto the edge in order to stay upright. "You and Mom were supposed to be the ones protecting me from the dangers of the world, rather than being the ones to throw me to the wolves. To teach me right from wrong, rather than to teach me to take whatever I wanted, consequences be damned. I was ten before I realized that stealing food from the grocery store was a crime. You warped me into someone who deserved nothing, because I didn't learn how to appreciate the value of life. Tell me, did you ever love me? Or was I just a toy for you to train?"

He scoffed, his face twisted into a sneer as if he smelled something rotten. "Love doesn't pay the bills. Love doesn't do shit for us in the world, girlie. I taught you that. I taught you to be strong. To be a survivor. Not to wither up and die when you didn't get your way. Love? There's no such thing. There's lust combined with a survival instinct. You think you love Sawyer? If you had, you never would've taken his money and left him."

How dare he disparage her feelings for Sawyer. It only proved that he had no idea what love really meant.

She slapped the desk with both hands. "You would've hurt him if I didn't."

He pointed the gun at her face. "Hell, yes, I would've hurt him. I would've made him suffer before I killed him. He had no right to take you away from me. No right then and no right now. You belong to me."

"Just because I'm your daughter—"

"You ain't my daughter," he said, coming around the desk to stand by her. "Not by blood, anyway. Doesn't make you any less mine."

Her chest hurt as if he'd slammed a bowling ball into it. "You're not my father? Mom—"

"She wasn't your mom, either." He shrugged off the significance of his statement with a brief lift of his shoulders. "We wanted you. We took you."

She collapsed into the chair behind her. "Oh my God. You weren't my parents? You kidnapped me?"

"Kidnap is such a messy word. Besides, when we took you home with us, your parents were already dead."

Tears slipped down her cheeks. "How did they die?"

"They weren't supposed to have been home. Had some charity event in Milan, and the three of you were supposed to leave on the private jet a couple hours earlier. They came home because you were sick and found me and your mom cleaning out their safe. Mom was their maid for a couple of months, while she scouted out the house."

Conning wasn't in her blood, because she'd never shared DNA with any of the Hunts.

Her real parents had cared about her. Loved her. She would've lived a completely different life if they hadn't died. Instead of a trailer, she would've grown up in a mansion. She might have gone to college. Would've had friends and a real family.

When she got out of here alive, she'd mourn the life that had been stolen from her.

Asa's comment about him not being her brother now made sense. "Asa knew, didn't he?"

Her father began pacing the floor, pulling at his hair. "'Course he knew. That boy knew everything. Too much. He thought he was so much smarter than me, but look who's smarter now? He always took what was mine." When he turned his gaze on her, she saw that his eyes had changed. One pupil was so large, it practically eclipsed the brown iris, while the other pupil had shrunk to a pinpoint. "He took you from me. He was in love with you. In love with his own mother. Disgusting. Why did you do it, Helen?"

In love with his own mother?

Eyeing the door, she popped up from her chair. Gun or not in his hand, she had to get out of there. "I'm not Mom. I'm not Helen. I'm Annaliese."

He grabbed her by the shoulders and shook her. "Don't lie to me, bitch! I can't believe you cheated on me after everything I did for you!" His hand flew at her cheek with a loud smack. "You're disgusting. Letting that boy touch you like I touch you."

She was confused. Who was he seeing as he spoke to her? Did he really believe she was her mother?

"What boy?" she asked, taking a step backward to get closer to the door.

Her question only worked to anger him, his body vibrating with immense fury. He shook her even harder. "What boy? You know what boy! I caught you with him. I caught you with Asa. Did you think I wouldn't find out?" He suddenly released her, and she toppled to the floor. He stood over her body, the gun aimed directly at her heart. "What were your plans, hmm? Were you and he going to kill me as I slept? I couldn't allow that to happen. That's why I had to do it."

"What did you do?" she whispered, dreading the answer.

"I didn't want to do it. I just didn't want you to leave me." He lowered himself to the ground, straddling her. He slid the barrel of the gun from between her breasts up to the middle of her forehead. "A shot through the brain, and it would all be over. But there was so much blood. So much blood. And you weren't dead. You begged me to call an ambulance. I made you promise you'd never leave me. But you lied. And I couldn't take you with me. I had to leave you all alone."

She trembled violently. "Oh my God. You killed Mom."

His face dipped down and hovered over hers. "I didn't want to, but the voices made me. They told me if I killed you, I'd never lose you. But they've gotten louder and louder. They never shut up. And they were wrong. You left me. Asa knew he done me wrong. Thou shalt not covet another man's wife."

"How long had they been…?" She couldn't bring herself to say the words.

He frowned and got to his feet, as if he wasn't sure how he'd gotten on the ground in the first place. "Not sure. How long had he been her favorite?"

As long as she could remember.

She noticed he'd said "her" and not "you." He knew she was Annaliese.

"Did anything happen between Mom and Mitch?" she asked, sick to her stomach. Wobbling, she got to her feet.

Her dad tipped his head as he thought about it. "I don't think so. Tell you the truth, I never asked. He was such an angry child. And he turned into an angry man. He didn't know how to take his beatings like you did." He shook his finger at her. "I know that husband of yours is into that BDSM shit, so I'm assuming you are, too. Guess you liked what I did to you, huh? Maybe I should've locked you up in a dark closet without food or water for a couple of days to teach you a lesson. That's what my daddy did to me. Believe me, once you sit in your own shit and urine for days on end, starving and thirsty as hell, you learn not to piss off the old man."

She rested up against the wall, using it for support, and slowly inched toward the door. "What happens between my husband and me is none of your business. But just because someone enjoys the pain aspect of BDSM doesn't mean she enjoyed getting hit and kicked by her father. There's a world of difference between the two. My husband has never harmed me and has always respected my limits. You broke my ribs. You beat me out of anger. Don't ever confuse yourself with my husband. He's the greatest man I've ever known. I love him. But I hate you."

He suddenly began smashing the butt of the gun into his head over and over until blood dripped down the side of his face. "It's time for us to be together, Helen. Asa is gone. Mitch is gone. There's nothing left for us here in this world. But we can be together in the next. This time, I won't chicken out. I'm going to kill myself too. This time, we'll go at the same time."

"I'm not Helen," she shouted. "I'm your daughter, Annaliese. And I don't want to die."

She ran toward the door, praying he wouldn't shoot her in the back. Her fingers covered the doorknob and pulled, but nothing happened. She'd forgotten Asa had locked it. Her shaky fingers attempted to turn the lock.

"I wouldn't open the door if I were you," he warned. "It's connected to the bomb I built. It started counting down the minute Asa closed the door. We've got about ten minutes left before it goes off, but if you want to go sooner, feel free to trigger it. I'm good either way."

She jumped back and confirmed a thin black wire was wound around the doorknob. Her gaze followed along the length of the wire until it came to a metal briefcase in the far corner of the room.

"Don't believe me?" he asked in a singsong voice. "Check the suitcase, but be very gentle when you open it. You wouldn't want it to accidentally go off. You thought you married a no-good idiot, but could an idiot build a bomb strong enough to take out this room? Would an idiot know how to wire the door so that no one could go in and out? It's time for you to admit you underestimated me, Helen."

She believed him about the bomb, and there was no way she was going anywhere near it. "Fine. I underestimated you," she said, not wasting her time convincing him she wasn't Helen. "Now, will you disarm the bomb and let me go?"

He covered his ears. "I want to, but the voices, they won't let me. They're getting louder and louder. Shut up, shut up, shut up!"

What voices?

"What's wrong with you?" she asked, hoping he could hear her.

He took his hands off his ears. "The doctors say I have a brain tumor, but they're wrong. The voices show up on the MRI as a mass, and radiologists think it's cancer, see? I'm dying. Dying. Dying. Dying." He smiled at her. "But now, I get to die with you, so it has all turned out right in the end."

She was running out of time. Even if he arrived before the bomb went off, there was nothing Sawyer could do to save her. She was on her own.

She didn't want to die, but she acknowledged her chances of getting out of this were slim to none. Still, she had to try.

She collapsed to her knees, playing the role of a lifetime. Playing Helen. "I loved you once."

"Yeah. There were good times, weren't there?" He was lost in the memories, oblivious to her crawling across the floor toward her brothers. "Before things got so complicated, and it was just you and me against the world? Do you think you could love me again, Helen? Could we go back to the way it was from the beginning?"

"Yes," she said nodding, making her way to Asa. "But you first have to keep that bomb from exploding."

"I can't. The timer is running through an Internet app. If anyone tries to disarm it, it'll go off. The only way to halt it is by stopping the timer from counting down."

"So do that!"

"Need a computer for that," he said, regret in his voice, as if he would've stopped the timer if he could. "It's our time to go, honey. Just accept it."

Her brothers' blood stained her knees as she crept between them and snatched the gun from Asa's hand. She angled her body toward her father and rose from the floor. "I can't. I'm sorry." She released the safety and pressed the trigger.

The gun went off, jerking in her hands and knocking her backward.

She did it again.

And again.

And again.

Until there were no bullets left to shoot.

At least two of the bullets hit him, blood splattering on her desk as he fell to the floor. She tossed her gun aside and calmly walked over to him, first kicking him with her foot to test his reaction and then removing his gun from his hand in case he wasn't dead.

Her clothes and hands were covered in blood. Her family's blood.

She shook her head.

No, these men weren't her family.

She would never think of them as her family again.

Pounding shook the door. "Annaliese! What's going on in there? I heard gunshots."

Sawyer.

The pounding got louder. "Why is the door locked? Open it right now!"

She ran over to the door. "Sawyer! Stop! It's wired to a bomb that will go off if the door opens."

"Thank God you're alive," he said. "When I heard the gunshots I thought…I'll call the bomb squad."

"They won't get here in time." She caressed the door with her fingertips as if it were Sawyer. "I only have five minutes, and they can't get in here anyway."

"Then they can tell you what to do to disarm it."

She sighed. "My father already told me. There's nothing I can do. But there is something you can do."

"Anything," he said, his voice cracking. "I'll do anything."

"Leave."

There was a long silence. "I'm not going anywhere."

Stubborn man. She knew he'd say that.

"I'm going to die, but you don't have to," she said.

"I'm not leaving you alone."

"I'm not alone." Her gaze flew to the bloody mess lying around her. "My father and my brothers are here."

"Let her go, you assholes," he said in a snarl.

She sunk to the floor. "They can't hear you. They're all dead. My whole family is dead. Not that they were my real family."

"What are you talking about?"

"Never mind. It's not important." She sighed. "But I'll tell you what is. I love you, Sawyer. I always have, and I always will. I didn't want to leave you, but I had to in order to keep you safe. But now my father and brothers are dead, and they can't hurt you anymore. I've spent the last four years defending your life. Don't make me die in vain. Leave. Now."

His voice came sure and strong from the other side of the door. "I love you, Annaliese. I never stopped. And if you go, I go. You won't be dying in vain, because all I ever wanted was to be with you. A life without you is no life at all, so please, don't ask me to leave you. Because that's the one thing I'll never do."

She started to cry. "Sawyer…I wish I could see you."

"Got your phone? We could Facetime."

She laughed through the tears. Only her husband could make her laugh when they were about to die. "No, it's in Asa's car. But maybe one of my brothers does." She got up and went over to her brothers, rifling through Mitch's pocket until her hand bumped into a cell. "Found one. What's your number?"

She dialed as he recited it to her. Then she returned to her spot on the floor, sitting with her back up against the door. He answered, his handsome face coming in so clear, she could see the dark circles under his eyes. "Hi."

"You're beautiful," he said softly. "Hey, there's one thing more I want to know before we die."

"Anything."

"What's your natural hair color?"

She laughed again. "Blonde. I'm a natural blonde."

He smiled sadly. "I'm glad when I die, I get to do it while looking at you. Thank God for technology, right?"

"Normally, I'd agree, but it's technology that's killing us." How was that for irony? Technology would kill her techie husband. "The bomb can only be disarmed through shutting down the timer, and my father used some kind of app—"

"Let me see it," he ordered.

"What?"

"Let me see the bomb. Now."

"Okay." She scurried over to the briefcase, holding her breath as she released the latch and opened it. She turned her phone around, giving him a good view of the bomb.

"I'm hanging up," he said.

"So much for dying while looking at me," she said to herself.

"I can hack into the timer through my phone," he announced from outside. "Well, through the Internet."

Hope burst through her. "Hurry, we only have one minute left."

Her heart was about to fly out of her chest as she waited to see if her brilliant husband could save their lives.

"I picked up the signal," he said. "Now, I…damn it."

"What?"

"Firewall." He cursed loudly. "Let me try this."

She watched as the timer counted down. "Thirty seconds!"

"There. It's working. I'm in."

"Ten seconds!" she shouted.

Nine.

Eight.

Seven.

Six.

Five.

Four.

The bomb's clock went black, and the numbers disappeared.

"Did the timer turn off?" Sawyer asked.

She inhaled a shaky breath. "Yes."

"Then I'm coming in."

She quickly unlocked the door and then threw it open. Sawyer swooped in, and she jumped into his arms. His lips slanted over hers, desperate and hot. She held onto him, her fingers in that hair she loved so much.

It was finally over.

She was free.

Epilogue

Out of breath, Lisa flew down the hallway, her heels clacking on the hospital floor. She still hated hospitals—nothing would ever change that—but now she had some happy memories to replace the others. As she turned the corner, smashing the box in her hand on the wall, she heard a cry.

A baby's cry.

Her own eyes filled with tears when she walked into the private room and saw Danielle in bed, resting comfortably while nursing her baby. Cole sat in a chair at her bedside, joy and love shining in his eyes, eyes that would go completely blind in the next couple of years. Lisa was grateful he had the chance to witness the beauty of his wife and baby girl before that happened.

She and Sawyer owed their friends so much. After all, it wasn't as if she could explain away three dead bodies in her office. Logan and Cole had both called in favors from the FBI, and Kate had represented her in a plea deal. With full monetary restitution given by Sawyer to all her victims and the black list in the government's hands, Lisa had avoided prison time.

She no longer had to look over her shoulder.

"She's gorgeous," Lisa said, smiling down at Danielle.

"She is," Danielle agreed. With the baby asleep, she tucked her breast into her nightgown. "Would you like to hold her?"

"I'd love to." She set the gift down on the foot of the bed and accepted the tiny bundle from her friend.

"Rosa Grace, meet your Aunt Lisa."

Although she now went by the name Annaliese Hayes, everyone other than Sawyer and the guys in Vegas called her Lisa.

The baby's eyes were closed, her face pinched and her pink lips pursed as if sucking even in her sleep. Wisps of dark hair covered her head. "Beautiful name."

"We named her after Roman and Gracie," Danielle said weepily. "If they hadn't been there, I don't know what..."

"What happened?"

"Cole was downtown at a meeting when I went into labor. It all happened so fast. One minute my water broke, and the next the baby was coming."

"There wasn't time to get her to the hospital," Cole added, dabbing at his wife's tears with a tissue. "Gracie and Roman worked together to deliver the baby."

"Oh wow. When she called me, she didn't say a thing." Which was very strange for a woman who never stopped talking. "Where is she now?"

"I'm not sure," Cole said. "She and Roman followed the ambulance to the hospital, but I haven't seen them."

Kate walked in with Jaxon by her side and a present in her hands. "Hmm. Maybe they've finally pulled their heads out of their asses." She laughed as she came over to see the baby. "She's so small. And she looks just like Cole."

Jaxon swept his thumb down Kate's cheek. "Someday."

Kate nodded, a small grin on her face. "Someday."

Jaxon crossed the room and thumped Cole on the back. "Congratulations, Cole. You've got yourself a beautiful family."

"That I do," Cole said, shaking Jaxon's hand.

"Rachel and Logan are on their way up," Kate said. "She panicked because she hadn't gotten you a gift yet, so they stopped in the gift shop."

"That's ridiculous," Danielle said. "I don't need anything other than my family and friends. That's all I ever wanted."

Kate's eyes widened as she looked at the door. "That is the biggest teddy bear I've ever seen."

Lisa turned her head to see Logan march in holding a four-foot brown teddy bear. Rachel was by his side.

"Cute, right?" Rachel said. She took a step to the right. "And look who we ran into on the elevator."

Sawyer.

In a business suit, her husband strode straight for her and hauled her into his arms.

She buried her nose in the crook of his neck, inhaling his scent. He'd only been gone a week, but she'd missed every moment they were apart. "I thought you weren't flying home until the weekend."

He kissed her soundly on the lips. "I finished signing all the paperwork this morning and thought I'd surprise you."

"So it's official?" Rachel asked.

He took Lisa's hand and faced their friends. "I'm no longer CEO of Hayes Industries. I'll still remain on the board, but I think our new CEO will do better in the role than I ever could, because unlike me, he wanted the job. And I turned over Paradise Lost, including the club, to the guys."

Hunter, Oz, and Rowan had all moved into the hotel that housed Paradise Found. From what they'd told her, they had plans to make the club's focus on ménage, rather than BDSM. But not one of the guys had any business experience. "Do you really think they'll be able to handle running a sex club?"

"I'm going to send two of my slaves to help them," Cole volunteered, sharing a secret look with his wife.

They were up to something.

"Does this mean we're getting a nursery at Benediction?" Logan asked, pointing at the baby.

"No," Danielle said. "Cole's hired a nanny to stay with Rosa at the new house whenever Mommy and Daddy need some playtime. Which I'm sorry to say won't be for at least six weeks."

Her friends continued talking about Benediction as Sawyer bent to whisper in her ear. "You look incredible with a baby in your arms. We haven't been careful lately, but are you ready to start trying?"

She turned to him. "I can't think of anything I'd like more than a mini Sawyer running around."

"Good. Because I want at least three."

"Three?" She smiled up at him. "That's doable."

"Good. How about we get working on that right now?"

"Now?" she asked as he took Rosa from her arms and handed her to Rachel.

He took her hand and yanked her toward the door while all her friends laughed knowingly. "We'll be back," he said to them with a wave over his shoulder.

They sped past the nurse's station and down the hall until they came to a door marked *Custodial*. He turned the handle and tugged her inside, pulling a string to turn on the dim lightbulb. His lips crashed into hers, the force of it slamming her backward into shelves of supplies.

A week without him had seemed like a lifetime. The damned sadist had made her promise not to make herself climax while he was gone, and then he tormented her by sending a video of him masturbating, his big hand wrapped around that gorgeous cock of his and her name falling from his lips as rope after rope of come spurted from the tip onto his stomach.

Right now she was so horny that if he didn't fuck her soon, she would likely go off without him even touching her pussy.

"Sawyer, we can't have sex in here," she said, giving a weak protest, although at that point she didn't really care about propriety. "Anyone could walk in on us."

He smiled wickedly. "Exactly."

She laughed. "You're such a kinky Master."

He stalked to her. "I have to be when I've got such a kinky girl. I bet you're already wet for me, aren't you?"

"I was wet for you about two seconds after you walked through Danielle's hospital door."

He motioned with his hand. "Let me see. Show me. Lift that skirt of yours."

Looking at the door, she paused only for a second before deciding the risk was worth it for the reward. She hiked her skirt up to her waist.

Sawyer's eyes went liquid. "No panties? You dirty girl."

"I'm not dirty yet, but hopefully I will be soon."

Sawyer braced his arms above her head, trapping her against the shelves. "What are you thinking about, I wonder? Maybe my come dripping out of you, running down the inside of your thigh while you pretend to your friends that we weren't just in the closet fucking?"

Her pussy clenched from his filthy words. "Sawyer, our friends are almost as kinky as we are. They're going to know what we were doing. In fact, it wouldn't surprise me if they came in here to do the exact same thing."

He took a step back and folded his arms across his chest. "Well, then we better get to it so they have something exciting to walk in on."

"What do you want me to do, Master?"

He held out his hand. "Fuck yourself on my fingers."

That was a new one.

Her pussy dripped as she took his hand and pushed down both his thumb and pinkie, bringing the other three inside her pussy. A loud moan passed her lips. Anyone walking by the supply closet would know exactly what was going on inside. The fact that they could get discovered at any time only made it that much more exciting.

She moved them in and out, faster and faster, her hips punching in time to greet each thrust. Heat banded around her core, pulling tighter and tighter until she hovered on the precipice of climax.

"That's right," he crooned. "Take what you need from me. I can feel your hungry cunt sucking them in."

"Oh God." She jerked forward into Sawyer as the orgasm crashed into her. Aftershocks shaking her body, she tilted up her chin. "Fuck me."

"Such a greedy girl." He took his fingers from her pussy and sucked them clean. "Good thing for you I happen to want the same thing." He quickly unzipped his pants and twirled her around, his cock inside her before she could take her next breath.

He pistoned in and out of her pussy, his hand on her spine. "The guys invited us out for the grand reopening. Think you might want to go out there with me?"

She peered over her shoulder. "I don't know. Are you asking if I want to fly out to Vegas to have an orgy with your friends? Hmm. Hard decision." She laughed when he smacked her ass. "Uh, yeah."

He pulled her hair, its color now back to her original blonde. "I fucking love you."

"You'd better." She arched a brow at her husband. "Because I am the mother of your future children."

"You're more than that," he told her. "You're my life."

Five minutes and two orgasms later, they returned to Danielle's room. The baby was back in Danielle's arms, a nurse by their side giving Danielle a little cup with pills in it. Roman and Gracie were now there, standing on opposite sides of the bed from one another.

"Oh good, they're here," Danielle said to the nurse. Then she waved her hand at Lisa and Sawyer. "Get over here. The nurse is going to take a group shot of all of us with Cole's camera."

Lisa was sweaty and sticky, but how could she refuse her friend? She and Sawyer joined the others by Danielle's bedside and smiled as the nurse snapped a photograph.

She held onto Sawyer's hand as she watched Danielle open her gifts. Cole took picture after picture, Lisa in several of them. She no longer had to worry about keeping her face out of the press or avoiding photographers.

The people in this room were her family. Someday when she was ready, she would contact her birth parents' relatives, but for now, she had all the family she needed.

She looked up at her husband and placed a hand on her soon-to-be growing belly.

Well, maybe not *all* the family.

Have you read all of Shelly's sexy and suspenseful novels set around Benediction?

If not, you must be dying to find out how the other couples met in…

WHITE COLLARED

(Kate and Jaxon)

RED HANDED

(Danielle and Cole)

BLUE BLOODED

(Rachel and Logan)

Available now in print and e-book from Avon Red Impulse!

About the Author

SHELLY BELL writes sensual romance and erotic thrillers with high emotional stakes for her alpha heroes and kick-ass heroines. She began writing upon the insistence of her husband, who dragged her to the store and bought her a laptop. When she's not practicing corporate law, taking care of her family, or writing, you'll find her reading the latest smutty romance.

Shelly is a member of Romance Writers of America and International Thriller Writers.

Visit her website at ShellyBellBooks.com.

**Give in to your Impulses . . .
Continue reading for excerpts from
our newest Avon Impulse books.
Available now wherever e-books are sold.**

An Excerpt from

HARD EVER AFTER

A Hard Ink Novella

By Laura Kaye

After a long battle to discover the truth, the men and women of Hard Ink have a lot to celebrate, especially the wedding of two of their own—Nick Rixey and Becca Merritt—whose hard-fought love deserves a happy ending. As Nick and the team shift from crisis mode to building their new security consulting firm, Becca heads back to work at the ER. But amid the everyday chaos of their demanding jobs and upcoming nuptials, an old menace they thought was long gone reemerges, threatening the peace they've only just found.

Wearing only her bra and jeans, Becca sat in a chair in the middle of Nick's tattoo room. Since the shop was closed while Jeremy focused on getting the construction on the other half of the building started, they were the only ones down there. The driving beat of a rock song played from the radio as Nick moved around the room getting everything ready.

Cabinets and a long counter filled one wall, which was otherwise decorated with drawings, tattoo designs, posters, and photographs of clients.

Becca had seen Nick work before and loved the dichotomy of this hard-edged, lethal soldier having a soft, artistic side. He was really freaking talented, too.

He handed her three sheets of paper. "I worked up a couple different fonts. What do you think?"

She shifted between the pages. "This one," she said, settling on the cursive design that best interweaved the letters in the words *Only, Always, Forever.*

"That was my favorite, too," he said, giving her a wink. "How is this for size? Bigger? Smaller?"

The total design as he had it on the sheet was about four inches square, the words stacked atop one another. "This looks good to me. What do you think?"

Nick nodded and came behind her. He folded the sheet to focus on the design, then held it against the back of her right shoulder. "Yeah. This is a good size for the space. Gonna be fucking beautiful." He leaned down and pressed a kiss to her skin. "Let me go make the stencil, and we're ready to go."

A few minutes later, he cleaned her skin, affixed the stencil, and let her look at its placement before getting her settled into the chair again.

He pulled her bra strap off to the side. "Ready?"

"Very," she said, butterflies doing a small loop in her belly.

The tattoo machine came to life on a low buzz. "Just relax and let me know if you need a break, okay?" he said, dipping the tip into a little plastic cup of black ink.

"Okay." His gloved hands fell against her skin, and then the needles. Almost a scratching feeling, it didn't hurt nearly as bad as she thought it would. And just like when he'd drawn on her with skin markers, she was already dying to see what it looked like.

"How you doing?" he asked in a voice full of concentration she found utterly sexy. Just the thought that he was permanently altering her skin—just like he'd permanently altered her heart, her life, her very soul—sent a hot thrill through her blood.

"I'm good," she said, relaxing into the sensation of the bite moving across her skin. "Is it weird that I kinda like how it feels?"

He didn't answer right away as the needle moved in a long line. He pulled the machine away and wiped at her shoulder. "Not weird at all," he said, his voice a little gravelly. "Some people like the sensation and even find getting tattoos addictive."

"I can see that," she said. He worked without talking for a stretch, and the combination of the quiet intensity radiating off of him, the driving rock beat, and the buzz of the machine was heady and intoxicating. She found herself breathing a little faster and wanting so much more of him to be touching so much more of her. If she thought he was sexy putting ink on someone else, it was nothing compared to how she felt when he was doing it to her.

"What are you thinking about so hard?" Nick asked, his breath caressing her bare shoulder.

"Really want to know?" she asked, already smiling at what his reaction might be.

"Always," he said, wiping at her skin. He dipped the machine in the ink and leaned in again.

"How turned on this is making me." She really wanted to turn to see his expression but knew she wasn't supposed to move.

He pulled the machine away again. "Jesus, Becca. You're killing me here."

She grinned. "I asked if you really wanted to know."

An Excerpt from

WILD AT HEART

By T.J. Kline

Bailey Hart has never felt at home in her small town. So when her band gets their big break in Los Angeles, "Wild Hart" can't run fast enough . . . If only there weren't so many reasons to stay. After a harrowing stint in the Oakland Police Department, Chase McKee has returned home a hero, and yet he feels anything but. And when he finds out Bailey might be leaving for good, the feelings he's always harbored for his best friend's cousin just won't stay hidden.

Chase picked up on the roar of the engine long before the motorcycle actually came into view. Reaching for the radar gun, he aimed it in the direction of the sound.

Ninety-two miles per hour. Did this guy have a death wish?

He'd no more tapped the gas on the cruiser when the motorcycle blazed past him in a midnight-blue streak. He flipped on his lights and siren and the bike immediately slowed as the rider glanced backward before pulling onto the shoulder.

At least he has some *respect for the law,* he thought acerbically as he stopped behind the motorcycle and ran the plates.

The registered owner's name came up on his computer screen and his eyes shot back to the rider.

"Damn it," he muttered, rolling his shoulders back and preparing for the battle he had no doubt was coming. Chase rolled his eyes and climbed out of the vehicle with a sigh of resignation. Crossing his arms, he greeted the most beautiful woman—and the biggest troublemaker—he'd ever met as she slid her helmet off her head and brushed stray hairs back into her low honey-colored ponytail.

"Funny seeing you here, Bailey. When did you get this thing, and are you trying to kill yourself with it?"

She turned her dazzling pearly whites on him, her blue

eyes flashing with mischief as she set the helmet on the seat behind her. Chase had been dying to ask her out ever since his return to town almost two years ago but she had no idea and, unfortunately, he needed to keep it that way. Her cousin Justin was one of his best friends, and if he knew Chase thought of Bailey as anything other than Justin's "little sister," Chase would probably have to arrest his friend for assaulting a police officer. Not to mention that he'd need to check himself into the hospital.

"Just picked it up last week." Her fingers ran lovingly over the blue gas tank between her thighs, and he felt his body immediately react. He stifled the response. "I guess I'm still getting used to how much power it has."

"Ya think?" He couldn't help but chuckle at her understatement as he clicked the top of his pen and started writing out a speeding ticket. "I need your license and registration."

"Aw, come on, Chase. Really?" She bit her lower lip, looking up at him from under her thick, dark lashes, and he felt the heat of desire trickle down his chest and center low in his belly. "I'll slow down. I swear."

"And you'll never do it again, right?" He didn't believe her for a second. Everyone knew Bailey's reputation as the wild child of the Hart family. She didn't just march to the beat of her own drum, she conducted the entire orchestra to a tune of her design.

"You know, you should come by for dinner tonight. I'm fixing enchiladas for them. We're hoping the spicy food will put Jules into labor. There'll be plenty if you want to stop by."

A flirtatious smile spread over her full lips and her eyes sparkled like sapphires. Chase felt the sizzle of heat come to life again. If he didn't know her better, he'd think she was flirting. That was the last thing he needed right now. He turned the pad toward her and handed her the pen, indicating she should sign the line. She stared up at him expectantly, practically batting her eyelashes.

Chase cocked his head to the side and gave her a lopsided grin. "Plying me with dinner isn't going to get you out of a ticket, Bailey."

Her eyes narrowed as he tapped the pad again. Bailey jerked it from his hand and scribbled her name, slapping the pen against it irritably when she finished. He ripped her copy of the citation from the pad and handed it back to her with the other documents. "You *do* realize trying to bribe an officer is a felony, right?"

She cocked a brow at him as she slid her helmet back over her head and slipped her sunglasses on, starting the engine. "Who said anything about bribing you? Maybe I was trying to poison you."

Chase couldn't help but laugh as she eased the bike back onto the road. "Murder One is a felony, too," he yelled after her.

Damn, that woman could turn him on faster than she did that bike.

An Excerpt from

THE BRIDE WORE STARLIGHT

A Seven Brides for Seven Cowboys Novel

By Lizbeth Selvig

Once comfortable on stage in front of thousands, Joely Crockett is now mortified at the thought of walking—or rolling—down the aisle at her sisters' wedding. Scarred and wheelchair-bound, the former beauty queen has lost more than the ability to walk—she's lost her fire. But when one handsome, arrogant guest accuses her of milking her injuries and ignites her ire, Joely finally starts to feel truly alive again, and soon it's impossible for her to resist her heart's desire.

"You look lost."

She started at an unexpected, masculine voice and swung her gaze to the dining room doorway. Her mouth went dry as a summer drought, and her pulse hiccupped before it began to race. The man who stood there with a hot smile and a confident demeanor owned a pair of the sharpest hazel eyes she'd ever seen, sandy-gold hair the color of a palomino stallion, and a jaw and cheekbones strong enough to have been chiseled out of Wyoming granite. Most unsettling of all was a smile that likely could have charmed Sunday school teachers out of their knickers—in any era past or present.

After she'd stared for an impolite number of seconds, Joely lowered her eyes and cupped her chin so her thumb rode up the left side of her in order to hide the scar. She'd convinced herself it made her look thoughtful and masked the self-consciousness she'd never suffered before the accident.

"I might be lost," she said. "But I'm probably not."

"You're Joellen."

"Not unless you're angry at me."

He raised one amused brow. "I'm not."

"Then it's Joely."

"I admit it; I knew that. What I don't know is how a pretty

little thing like you could possibly be sitting all alone like this in a house full of women."

She stared, not sure whether she was annoyed at the "pretty little thing" epithet or surprised at his mind-reading ability, since she'd been wondering the same thing.

"My whole family is in the kitchen through that door. I could ask you the same thing. What's a patronizing cowboy like you doing in my mother's dining room knowing my name when I don't know yours?"

The grin widened, and he strode into the room, dark denim jeans fitted nicely on his hips, a subtle plaid shirt tucked at the waist, and a casual brown sport coat giving him a touch of western class. He reached her in three strides, his cowboy boot heels beating a soft, pleasant cadence on the oak floor. "Alec Morrissey," he said, holding out his hand. "Alexander if you're mad at me."

The name left her stunned again. She knew it. Anyone who followed rodeo knew it. But he couldn't be *the* Alec Morrissey—the one who'd won three PRCA titles and then dropped out of sight half a dozen years ago . . . She shook her head to clear it before she could blurt a question that would sound stupid. She kept her hand over her scar by pretending to scratch her temple and took his hand to shake it. His firm, dry masculine grip sent a small warning shiver through her stomach.

"I'm not," she said.

"Not what?"

"Not mad at you."

"Ah. Even if I'm patronizing? Or if I admit I'm not a real cowboy? Which I'm not, by the way. I wear the boots because they're comfortable."

She wanted to tell him she'd only forgive him if he promised never to call her a pretty little thing again. Her father had called her that, but not in a proud papa kind of way. It had been more a "you're my delicate little flower, don't worry your pretty little head over such things" kind of way. But based on the confidence this man exuded, Joely doubted she could tell him to do or not do anything.

"Well, I can't lie. I'm disappointed about the cowboy part. But if you swear to quit being patronizing, I won't be mad."

He pulled out a chair beside her and sat backward on it, comfortable and easy, looking as if he'd lied about not being a cowboy and straddled seats and saddles every day.

"Ma'am, if calling you pretty is patronizing, I can't swear because any promise I made I would break every time I saw you."

[illegible]